a novel of magic most foul

The Twisted Tragedy of

MISS NATALIE STEWART

LEANNA RENEE HIEBER

sourcebooks
fire

Published by Sourcebooks Fire, an imprint of Sourcebooks, Inc.
P.O. Box 4410, Naperville, Illinois 60567-4410
(630) 961-3900
Fax: (630) 961-2168
teenfire.sourcebooks.com

Library of Congress Cataloging-in-Publication is on file with the publisher.

Printed and bound in the United States of America.
VP 10 9 8 7 6 5 4 3 2 1

To those who were born melancholy,
and those who have melancholy thrust upon them,
may you find your true, beloved community.

Chapter 1

Isn't that the man wanted for those murders in New York City?"

I tried not to let my face betray the panic flooding through my body. I'd thought once we made it out of New York City and onto the train we'd be safe.

A man in a dusty suit and cap had a conductor by the elbow, pointing at the cushioned benches where I sat with Jonathon. The wide-brimmed felt hat he'd been keeping low over his head had fallen back, revealing his face. It was a face hard not to notice. I nudged Jonathon awake, trying not to be too obvious about it. He blinked sleepily. If he hadn't been wanted for murder, I might have thought he looked adorable.

"Hello there, beautiful," he murmured in his refined London accent.

"Look sharp," I whispered. My anxious tone doused his smile. "Someone recognized you. Whatever I say, just…nod in agreement."

I could feel my voice fumble in my throat. *Oh no. Words, do not fail me now.*

"Miss? Sir?" The conductor approached, swaying slightly as the train curved around a bend and plunged into a tunnel cutting through the mountains of Pennsylvania. Jonathon's accuser hung back, his haggard face scared. I wondered if I looked scared too.

"Yes? Hello," I said softly. *Just focus on one word at a time.*

"You…and this gentleman here," the conductor said carefully. "Are you acquainted?"

"Oh, yes," I said with a sad smile. "Cousins. We're off to see our uncle on his deathbed. We hope we make it in time…" I turned ruefully to Jonathon, who nodded, squeezing my gloved hand in comfort. The conductor glanced back at the man who was gesturing toward Jonathon. A few other heads, men in top hats and ladies in feathers and ribbons, turned our way.

"Is there a problem, sir? Do you need to see our tickets again?" I rummaged in my bag. Jonathon reached into his coat pocket and held his out.

"No, no, it's just…there were murders in the papers, in New York—"

"Oh! That madness in the Five Points?" I shuddered. "Horrifying, isn't it? What about it?"

"He looks just like the man in the sketch!" the man hanging back shouted. There was a murmur of shock from the compartment. That would teach us to not pay the extra dollars for a private compartment. But runaways have limited spending cash. Jonathon assured me of finances secure in England that demons could not have seized, but those were of little use at the moment. Mrs. Northe had been generous to us both, but we'd played things safe. A tired-looking woman reached a hand up, begging the man to sit and leave things to the authorities.

"I know the likeness is unmistakable," Jonathon broke in. "That's what I thought, too. I promise you, the last thing a man wants to look like is a murderer."

I stared at him. Jonathon Whitby, Lord Denbury, had just spoken in an uncannily perfect American accent. Impressive.

"But," Jonathon shrugged casually, "I'm not British. I'm from New York. And my eyes aren't dark like his. See? It's a difference one really can't mistake." He widened his ice-blue eyes for effect. He was right to bring it up. In that respect he was a far cry from the rough portrait that sensation-driven papers had been eager to publish. The conductor looked embarrassed.

"Don't worry," Jonathon added. "I'm used to it. I've been stopped a few times since the sketch. But if you could just let me and my cousin go in peace to our family, we'd sure be grateful."

That was no lie. All we wanted was to be left alone.

Nor was it a lie to say that Jonathon wasn't the murderer.

But telling a train car full of people that a demon had possessed his body wouldn't have helped. It's why we were fleeing. We couldn't trust the police to believe us either.

"Sorry to trouble you both," the conductor said, tipping his hat. The man who had caused the disruption looked at Jonathon warily and finally heeded his wife's urging to sit down again and drink a beer. Awkward silence descended. There is nothing more unnerving than a train car full of people staring at you. And I've stared down a demon, full in the face. The decision of whether we would stay in that car was mitigated by the announcement that we would soon be arriving in Chicago.

Thank you, Chicago, for your kindness.

While I'd risked my life to save his, Jonathon Whitby, Lord Denbury, could yet be the death of me. But here I am, at his side. What is wrong with me?

Well, look at him.

A girl would be kidding herself if she wouldn't attempt the impossible for a face like his. The gas-lit sconces of the train cast him in a golden light. His black hair, slightly wavy, framed features carved in classic lines. Shocking blue eyes could cut the breath out of a person as if his gaze were a surgeon's knife. The train's whistle blew as it pulled onto tracks in a crowded station.

"We've got to mail your diary back to your father," Jonathon murmured in my ear, regaining his delicious

4

accent again. "A telegram cannot possibly explain every-thing, and otherwise he won't know what's happened to you. I'd rather he not kill me when I ask to court you properly."

I bit my lip at the word "court" and blushed to the tips of my ears.

We disembarked onto a platform that was too small for the crowds. Signs promised that a new Union Depot would be opening next year. Chicago clearly needed it.

Jonathon helped me down the train stairs, and my blush heightened as I thought of all the kissing parts in my diary that I hadn't thought to redact. It was too late. We only had twenty minutes before the next train.

No matter the contents, the diary was the only way to explain what really had happened. Even if Father couldn't believe the account, we needed to try to make things right with him. Unless Mrs. Evelyn Northe, our benefactor and all-around guardian angel, could make him believe in what sounded impossible. She'd thought of most everything, so perhaps she'd even solve the crimes in our absence.

The station was hectic, but the postal counter was clearly marked and we eased our way to the ornate brass counter. As we bought an envelope and postage, the clerk gave us such an odd look that even Jonathon noticed.

"Is there a problem, sir?" he asked, again in an American accent.

"No, sir, it's just that…"

"She's very pretty, I know, but you needn't make it so obvious that you think so too, sir," Jonathon chided. My blush returned.

"No, sir, I mean no offense. It's just…" The poor man, who was now as red as I was, slid a note across the counter. "This came in earlier, so you see I'm just…"

I glanced at the note, transcribed from a telegraph onto Western Union labeled paper.

New York City Police Department reports missing girl. Natalie Stewart. Age 17. Auburn hair. Green eyes. Pretty. Presumed traveling alone? Mute.

Jonathon read over my shoulder and didn't miss a beat. "Sarah here, while I agree she fits the description, isn't traveling alone but with me—her cousin."

Father must have reported me missing before Mrs. Northe could get to him. But Father didn't know I could speak, that saving Jonathon had cured my voice. Speech still wasn't always easy, but talking would further disprove the cable.

Words. Come on, Natalie. I took a deep, long breath.

"And I'm hardly *mute* now, am I?" I replied, sliding the paper back to the clerk. The man still looked wary but didn't immediately call for the police. I tried to steady my shaking hand as I addressed the envelope and handed him the package.

"But whoever she is, I hope you find her," Jonathon offered with a winning smile. He sounded as if he'd grown up here. He was so aware of his details and yet so unruffled that the man would make an *excellent* spy.

"Have a lovely day," I offered.

"And you, miss. Sir. Travel safely." The clerk nodded to us, throwing the package in a bin.

As we turned away, Jonathon grabbed my elbow. "What if he sees the Stewart name on the package? Won't he—"

"I sent it to Mrs. Northe. Without a return address," I replied.

"I could kiss you for your cleverness," he replied near my ear, smirking at me and dropping the American accent for his tantalizing British one.

"No, no, none of that," I giggled. "We're *family*, remember?"

"Kissing cousins?" he grinned. "I thought you loved Edgar Allan Poe. He married his cousin."

"True. And she died a tragic, early death. Stay sharp. We're hardly out of the woods," I said, trying to stay serious and on task. But it was hard to remain focused with that half-dimpled smirk of his and the heat of his hand on my elbow.

"No, there are no woods here," Jonathon said, looking around him and up at the soot coating the station beams.

"The woods are ahead of us in the wilds of Minnesota. Wait, what are you—" he cut short as I dragged him suddenly in the opposite direction toward something I saw across the station foyer.

"I've an idea," I declared, stepping into the light of a general store selling everything a traveler might need, have forgotten, or have lost. I went to a rack of eyeglasses on display.

"I told you, you oughtn't have dozed off on the train with your glasses *on*, Humphrey dear. Slid right off and underfoot," I crowed for the shop-girl's benefit, plucking a wide-rimmed, clunky pair of glasses from a display and sliding them onto Jonathon's face.

"Oh, those look nice," the lady said, bored, as if that's what she said to everyone who put something on their nose. And no they didn't; they looked hideous.

Jonathon thought so too. I could tell from the clench of his jaw and the flash of his blue eyes beneath the thick, fishbowl glass. I wanted to roar a laugh but held it back admirably.

"We'll take them," I said, rummaging in my reticule for one of the larger bills Mrs. Northe had sent me off with. The bored clerk took it.

Walking away, Jonathon fumbled for me, his case and my knapsack on one of his arms, reaching for me with the other.

"I can't *see*," he hissed, his British accent particularly

8

sharp in annoyance. "These things are for a blind man. I have perfect vision—"

"Yes, but they entirely distract from your handsome face, my dear Lord Denbury, and that is a distinct advantage," I replied, steadying him toward the westbound platforms.

"You'll have to guide me closely," he declared.

"And is that so bad?" I teased. He offered a rakish grin that even the glasses couldn't make unattractive.

"I'll suffer the fashion if it means you'll cling to me."

I giggled and slid my arm around his, entwining our fingertips. My blush returned.

"Humphrey, though? *Really?*" Jonathon scoffed. "At least I gave *you* a normal name with Sarah. I could've gone for Irma or Wilhelmina, something stuffy and matronly." He stumbled as we took a step up onto the platforms, the bags swaying.

"Oh, but I love the name *Mina*," I replied airily, guiding him toward our train.

"*Wilhelmina*. I didn't say Mina. *Wilhelmina* Irma Persnickety and her blind cousin, Humphrey Fitzwilliam Persnickety," he said, reaching out as if he were falling and finding my face and petting it. I let loose the laugh I'd held back earlier.

"Fitzwilliam? Oh, no, you're not allowed to allude to Mr. Darcy. Darcy would not be caught *dead* in those glasses," I teased and jumped aside as Jonathon crowed in protest. I ran a few steps ahead, thinking of the most random name I could come up with. "You're helpless without me, Humphrey...*Pindarus* Persnickety."

Pained by the name I'd plucked from *Julius Caesar*, he shook his fist in the air quoting, "Pindarus? Where art thou, Pindarus?" He slid his glasses down his nose to look at me. "If you dare match wits with me about Shakespeare, I'll rename you one of Lear's daughters. How about Goneril?"

"That sounds like some horrid disease." I tried to shush our laughter, afraid we'd attract unwanted attention, as I moved to Jonathon's side to guide him up the train stairs. "Where are we going again, *coz*?" I asked, checking our printed schedule.

"St. Paul, Minnesota, to throw ourselves at the mercy of my friend Samuel Neumann," Jonathon replied.

My smile faded. Passengers jostled around us. More trains pulled in, making the air wet with steam and smelling thickly of coal. Jonathon set his case and my bag down, and removed his glasses to adjust their thick bridge. A train whistle screamed.

"Jonathon," I murmured. "I'll be at the mercy of two men. One I don't know. You, I barely know. And...I have to ask. Am I a reminder of terrible things? In the light of day, in a world free of magic—"

His gloved finger lifted my chin gently. The lamp post above us cast his elegant features partly into shadow, but his eyes blazed into me and stopped my breath as they so often did. "Here in the light of day I care about you more than ever. You're the angel that freed me from a curse, not a reminder of it." He smiled, putting on the ridiculous glasses again. "If you're worried about me falling *further* for you—"

I laughed, giving him a swift kiss on the mouth. "I'm not. Just…keep falling for me." With a look I hoped was flirtatious and alluring—I was still practicing my feminine wiles—I picked up my skirts and darted up the train steps.

"I will most certainly keep falling if you don't help me up these stairs," Jonathon called. With a giggle, I aided him up and into the aisle between the compartments. "A *private* compartment, if you please, Miss Persnickety," he said pointedly. "Let's avoid another incident like we had on our last train."

"A *private* compartment?" I breathed. A thrill raced up my spine at the prospect.

A conductor with the logo of the Chicago, Milwaukee, and St. Paul Railway prominent on his vest and hat came to collect our tickets.

"We'd like a private compartment, please," Jonathon stated.

"Of course, sir." The man eyed us. "Newlyweds?"

Jonathon and I scoffed at the same time. "Cousins," I replied. The conductor just eyed us some more and showed us to a small compartment with frosted glass doors.

"Where to?" the conductor asked as we entered the

narrow compartment, which had two small beds and a long bench.

"St. Paul," Jonathon replied. The conductor stamped our tickets and slid them into a clip by the compartment doors. I bobbed my head at him as he closed the doors, and we were alone for the first time since our hasty flight out of Manhattan.

"Think he believed us?" I asked.

"Not for a second." Jonathon took off his hat, threw his glasses onto one of the beds, and pulled me into a deep kiss.

Next thing I knew, we were in a mess of entangled fabric, my skirts around his legs and the bones of my corset pressing hard against the bones of my rib cage.

I was afire with the dangerous thrill of something that we shouldn't be doing, wondering just how far I'd dare go. Before I'd rescued Jonathon, he'd been trapped in a portrait. The demon might have had Jonathon's body, but his soul was free. We had met in the world of the portrait. Sometimes in dreams. There, we had first tasted passion. But flesh-and-blood was *far* sweeter. It was so scorchingly real that I almost couldn't breathe. Well, perhaps my corset *was* laced a bit too tightly…

Jonathon, balancing on one hand, nearly had his cravat free when the train rolled out with a lurch. He lost his balance, tumbling away from me and onto the floor of the car.

My cry of concern joined his laughter as he lay splayed on the floor, the silk of his neckwear pushed aside and revealing the hollow of his throat and a few undone buttons of his vest. I shifted on my elbow to look down at him.

"I could kiss you forever," he said, gazing up at me hungrily. "But I'd want more."

My nerves fluttered, my voice failing. "I…can't…not that I don't—"

He sat up, face to face with me, pressing a bare fingertip to my lips. "I know what a woman's virtue is worth. I'll wait as long as it takes. I know what you're worth—"

I turned away. While his gentlemanly words were indeed comforting, another boundary worried me more. *Worth*.

"Worth has a whole new meaning with you, Jonathon. You're from generations of nobility. I'm the daughter of a museum curator. I have nothing to offer you. You could ruin me, and no one would—"

"I'd never ruin you, Natalie. And what, saving my life isn't dowry enough? To hell with class, society, and expectations. I'd have wanted you no matter how I met you."

"Our paths would never have crossed if not for the painting and the dark magic."

"And if I had to, I'd suffer everything I went through again just to meet you," he declared. "My soul split from my body, the curse, the prison, the scars, the sleepless nights—I'd suffer it all again for you."

I stopped him with another kiss, slow and passionate, running my fingers through his black locks, but careful. Tender. These sorts of kisses were generally reserved only for the engaged or married, but kissing Lord Denbury was its own point of no return.

Finally breaking away, he stared again into my eyes. "Do you trust me?"

"Why do you ask?"

Jonathon furrowed his brow, sliding away to lean against one of the beds.

"With everything that's been assumed of me, I just… don't want you to be frightened of me." An awkward discomfort I'd rarely seen from him now surfaced.

"I do…trust you." There were times when words came so easily. Other times not. Selective Mutism meant that for most of my life, I hadn't spoken. I was four when I stopped speaking. Words, out loud, are still quite new to me. And evidently they fail most often when I'm self-conscious. But believing in him steadied me. "I wouldn't have risked what I did if I didn't believe in you."

Jonathon grimaced. "Am *I* a reminder of terrible things? When you look at me, do you think of the demon?"

"He looked like you. But wasn't you. His eyes were the reflective eyes of an animal. When I look at you, I see…" I blushed. "Wonderful."

Jonathon smiled a moment before his expression turned

calculating. "That's what gave him away to you? The eyes? What else?"

"His voice was lower, his cadence uneven. He was rude. But his eyes were yours, until I looked straight at them. That's when the difference was clear. Looking into his eyes, I saw the abyss. Why?"

"I may need to become him." Jonathon looked at me as I swallowed hard. "I may need to act the part." I started shaking. That might do my head in, watching Jonathon play his evil half. "Trust is the only thing that's going to get us through the coming months," he added, collapsing upon the uppermost bed. "So that's all I'm going to ask of you."

"You have my trust," I said quietly, even if the last thing on earth I wanted to see was him playing the part of a fiend.

The reply must have soothed him, for several moments later I could hear the even breaths of his slumber. The poor thing hadn't had much chance to sleep in recent days.

I watched him for a long time, the gaslight of the compartment flickering across his fine features, his long black lashes hiding his oceanic eyes from me, hiding the dreams we might share if we both were asleep. It was true about trust and the future. So many terrible loose ends. Too many. But we'll sort them out. Together. We've no choice.

Chapter 2

Seeing more of the country was lovely, if only from train windows. Before this I'd never been further than New Jersey; there was never any need. New Yorkers believe New York is the center of the world, and I maintain they are correct. But if one is to *rightfully* claim that New York is the center of the world, it adds credibility to know something of the rest of the country for comparison.

However, there's something to be said for the train cutting dramatically in and out of mountainous steppes, the gently rolling hills in parts of Ohio, and the plains of Indiana and Illinois, interminable miles of fields with the occasional city sprouting up out of nowhere.

The great speeds of the trains surprised me. One could get entirely across the country in mere days. It was freeing and thrilling to think that in our modern day, our vast country was laid open to us if we could afford the tickets. It's so close and crowded in Manhattan. There's such breadth out here that it's a whole other world. I'd never appreciated the sheer scope of America until now.

More hills again in Wisconsin, the land so green, the fields speckled with herds of cows. Jonathon had slept right through the towns, all with names that sounded native. Signs visible from the train windows named countless dairy farms. Jonathon looked so peaceful that I hated to disturb him, but the thought of dairy farms roused my appetite.

I bought an apple in the dining car and sat near neatly dressed ladies with cultivated speech. Three generations, it appeared. The elder matriarch eyed me.

"Traveling alone?" she asked with disapproval.

"Oh, no, my cousin is sleeping. Last-minute journey. Off to a funeral."

"I'm sorry," the youngest said. "Where are you from?"

"New York City," I replied.

"So are we," she said. "And I can't *wait* to get back."

"Yes, but I'm enjoying the journey," I replied. "I've never been west. What's St. Paul like?"

She looked at me with an unenthused gaze. "I hear it's quite the industrious little city full of hard workers. I'm told they put a park atop a hill before Central Park was a gleam in anyone's eye. Nothing compared to New York, though," she was quick to add. "Nothing *ever* compares. Certainly not that slaughterhouse town of Chicago."

"There you are, *Wilhelmina*," Jonathon said, sliding the thick glasses onto his nose and bumping against the ends of tables before taking me by the hand.

"And here is my cousin now. Please excuse me."

The grandmother looked us up and down, as if we couldn't possibly be related, and sniffed. "Safe journey, my dear."

As I led Jonathon away, he murmured. "I'm hungry too, but please, another car. I didn't take too many of the privileges of my station, but I've a weakness for fine food." He offered his arm, and I led him toward First Class.

I tried not to look like a fool gaping at the gilded details and lavish settings of the elite car as we slid back its carved wooden doors with beveled glass. We were met by a gloved waiter and shown to brocaded seats and a table set with the finest crystal and silver table settings. I'd never even been *into* such a train car, let alone seated in one. I didn't want to trouble Jonathon about luxury, but he was a displaced noble and I was a middle-class runaway with only as much in my bag as Mrs. Northe had packed for me, plus a bit of jewelry and my wits. But to hell with it, I wanted a lavish meal and to be *courted* by a British lord.

"You'll love Sam. He thinks the best of everyone," Jonathon began. "He and I met during lectures at the Royal Academy, sitting next to one another. He'd driven his family here mad with wanting to set up his own clinic, so they sent him overseas to learn proper surgery lest he put any more stitches into the family dog." I laughed as we were brought coffees in gold-trimmed porcelain cups. "We set up a clinic near Covent Garden, the theater district in London. My parents didn't care what I was doing as long as I wasn't out whoring or gambling like my uncles…"

A shadow crossed over his face as he said the word "parents." Now eighteen, Jonathon was an adult, not an orphan, but his parents were recently deceased. Having lost my mother, I knew the pain, but his was fresher than mine.

"Those were amazing days, that summer with Sam, Nat, and me at the clinic. Nathaniel, you'll have to meet him, too, the *nutter*," Jonathon chuckled. "He's an actor, but he has a habit of collecting melancholy folk who sometimes don't take care of themselves."

I wanted to meet everyone in his life. I missed my friends Mary and Edith from school, and Rachel, too. They'd all die to see Jonathon. Here I was, living an adventure we could only have dreamed up. I'd happily trade in the darker side, though. I even missed Maggie, Mrs. Northe's niece. I'd hoped to become great friends with her, but it hadn't quite worked out. I wasn't going to give up on her, though. Somewhere inside Maggie lived a nice girl; I'd have to try to find her.

"Will your friends believe the supernatural parts of our story?"

He snorted. "Sam? Never. Nat? It would prove everything he hopes is true. I'll end up in his show if I'm not careful. I've so much business left to deal with. Mrs.

Northe gave me the address in London of a solicitor who will help me. I should just go."

I opened my mouth to protest, then closed it. I didn't want him to go, of course, but it wasn't up to me.

We dined like a king and queen, and were treated as such. For the first time I felt what it was like to be a normal girl, not a mute girl, not one of society's "unfortunates," but a *fortunate* girl with every opportunity offered to my sex. We kept the shadows at bay and spoke of travel. He was as curious and insatiable as I was. He wanted to see the world with *me*. Together it seemed like anything and everything might just be possible.

Back in our private compartment again, I was exhausted, having been unable to doze easily. Subtly loosening the stays of my corset, I laid my head upon Jonathon's knee. He ran his hand over my hair. My thoughts wandered to that one exquisite trespass within the painting, where I'd felt his fingertips upon my skin directly, and I longed for it again. But nerves had me blushing and sitting up again in the train car, unable to look him in those breathtaking eyes. I went to my bag, dabbing a cream onto my hands rather than just wringing them nervously. I glanced at Jonathon. He was deep in thought.

"We need a signal," he said. "A word. To know when something is wrong. Something innocuous in conversation that no one would suspect."

I breathed in the rosewater scent of the cream Mrs. Northe had packed, something exquisite and French with matching perfume. "Rose," I said. "They're one of my favorite flowers. That's a harmless enough word. Rose."

"A shame to associate one of your favorite things with danger."

"Well, you're one of my favorite things. And you're associated with danger."

"Fair enough. If we can't speak, the signal will be pulling on the left side of our collar. Either the word 'rose' or the left collar means we play the lie that either of us tell. Agreed?"

"Agreed."

"Let's hope we don't have to use either signal any time soon."

Chapter 3

There's a fine stretch of homes upon St. Paul's Summit Avenue, where a tree-lined mall divides a cobbled street. It was here that the carriage Jonathon hired at the train station pulled in, under a pillared portico against a Georgian edifice with candles in the window. Ivy was kept carefully at bay upon the brick, though it was straining at the seams, as if ready at any moment to engulf the whole building in leaves.

I wish I could have sketched the face Dr. Neumann made upon seeing us at the door.

"I'm not a ghost," Jonathon assured his friend, holding out a hand. For the first time in public since the incident on the train, he retained his British accent. Samuel dodged his hand, throwing his arms around Jonathon with a joyful laugh.

"Nat wrote me that you were dead, suicide, some rushed burial—"

"Samuel, you know you can't believe everything you read in the papers—"

"Denbury, my friend, is this some miracle?" he asked, turning then to me, curiously wondering if I were a part of this surprise.

In that moment, when Jonathon nodded to me and I was about to be introduced, everything changed.

I noticed a man step into the hallway behind Samuel, a small man in a fitted tweed suit, perhaps around the age of thirty. His eyes were so haunted that I thought he might be a specter.

"I told you, my friend," the man said, with a quiet accent similar to Jonathon's upper-class standard British. "That with me, you would see many impossible things."

If I hadn't spent the last month so intensively studying Jonathon and everything about him, I might not have noticed his body tense. But I did.

"You speak truth, Dr. Preston," Samuel said. "Let's not dally here by the door. Denbury, you must introduce me to this fine young lady."

"This is Miss *Rose*," Jonathon said. I reeled to hear our secret code so soon. Something was wrong. His gaze flickered to the other doctor in the hall. "And she doesn't speak or hear, but she can read lips, so don't say anything rude. She's become…somewhat of a project of mine." He said the word "project" carefully.

I quelled a shiver. Jonathon turned to me, gesturing me to nod, that I'd been presented. I curtseyed briefly to

Samuel, who was looking at me not with pity, thank God, but with curiosity. I nodded toward the man in the hall. A moment of irritation flared through me—what, didn't Jonathon think I could speak for myself?

Jonathon had said his friend could be trusted. Clearly this doctor in the hall could not. What had he and his friends gotten wrapped up in?

"Let me send off my driver and take our bags while you seat Miss Rose in the parlor," Jonathon directed. "I assume she and I are welcome to stay the night? I apologize for not sending a wire, but things have been rather…complicated."

Preston's mouth curved slightly. I didn't want to stay a night here. Had we been followed? Anticipated here? I suddenly didn't want to be around anyone other than Jonathon. He was the only one I could trust. And clearly, he was treading carefully too.

"Of course my best friend is welcome in my home!" Samuel said. "I saved a stash of Earl Grey tea just for you." Jonathon gave a sound of relief as he darted back down the steps toward the hired carriage to pay the driver and deal with our bags.

Samuel gestured for me to enter. A fine wooden-paneled entrance foyer led to wooden pocket doors open to a pleasant parlor, open and trimmed in blue. "*Danke*, Mrs. Strasser," Samuel said warmly as his housekeeper wheeled in a tea tray to serve us.

With no obligation to speak, I considered Samuel. He was tall and fair with straight blond hair and an open, friendly face. If there was danger surrounding him, he evidently didn't know it. Jonathon had said Samuel thought the best of everyone. Such a disposition would have made him an easy target for the unsavory.

Mrs. Strasser was out of the room before anyone spoke again.

"Your friend is not the man he was, Dr. Neumann," Dr. Preston said. His tone was eerie and quiet, and he seemed to have purposely turned away from me. Not bothering to include me. That's right. I couldn't hear. Why bother addressing me? That was rather brilliant of Jonathon. I was perfectly poised to listen in while assumed to be the least threat.

I appeared busy with my tea but watched out of the corner of my eye. Samuel frowned. "How's that?"

"He's been through a…great deal," Preston continued. "My associates chose him, too, as you and I have been chosen. But unlike us, his body and soul were changed in the process. The body and the soul have distinct uses. We proved them separable in Lord Denbury's case."

"Separable? But—"

"Oh, don't worry, he's quite whole now. But that's not our department. We must stay focused on *our* goals."

I sipped my tea with dawning horror. Not only was this

doctor involved with whoever had cursed Jonathon, but he assumed Jonathon was still possessed. Was Samuel next?

"Your associates didn't hurt him, though?" Samuel said sharply. "You promised me our aim was to help the suffering, those in loss, those between life and death… like Elsa…"

"Of course," Preston assured quietly. "At least, that's what I was promised too. I'm doing this for my Laura, Samuel."

The two men nodded. I felt pain hang heavily in the air like humidity before the release of a storm. Doing *what*? And what poor women were at the heart of this?

"In our gilded age," Preston added, "with medicine, surgery, and physiology, it's all a thrilling frontier, and we must be at the fore. Everything is new, and we must seize the day."

He sounded like an avid student—possibly delusional.

Jonathon returned. I jumped up to fix him tea from the tray, trying to keep my hands from shaking. I hoped my very wide eyes as I handed him the cup signaled to take care, willing him to see that he had to play the demon. But something told me that, from the moment he'd seen Preston in the hall, he'd already known that. Had they met?

There was a strained silence as we sat, and I had to remember I couldn't turn to whoever spoke first. I could only read lips. Samuel broke the silence with a sigh.

"It's just so *bloody* good to see you," Samuel said to

Jonathon. "When Nat wrote you'd died…after your family…I'm so sorry—"

Jonathon waved his hand as if it were nothing. But I read the flicker of the muscle on his neck, the subtle clench of his jaw, the tightening of his chest that kept in the grief he'd not yet been allowed to process.

"I'm sorry we lost touch," Samuel continued. "I returned to the States to learn my family was moving west. So were the Wells. And you know, wherever my Elsa would go, I must follow…"

"Ah, yes, true love," Jonathon said with an edge. Preston's eyes hardened.

Samuel looked up at a portrait of a lovely woman over the mantel. "We were supposed to be married this year. But she's slipping away. Comatose. None of the doctors understand…" Samuel clenched his fist on the arm of his chair. "*I* don't understand, and I'm supposed to be gifted—"

"Being exceptional only gets you so far, my friend," Preston said in that same voice just above a whisper that somehow the whole room could hear. "And even the most skilled physicians in the world cannot keep our loved ones from the grave."

Jonathon's cup rattled slightly. I imagined he had a lot to say about loss but couldn't. We had to play nice. Complicit. It was sickening.

So Samuel was losing Elsa, and Preston had lost a Laura,

but what did that have to do with splitting soul from body? Would they seek to put their love's souls into other bodies? Was that the bait that lured gifted doctors?

"What news from the home front?" Preston asked Jonathon. "And the New York branch? Settled into their offices?"

Jonathon chuckled low, a sound I didn't like. "To tell you the truth, I haven't been in touch. I'm in a brave new world, and I wanted to…explore New York to the fullest. I came west to…cool my heels. I was attracting attention I don't think is proper at this stage."

Samuel looked at Jonathon with concern. Preston only looked at him blankly.

"I know nothing about the wings of experimentation by the Master's Society," Preston replied. "Other than mine. But if you're in touch with the London office, tell them that while my work may be slow, it's sure. I won't be pressured for results. I don't want my careful work destroyed." Preston turned to Samuel. "They seem to forget sometimes that we're only human. Don't you forget it."

Samuel furrowed his fair brow. "How can we forget our humanity, and the delicacy of it, when we face death nearly every day in our profession?"

A flicker across Preston's haunted face made him appear older than he was. "Because it's easy to get lost in the work, my friend. It's so important to us. My department has doctors working in three major cities questioning when a dead body is really dead, all of us prodigies under thirty. Our associates treasure the fire of youth as much as anything. But with fire, there's smoke. And in the thick of smoke, one can lose his way…"

Was this a warning or was Preston talking about himself? I sat watching the conversation, glad to be ignored because I wasn't sure I'd manage to say the right thing. Occasionally Samuel stared at me as if I didn't belong or something didn't add up.

"Why are you here?" Jonathon asked Preston coldly. "I won't tolerate being followed."

"Calm yourself. My being here has nothing to do with you," Preston scoffed. "The Mayo family brought me this direction. Then I found out that Samuel had left your London clinic and thought I'd seek him out since we've so much in common."

"I am sorry to hear about Elsa," Jonathon said quietly. Samuel nodded.

"Mayo," Preston said in his uncanny whisper. "True luminary of our craft. That family may change the whole profession. I know genius when I see it. But when I return to New York, *I* shall be the one to prove that death will not be the last word…"

I looked into my tea to hide my anxiety. Preston was based in New York? The Master's Society had *offices* there?

"So with that, I must be off." Preston rose. "I dare not

miss tonight's presentation. I've much to learn about tissue in particular," he said jauntily. "Now *I* just need to know how to keep it fresh after the spark of life has fled. Tend to your friends, Samuel. I'll see myself out."

I saw Jonathon fighting the same shudder I fought. Samuel looked at Preston as if he held all the hope in the world, not as though he'd just said something terribly creepy.

Preston bowed to each of us and exited the room. Mrs. Strasser stood in the hall with his hat and light cloak, holding them out far in her hand as if she didn't want to be too close to him.

I turned to see that Samuel had crossed the room to sit on the arm of Jonathon's chair, turned away from me.

"Jonathon, I don't want your…*friend* to read my lips. Preston said you'd changed during your ordeal. What's she doing here? *Who* is she? Since I've known you, you've been too busy with studies, the clinic, and duties of your station to have time for a girl. Let alone a 'project.' What the devil does that mean? What sort of consort—"

"Don't jump to conclusions," Jonathon muttered. He paused a moment and glanced at me. "It means she's my ward. She has no one else. And in her condition, would you have left her to the work house or the brothel?"

Samuel measured up his friend while I held back a wicked grin. I always wanted some sort of torrid Gothic-novel affair in which I was haplessly thrust upon some young lord's mercies as his ward. And now I had it. But the thrill of a delicious guardian-ward intrigue was short-lived as I thought about all the *lies*... Jonathon didn't have to play the demon to his friend, did he? But could he be honest?

"Then you are still the man I know," Samuel said with quiet relief. He turned to me, and I made a show of focusing on his mouth. "You know, Miss Rose, the day I first visited the Denbury estate, Lady Denbury had just experienced quite the shock of finding three starving stray dogs sequestered in her son's room."

Jonathon grinned, showing a warmth and fondness that I hadn't seen on his face since we'd been sequestered in the private train compartment. "Those poor mutts." He shrugged. "They were starving and sick. So I fed them and cleaned them up a bit, and they were on their way, my estate none the worse. I'd have done the same for a person—"

"And you did. That was the point of the clinic. So here you are, Denbury, a guardian to this pretty young ward, and you remain the world's knight in shining armor—"

"Not exactly." Jonathon's warmth vanished. "Who I am in the world is terribly complex. Once we're gone again, don't say another *word* about me to Preston."

"You don't trust him?"

"You don't remember him?"

"No, why?"

"He came to the clinic one night. I turned him away."

"Why?"

"He was looking for *resurrectionists*, Sam. Burkes and Hares."

I shuddered. Earlier in the century, William Burke and William Hare had made headlines by murdering people, then selling the bodies to a doctor performing autopsies at Edinburgh College. Their names were most frequently used now to terrify young children into doing what they were told. Resurrectionists stole bodies out of graves, from morgues, or still alive from the street.

"Preston mentioned experiments of a revolutionary kind," Jonathon continued. "He spoke of a new age in the new world. It would seem this 'new age' has fine doctors in several cities and offices in New York," he muttered. "True, the field of medicine is wide open and anything could happen. Let's just try to keep our heads about it."

Samuel scratched his head. "Preston said his wife died in childbirth in London, and he quit his practice in grief. He was approached by an organization conducting experiments on tissue and the human spirit, and they sent him to New York. He told me he'd heard of us and that he could pay me a visit en route to see Mayo. When he found out about Elsa's condition, he brought me into his confidence about new developments that might shock the comatose back to life."

"A coma is not death, Sam. What did he want with *dead* bodies?" Jonathon asked sharply.

Samuel shrugged, honestly baffled. "I…don't know."

An uncomfortable silence followed. Samuel broke it by turning to me, making sure I was looking at him before he spoke. "I am so sorry. We must appear so rude. Come, please let me give you a tour."

Samuel showed us the clinic at the rear of the house, a wide room full of windows and sick beds with a view of a rear garden and the rest of the town below. It was empty at present, Samuel proud that he was able to send his patients home recovering.

"My family chose this area so that my work could be used to supplement my parents' missionary work," he said, sitting on a rear bay window. "I'm conflicted, though. They have their own faith, so why do they need another? Medicine, however, I believe in sharing. My parents only ask me to do what's comfortable. And for that, I'm grateful."

"Many wouldn't have given it such thought," Jonathon replied.

Samuel shrugged. "I've never suffered from a lack of thinking." I nodded in commiseration. Overactive minds were something we all seemed to have in common. "How long are you staying?"

"Just the night. I've affairs back in England to attend to." Jonathon's voice was hollow.

Just tonight? Where were we going next? Was I going to England too?

"That's a shame, Miss Rose," Samuel said. "I'd like you to have met a young patient of mine. He can't speak either."

Teaching others appealed to me. Since I regained the gift of my voice, I felt a duty to help others communicate. I'd never forget how hard it was to speak. How hard it *is*. Every time I open my mouth I shove fear violently aside, every word an act of bravery. It's exhausting. But never again will I return to silence. Except when playing a part.

"Could you show me to a postal office?" Jonathon asked.

Samuel readied for the trip downtown, showing us out onto a verandah as he disappeared into a rear carriage-house. It was a beautiful day outside, and the fine houses and promenade mall of green trees in bloom made the avenue a fairy-tale town. If only our situation mirrored the beautiful summer day. Jonathon edged me slightly into the shade, away from any windows, turning me to face him.

"I'm sorry to silence you. But I recognized Preston and light crackled around him, fiery, the aura of the demon. Samuel has no idea what he's gotten involved with. We'll return to New York by train tomorrow," Jonathon whispered quickly. "Preston might come back here, and I can't risk revealing I've 'recovered' from the curse. I must go back to England, and I dare not leave you here alone."

He raked his hand through his hair, anger and frustration flashing in eyes as blue as the sky.

"I'll come to England—"

"No."

Our discussion was halted as Samuel came around the drive with a four-wheeled calash attached to a strong white mare. He tipped his top hat as he sat upon the driver's bench, awaiting us in the street. Jonathon and I trotted down the walk, and he helped me up onto one of the leather cushions.

We traveled across elegant Summit Avenue and down a sloping hill. Such picturesque scenery was hard to reconcile with the cool and subtle dangers we danced with. As we traveled into the center of town, the city spread out into a plain of cobblestone streets and a mixture of buildings. There were a few lanes for promenading and even a small circular park. But there was no bustling roar, hardly the glorious chaos of energy one found in New York City.

Samuel dropped us at the post while he went on an errand at the pharmacy.

The postmaster approached Jonathon with an odd look on his face. He glanced from Jonathon to me and back again. Oh, no. It was the Chicago station all over again.

"I was hoping to ask if you could help me, but by that look on your face, can I help you?" Jonathon asked.

"Well, someone has an odd way of knowing what company I'd keep today," said the clerk, mopping his receding brow with a kerchief and inching his glasses up his nose. "I believe these telegraphs are for you." He beckoned for us to come to the counter bordered by brass rails and slots marked "post." He slid two envelopes across the counter.

One said:

> To a young British stranger, absurdly handsome, black hair, blue eyes.

The other said:

> To a young auburn-haired woman. Green eyes. Pretty.

Jonathon nodded to the postman and eased me away from any listening ears and over to an alcove filled with pens, paper, and supplies. We each opened the envelopes and read the telegraphs typed therein. Mine read:

> THE WESTERN UNION TELEGRAPH COMPANY
> A friend of yours appeared. We must look after her. Again, you remain at center of mystery.

And his:

THE WESTERN UNION TELEGRAPH COMPANY

London source confirms artist in permanent residence under
your name at Highgate. Source awaits you.

I took in the messages. "These have to be from Mrs.
Northe," I whispered. "But what does yours mean?"

"Highgate is a cemetery in London," he replied grimly.
"There must be a dead body in my family plot, the man
who painted my portrait. An artist in 'permanent residence'
indeed…" He leaned in to me. "But Natalie, I didn't *tell*
Mrs. Northe we were coming to St. Paul! How could she
have known? How could these have been waiting for us?!"

I smiled amid his anxiety as the truth dawned on me.
"She's *clairvoyant*, my love. Terribly handy in a pinch."

"Oh. Right. Well." He scratched his head, displacing one
wavy black lock. "Unfortunate if I want to keep a secret."

"Thankfully she's good at keeping them. Still, I'd have
thought she'd have sent nicer notes."

"Natalie, at a dollar a word, a telegraph isn't a medium
for niceties, but speed."

I'd had no knowledge or need of telegraphs, even if our
family could have afforded them. At such a price they
were a convenience for the wealthy alone. A dollar could
be a whole day's pay for many New Yorkers. I tucked the
telegraphs into the drawstring bag at my wrist as Denbury
began writing telegraphs of his own in return. I used some

of my remaining money to send a wire directly to Father, one that could not be mistaken.

"Please give Mother my love with her usual bouquet of black-eyed Susans," I wrote. We had a ritual of visiting her grave at Woodlawn in the Bronx, bringing a particular flower we bought from an old woman who'd seemed ancient for as many years as I could remember. Father would tell me how the flower symbolized my mother. I felt a pang for that old lady, those flowers, my father, that grave, and my city. New York City wasn't paradise, but it was home. We sent our messages, nodding our thanks to the baffled clerk.

"Everything all right?" Samuel asked from the carriage as the bell of the post-office door clanged shut behind us. I shrugged. Denbury offered a curt nod.

As we went up the hill again toward Summit Avenue, Samuel took a different route, turning back to us to say, "I'll show you our outlook. We've a park with many fine homes around it. It may not be as grand as your Central Park, but it's ours…"

A timber magnate owned an impressive estate alongside other industrialists, and the square of Irvine Park was lovely, replete with statuary. But it was the outlook between the mansions that was spectacular.

The view was magnificent. New York City is a crowded, close place. The only time you've a sense of vastness is in

Central Park or along the rivers, but even then, there's so much smoke and traffic. From this height the bustle on the river was miniscule, the trains long insects, the Mississippi mighty and commanding. I held in a gasp. It was as if we were flying above it all. Rivers are the heart of civilization, and it was as if we gazed down on the veins of human-kind at the mouth of the most famous waterway in our country. Here we were above the beginning. Jonathon's hand squeezed mine.

"Magnificent," he said. I nodded.

We ate a pleasant dinner, during which Samuel discussed cases with Jonathon and they spoke a different language of medical terms, medicines, chemicals, and physiology. It was impressive, and I took interest in the methods of deduction between symptoms and diagnosis, even if most of the terms were new to me. I resolved to examine a few medical texts so that I might keep up with such a conversation.

"Before it grows too late," Samuel said once we had finished dessert and coffee, "we must promenade along Summit. It's beautiful at dusk."

The sky was spectacular with stars. The quiet of the town was profound in comparison to home, which hissed and rushed at all hours. I longed to be alone and unhindered in this peace with Jonathon. I've spent so much time being frightened for him that I wondered what just wandering like a normal young couple on a perfect summer night would be like. Samuel's gaze was far away, and I wondered if he wished Elsa were here instead.

"I wish you could have met Elsa," Samuel broke the silence as we passed a grand home more darkened than the others, no lamps lit at the doors, no candles in windows. "She lived there."

"*Lived?*" Jonathon asked gently. "Isn't she still alive, friend?"

"Only a shell. Sometimes I wonder if she was just a figment of my imagination that I dreamed up in the days when we played as children. Our falling in love seems lifetimes ago. Dr. Mayo believes it's something to do with the spine. Tricky, the spine. I cling to hope, visit her, talk to her, take her hand as though everything is normal, yet I… *feel* her fading. That doesn't sound very scientific. But I'm beginning to think I don't really know anything. That I don't know what I do or don't believe."

"You don't believe in the supernatural," Jonathon stated.

"Could the supernatural cure Elsa?" Desperation edged Samuel's voice. "Is there a way I could know if she was all right? I lose sleep wondering if she suffers."

Jonathon glanced at me and spoke carefully. "In dealing with the supernatural, take care what…company you invite."

We were again at the doorstep. Seizing a paper and pencil on a small tray where calling cards might be placed, I wrote hastily: "In New York, I could direct you to someone who might try to contact Elsa's spirit to answer you. But yes, be careful."

Samuel stared at me for a long moment. "Thank you."

As we were shown up to our rooms by Mrs. Strasser, I noted Jonathon's room was just three doors down. Left alone in the hall, I thrilled at the possibilities, but Jonathon chilled me with business instead.

"Natalie, nothing would make me happier than running away with you, forgetting everything terrible that's happened. But there are clues back in London—this 'Society' Preston mentioned. I *cannot* sit idly by, not knowing what happened to my family, wondering what they wanted with me to begin with." I opened my mouth, but he continued. "You gave me my freedom, Natalie. Release me again. I'll return to you as soon as possible."

"Can't I come with you?" I whispered.

"What, and explain to your father that I absconded with you to another continent?" He took my hands in his. "Do you truly want him to kill me? No. Return to Mrs. Northe. She's the only one we can trust—"

"What if she's been targeted too? And isn't it too soon? The magic too fresh—"

"She'll know what to do. Don't argue with me, please. I allowed you to come this far. No man would place his treasure in any further danger."

Moving in to kiss me, he had just pressed his lips sweetly

to mine when we heard footsteps hesitate at the landing. Wishing to avoid what might be a ferocious German scolding from Mrs. Strasser, Jonathon cupped my cheek fondly in his hand before reluctantly retreating down the hall toward his room, his scorching gaze upon me to the last.

I ducked into my room. I heard Mrs. Strasser's slow tread down the hall after I'd shut myself in. She paused at each of our doors to listen for any telling noises.

Crawling into bed in my nightdress, I felt the uncertainty of the coming days settle over me like a damp cloud. What would Father say upon my return? And how long would I have to be secretly courted by a man secretly pretending to be a demon? When he played the fiend, would I forever be reminded of that creature that nearly killed me?

The thought of the demon must have triggered something. I found myself scratching at my wrist. The skin around it was nearly rubbed raw, and a scratch mark was visible in a thin line of blood. A marking. A letter. No.

A rune.

Runes like those that had been carved into the demon's Five Points victims, onto the painting, onto Jonathon. Now onto me as I sat stewing in a bed in Minnesota. Runes were just an ancient alphabet. But in this case, the letters channeled something more. I turned my arm one way, then another, seeing if it was trick of my eye. I closed my eyes and opened them again. The mark remained.

I couldn't remember what this letter represented. But there it was on my arm. Delicately written in blood. "Natalie, you're exhausted—you're seeing things," I whispered to myself. "Besides, I'm done with you, dark magic. I renounced you."

I looked down again to find the marking had faded. Convinced that it had been delirium, I eventually realized I couldn't hold out against how little I'd rested on the train, and I fell into a deep and dreamless sleep where even Jonathon could not find me.

Chapter 4

I awoke nearly at first light, lying in bed, kicking at the sheets, and sick to my stomach. I lifted my arm to see if any mark remained. Smooth skin.

I resolved to look up the mark in Mrs. Northe's book on runes. I made note of the figure in a fresh diary she'd placed in my bag with the inscription:

A Gift to Miss Natalie Stewart, whereabouts unknown. Dream well, dear girl.

Love, Evelyn Northe

Dream well. Did that mean pleasantly or prophetically?

I tried to make myself presentable. Bless Mrs. Northe for sending me off with a nice tea gown; she did have an eye for clothing. Someday I hoped to have enough options that I might not be seen in the same array of things for a whole week and a half. That would be luxury. I tucked a few errant tresses behind my ears and pinched my cheeks for some color.

I pulled out the rosewater toiletries. Miss Rose indeed. The finery made me feel better, and I needed all the help I could get. I glanced in the long mirror of the armoire to see wide green eyes staring back at me that appeared older, wiser, and more harrowed than they had mere months ago.

My footfalls at the top of the stair must have alerted Samuel. He popped his head around the corner with a smile, bounding up the stairs onto the landing beside me and extending an arm to escort me down the stairs.

"And how are you this fine morning, Miss Stewart?" he asked, sure to bend his face into my view so I could read his lips.

I grimaced and thought about the question. Everything I was worried about must have passed over my face. I shrugged.

Samuel looked at me blankly for a moment before replying: "Well, the good news is that your hair smells like rosewater."

I stared at him, and suddenly I smiled. My shoulders relaxed. What a kind soul. How, then, could he be blinded by Preston? Clearly, grief could keep strange company.

Bread, butter, and coffee were laid out for us. The day outside the wide windows was bright, the trees green. I could hear birds singing, and I recalled glorious summer days in Central Park. I hoped I'd have the presence of mind to enjoy them this year. My reverie was interrupted by the entrance of Jonathon, freshly groomed and breathtaking as ever, but with suitcase in hand. Back on the run again, the two of us. Mrs. Strasser had put my things by the door.

"Will your ward be traveling with you to England?" Samuel asked. "Miss Rose would be welcome here."

"Thank you for the offer, Samuel, but I've made arrangements."

"It's Preston, isn't it? He changed your attitude immediately."

Jonathon gave a little laugh. "Nonsense."

"Denbury, you once praised me on my attentiveness to a patient's symptoms. I couldn't miss the icy pall that came over you when he entered. He means well—"

"Does he?" Jonathon said sharply.

"He's a grieving man, just like me. All he wants is to help others rouse their loved ones again."

"We can't cheat death, Samuel. None of us can. Even science, the all-mighty savior, can't. We took the Hippocratic oath including the promise to do no harm. Don't deal with devils, Sam."

"Why? Because they haven't treated you nicely? Preston told me you're involved with his associates—"

"Nothing is as it seems, my friend. And if you say *one more word* about me to Preston or anyone he knows, it may end in my death. Truly, this time. Yours too. Maybe Miss Rose here if we're not careful."

"I'm sorry…" Samuel said softly. "If I thought I was bringing some sort of ill luck upon anyone, least of all you—"

"Oh, no, I think we were targeted, my friend, but not for ethical reasons."

"Preston said you're not the man you were. What do I trust or believe? Preston and I bonded over grief. Over tragedy. Over young lives ruined too soon. Surely you of all people can understand that."

"Grief can make you vulnerable and lead you down a path from which there is no return," Jonathon said darkly, his gaze downcast, his face coloring in shame.

The day Jonathon's parents died, he'd been persuaded into an opium den. From there, he'd been taken prisoner, and the curse began. He couldn't forgive himself for it.

Jonathon sighed. "I'm sure Preston, like me, is being used. Just…extricate yourself from his acquaintance. Tactfully. But by your own wits, not by anything I've said," he warned. Breaching the icy gulf, Jonathon embraced Samuel by the door. "We'll be in touch," Jonathon said.

Samuel looked at one of us and then the other. "Travel safely."

"Indeed. And…give Elsa our best," Jonathon said. "Keep faith, my friend."

So. Here we were again on a train. Jonathon had been quiet for hours, staring out the window, brooding, and scowling.

"You're worried about him," I said.

"I'm worried about everything: Samuel, what I've yet to

face in England, you, everyone. I wish I had some sense of security." He returned to silence.

The lazy motion of the train had me nodding off. And once I did, the nightmares returned. I suppose this was a day-mare, as it was daylight outside when I fell into the fitful sleep that produced yet another traumatizing vision.

A long corridor, a hallway, with doors on each side. The floor is slightly damp. Perhaps a basement. The lamps are trimmed too low. I hear a distant sound of moans. This is not a place of happiness but torment. As I pass each door, they recede in number; 10, 9, 8, etc., and either no light or only dim light comes from the other side of the door. There are sharp smells, medicinal but below an astringent scent, like something elderly, decaying.

And just as I arrive at the end of the corridor, glass doors on each side of me and a brick wall ahead of me, I glance to my right. My heart stops as a yellowish hand suddenly slaps the glass, splaying out as if in pain or trying to reach for someone. There is a whooshing sound of exhaling breath like a last breath. I try to scream, but nothing comes out, my voice again unreliable.

A door opposite flies open.

Inside the dim room is a girl in a white dress trimmed with lace, dark hair pinned up but askew, hands folded tightly on a circular table. Her face glitters with tears. The room is freezing cold, wind in the air where there should be no flow.

Wait, I know that girl. That's Rachel. Rachel Horowitz, my friend from the Connecticut Asylum. She left school to tend to her aunt in the city, and we lost touch…

"Rachel," I say but then remember to greet her in sign language instead.

"Help," she signs in return. "Help me. Make it stop."

Her face distorts with horror, as if she sees something behind me that I cannot. Suddenly I am shoved hard back into the hallway by an unseen hand and the door slams in my face, shutting Rachel away again.

The ghostly shove backs me up against a door. A knob jabs against my corset boning. I turn to the door, put my hand upon the knob—Wait, I know that door. I open it to find Lord Denbury's study, the study from the painting, and this was the way my dreams always let me in.

But the room of his prison lies in cinders.

His study has been burned to bits, leaving only smoldering beams. The books are all unbound, pages in the air and falling like dead leaves. Where I used to look out of the frame, out onto the world, there is only blackness. The frame itself, the device used to trap and hold Jonathon's soul, smolders with dying fire, yet the runes carved around the edges burn brightly.

There is a pile of ash on the blackened Persian rug in the middle of the room, a pile of ash where Jonathon would stand. And whispers. So many whispers, the growing sound of chanting that rises in the air like thunder. Words I can't make out. A rite. A spell, perhaps. The room darkens as searing pain shoots up my arms…

I awoke with a guttural sound in my throat, sitting up in the gently swaying sleeper car, feeling something ugly and ungainly like when I first tried to speak, and I croaked out, "Jonathon," before blushing and remembering myself. He turned to me, propping himself up on his bunk with one elbow.

"Yes, my dear?"

I hesitated.

"What is it?" he urged.

"Do you think clairvoyance may be contagious?"

Jonathon thought a moment. "You're dreaming up clues again, aren't you?"

While trying to reverse Jonathon's curse, I'd dreamed various clues related to murders the demon had committed. Perhaps I just needed to give in to the fact that I was, at least while dreaming, a bit psychic. The idea didn't frighten me if it could be useful.

"I dreamed of a friend from school. Someone I haven't thought of in a while. But I realize, in seeing her, how much I miss her. I think it's the girl Mrs. Northe mentioned in her telegraph."

"Well? Tell me about her."

"Rachel was one of those girls who bore her disability—she

can't speak or hear—so graciously." I smiled. "It would have been annoying if she wasn't so darned sweet. Shyness made her seem more fragile than she was. But she noticed *everything*. I told her she'd make the perfect arch-villain. No one would suspect her in a million years. She smiled and blushed at everyone she met, the perfect foil.

"She was greatly amused by the idea of being an arch-villain. I was the first to get her out from under her rock," I said. "I passed her notes in class that made her laugh. Then one day she confessed that while she couldn't hear nor speak to the living, she heard the dead. That's when I knew she was a true friend."

Jonathon took a sharp breath at that. "We must attract the haunted to us, Natalie."

I shrugged. "I told her I envied her," I continued. "I was jealous that she could hear the dead when I had always wondered about Mother. She told me she'd gladly give up the gift and give it to me instead. It was likely more of a burden than she ever let on."

"I'm sure it was. What were *you* like in school?"

I thought about myself, my friends, my circumstances. "Rachel was fearfully obedient and always watching. Mary was a helpless romantic obsessed with saints. Edith did all our math homework. *I* was a restless prankster. They all kept waiting for the day I'd start speaking, as if my whole time there had been one big stunt. But I really did have a hard time with my voice. It took you for that," I said, running a hand over his as he smiled. "While I was good at my studies, I preferred changing out Sister Theresa's communion wine for whiskey."

Jonathon laughed. "I bet you were the most popular."

I rolled my eyes. "Winning the popularity contest among the 'unfortunates' at the Connecticut Asylum for the deaf and mute isn't something to write home about. Maggie and her snotty friends sure would have a laugh over that, now wouldn't they?"

"I'd have still fancied you if I'd been there."

"You're just saying that. Now, your turn," I murmured, suddenly blushing with what I wanted to ask. "Samuel mentioned you hadn't the time or inclination for a sweetheart. Is that true?" Jonathon raised an eyebrow. "I suppose it's not ladylike to ask—"

"No, it's all right," he said, bemused. "There were a few girls at balls, all of us curious about whether chaperones were really paying attention, a stolen kiss here or there, mostly for sport. Most young ladies found my scientific obsessions boring or frightening. All of them were being pushed to marry, so they preferred talk of courtship over medicine. It wasn't their fault. I've always been free to pursue my interests, but girls your age are forced to appear as though finding a husband is their sole preoccupation."

"But it isn't," I defended. "We've other interests."

"I know that now. And now I've finally found a girl who interests me."

I smiled. He snatched up my arm, kissing me on the open patch of skin between my glove and my sleeve. Where the rune had appeared...I bit my lip. "It's good you're going on to England to further break the spell. The dark magic might still be hanging on to me."

"Why? What happened?"

"A mark. On my wrist there. It faded. Surely I was just seeing things, exhausted—"

"Don't assume anything is your imagination," Jonathon said sternly. "Tell Mrs. Northe. She'll help counter any aftereffects and take care of you until my return."

I nodded. "If what I just saw in my nightmare is a clue, Rachel is in immediate danger. She's my first concern upon arrival. Mrs. Northe's telegram said I was again at the center of the mystery."

"Mrs. Northe won't be deterred."

It had occurred to me too, that all this revolved around Mrs. Northe; she is both a mother and harbinger of doom to us all. She uses us without giving us any proper training as to what we might encounter. And she's getting closer to my father, maybe Rachel. What might she inadvertently bring upon my friends and family? Did spiritualism bring more than one bargained for, even if one was trying to practice it in the best way possible?

I stared at Jonathon, suddenly terrified for him. "In my dream, I visited your study again, the one from your painting, but you weren't there and everything was in cinders."

"That's a good thing. Of course I wasn't there. I'm free. I doubt your dreams would operate the same way now that I'm released. I'm glad for the ashes. I wanted to torch that canvas. I would've, too, if I hadn't been worried about burning down the Metropolitan Museum of Art. I don't want anything left of that horror but dust. You're dreaming of our vindication, not an omen of worse to come."

I took his assurances and fell into his arms, and we watched a glorious sun set from one state to the next.

Chapter 5

The Germans have a good word for nightmare, or a nightmare dreamscape.

Schreckensvision.

The word itself is like shrieking when what enters your vision is too terrible to describe, and a long cry is the only thing to do. But I'll try to put words to the terrible.

If one could find a profession in nightmares, I'd have quite a career.

The hallway again, all medicinal sharpness and low-trimmed lamps. My every sense alive, I feel the damp moisture of the cool basement humidity on my face and on my arms below the sleeves of my robe. I'm traveling a frightful corridor in my dressing gown. I see a door marked with a word to chill any sane soul: MORGUE.

I *really* needed to stop reading Edgar Allan Poe before bed.

I enter the room, which is gray-white and cold.

There are bodies under sheets, laid on tables. Four of them, vague human shapes below the sheets. They are either being kept for family before transferred to a funeral parlor, or perhaps they'll be used as cadavers for science. Who knows?

Regardless, the vision was unpleasant. I hadn't been in a room with a dead body before, much less several, so my mind could only imagine what the stale smell of beginning decay was like. It was an unwelcome detail nonetheless. My dreams are nothing if not thorough.

And then, all at once, the dead bodies sat up.

Their white sheets slid down to reveal bare, gray flesh. With a raspy gasp, their blue mouths fell open.

And as they began to shriek, the bodies turned to me with sightless eyes, and yet they knew I was there or that I would be coming.

And I, like those bodies, shot up upon the train, glad to be alive and not under a morgue sheet myself.

With a gasp, I opened my eyes. I was on the train. With a cup of tea in hand. Jonathon had nodded off to sleep in our compartment shortly after nightfall. I, however, had been too restless for sleep. I'd made my way to the dining car for a calming cup of mint tea. Apparently it had soothed me right into sleep; unfortunately, it hadn't been able to lull my dreams.

An older woman a table away must have noticed my frightful expression. "Bad dreams?" she queried.

"Always," I replied.

"I advise you to pray."

"I do."

"Good, then."

I was relieved by the mercy of not being questioned further and excused myself to attend my sleeping "cousin." The moon had turned wide expanses of cornfields into dark plains of rustling velvet.

Mrs. Northe once told me that the spirit of my deceased mother told her that "the mysterious and wondrous and, yes, the truly terrible" would be laid at my feet. And that it would be best if the world left me to it. She had spoken grandly of a future, but what sort of future was this, veiled in nightmare? Is this what my mother wanted for me?

I'm seventeen. Eighteen in nine months. What match am I against dark forces?

There have been such advances since the transcontinental rail was completed more than a decade ago. Some trains reach eighty, nearly a hundred miles an hour on their express routes. It's nearly inconceivable that the whole of the country is laid open so swiftly.

Ever eastward, the behemoth steam engine roared me home. With every mile the towns grow more populated, the gravity of New York City calling souls from every walk of life. It was as if everyone in the whole world, if they strained to hear it, could feel the heartbeat of New York. Gazing out the windows, I saw the density of the city exploding around us as if we were plunged into a forest of brick and cast iron.

All tracks led to Grand Central Depot. From there, Jonathon and I will part ways. The thought has cast a pall over the entire trip; neither of us has wanted to speak of it.

As if Jonathon could hear my thoughts, he turned to me. "I'll miss you," he breathed as he brushed his lips against mine. I caught that tantalizing taste of bergamot from his Earl Grey tea.

This parting was inevitable. The pit of my stomach wrenched. I had to let him go to England alone, but since his welfare had been my personal responsibility since we met, letting him go was not easy. But he was no longer trapped in a painting, and I couldn't treat him as if he were. "*Promise* you'll return to New York—" I choked out.

That was my great fear: I'd lose him to London and he'd never come back, as if he were a dream that never really existed after all.

"You've got to show me Central Park, remember?" he said. "And all our adventures? At least ten world tours? It'll take years. We've so much to do."

He pulled me into his arms, as if the tighter he held me, the surer he would be to return. "If you *don't* come back, Jonathon Whitby, I will hunt you down—"

He drew back with a laugh. "Oh, I know you will. In disguise, no less. Wielding a dagger. I know better than to cross you, Natalie Stewart. You're too clever for me by half! And I love you for it."

Love. I blinked back tears. We gathered our belongings and opened the train car, our last vestige of privacy for a long while. It took everything inside me not to shove him back inside, lock the compartment, and hide us away from the world and everything in it that could harm us. But Jonathon, full of determination, was already heading down the aisle.

"I miss you already, so you'd better write soon," I warned, watching him move further up the aisle, a hat low over his beautiful face. "And keep a low profile."

He reached into his breast pocket and pulled out and put on the ridiculous eyeglasses. "Of course, my *Wilhelmina…*"

I laughed. The depot clattered and roared, thronged with passengers from every walk of life. Cornelius Vanderbilt needs to expand his station here, much like in Chicago. Jonathon stepped back to take my hand and lead me down the train steps onto the platform.

"Will you be all right to go home on your own?" he asked.

I nodded, gesturing to the streetcar line. "Shop girls and garment workers. It's the close of their shifts. Working- and middle-class girls, we ride together all the time with strangers as chaperones. Although I wish you could just stay the night—"

"This isn't the time to meet your father. I want to be on

better footing." Glancing at the large clock on a depot truss, he sighed. "I'll just catch the next departure."

"Go…" I say quietly.

"Kiss me," he demanded. I obliged. We got a scolding from a woman in a Salvation Army uniform. We kept kissing. A train whistle screamed. He pulled away.

"Keep busy." He flashed a grin, stepping away and up the platform. "You're less troublesome when you're busy."

"I am *not* troubleso—" My protest trailed off at his grin. He was absolutely right.

He blew me a kiss. I caught it and sent one back. He caught it and turned away, putting my kiss in his pocket and disappearing into the crowds.

The tears I had held back now rolled down my cheeks. I loved him more than I could say. Indeed, I hadn't even said those three words to him during this journey. I wanted to call to him, but the station was so loud and my voice failed.

"I love you," I murmured with a fervent prayer that he'd return to me in one piece.

Chapter 6

There were the sights of home first. Then the sounds. Ah, the hiss and scrape of the elevated rail on Lexington Avenue. The clang of trolley-car bells, the myriad clops of horse hooves and carriage wheels, the city of eternal motion, a city that barely rests. The city of humming noise. Music to my ears.

I realized then that I could never choose quiet over this thrum of life. But I truly appreciated having had the opportunity of experiencing otherwise. Just like a person chooses a partner and friends, perhaps given the chance, one chooses the home of his or her heart. Or has it affirmed. Even if New York would not have me again (I wasn't sure I would be welcomed home), I'd try to have New York once more.

Block by block, my pulse quickened. My hand shook as I put the key in the lock of my own home. It wasn't that I was frightened; I was nervous.

What sort of daughter brought curses, mediums, magic, and nightmares into her home?

Still, I was home, a place of safety and love. While my

condition of mutism made life difficult and painful for me, leaving me often alienated, I knew I was loved in this house. This quiet home, while touched by loss, was safe shelter. So as I turned the key in the lock, I thought about how much I feared to bring anything untoward to this sanctuary. I feared supernatural influence. I had to at least warn my father about what we were being dragged into.

Bessie poked her head around the banister and gasped a few choice phrases pulled from both her mother's—descended from slaves—and her German father's—descended from farmers—sides of the family. We weren't wealthy enough to have servants, and my father chafed at the idea of them anyway. But Bessie had been a friend of my mother's, and after her husband died helping build the Brooklyn Bridge, she was refused compensation for his death due to the color of her skin. With no place to turn, she had asked my father if he or any of his associates might need help around their homes. I was away at school at the time, but when I returned for the holidays she had seamlessly become a fixture in our home.

Bessie didn't run to hug me—I thought she might have swatted me—but went to the back of our flat and declared me to my father before I could even surprise her with a spoken hello. In fact, as I stood there in the entrance room that served as a modest parlor, the hello died in my throat, as if I'd forgotten how to speak again, as if all my advances were for naught. My hands clenched and unclenched in the muslin folds of my skirt.

Father appeared in his beige linen summer suit, freshly cleaned, one he usually saved for company. He was well-groomed and sported a loose, blue silk ascot. I stood at the door like a guest. He moved toward me warily, as if he thought I might bite.

What was wrong with me? A moment of truth: Lord knows I'd spoken when my life was on the line, but all Father had wanted was for his daughter to be normal, to communicate, to not be flawed, and here I was, healed. Yet nerves rattled me and I couldn't seem to prove my progress to him. Perhaps because it was so personal, perhaps because losing what I'd gained was my greatest fear.

"Natalie…" He approached. "Tell me you're here to stay. *Tell me.*"

If he was angry, he kept it well hidden. In that moment he sounded desperate. And it was that sentiment that had frozen me.

"Mrs. Northe told me everything," he continued, "and while I hardly believe it, I choose to believe that you did act for your safety, rather than as a fool girl in love."

He grabbed me by the arms and hugged me. And once I was spared from having to look at him, then the words came out in a torrent.

"Father, I-I'm sorry for everything, but yes, all of it was

true. But I'm scared what I might be bringing upon you. There are so many odd goings-on, and I'm not sure the danger has passed yet. Mrs. Northe is caught up in it too. I adore her, but I'm also frightened that if you court her…I'm just not sure, as well-intentioned as she is…I'm afraid we're omens of terrible luck—"

"Ill luck? I'd hope you'd think better of yourselves, and of me, than to assume that," came a voice from another room into ours. *Her* voice.

Father drew back sheepishly. I turned red.

"Mrs. Northe, I'm…"

"Sorry, I'm sure. And since I'm in your home, you ought to call me Evelyn, shouldn't you, or do you fear familiarity with me, after all I've done to help you?" Her tone was distinctly hurt.

She stood at the sitting-room threshold, a vision. She was tall and elegant in thin charcoal silks, skirts gathered into a bustle at the back, a long-sleeved bodice with many buttons accentuating her slender limbs, and black trim around a small V-line waist. Her long neck was accented by a wide black choker, and dark blond hair with a few strands of gray was piled artfully atop her head. She stared at me, hazel eyes wide and luminous with fierce intelligence and self-assurance. She was compelling and breathtaking and everything I wanted to be someday.

My emotions upon seeing her were complex: hesitation

against admiration, fierce longing for her to be a mother-confidante and a best friend, envy at her ageless statuesque beauty and her ease and confidence in the world, and fear for the things we'd been a part of together. I hated to wound her with my words, and yet she herself had said that sometimes darkness attracted darkness. What if she'd become some sort of inadvertent collector?

"There is some sense in what you say, Natalie," she continued finally. "I will give you that. But I ask you to give *me* a bit of credit."

I nodded. There was nothing I could say.

"It's good to have you home, child," my father said, and that was likely the best thing to say. But here came the anger, and I couldn't blame him. I'd flouted every rule society demanded of a proper young lady. "But you are under *my* roof. You have always been under my roof and under my guidance. Don't think this little adventure of yours has liberated you into an adult who does not still need the permission of her father. Until you are married off to a man *I approve of*, you are still subject to my will, young lady. Is that *perfectly* clear?"

I stared at him, at the green eyes and high cheekbones I'd inherited from him, at the smile lines around his mouth and the few gray hairs around his temple—a few more since I'd left—and I saw a man who had tried hard to do right by me, even if he was often at a loss.

There was a comfort in this, his laying down of the

law. It meant he cared, that I was never alone. Despite his hard tone, I smiled. It was good to be loved. Good to be a daughter. He must not have expected my smile, but I hadn't realized until that moment just how much I'd missed him, missed that chiding fatherly voice, and he found himself smiling back at me.

This eased us into a modicum of comfort while Bessie brought us coffee, pausing only to touch my cheek fondly, a glimmer of a tear in her eye. Perhaps she'd been afraid she'd lost me, too. The coffee could only distract us for so long. There were a thousand questions.

"So. This…*Lord Denbury* of yours. Is he…with you?" Father asked warily.

I suppose that question could have meant many things.

I replied carefully. "He is in London, dealing with the unfortunate affairs that robbed him of his estate and spread lies about his death."

"Ah, but will he reveal himself as who he is?" Father queried. "The case here was closed, but uneasily. Mrs. Northe saw to wrapping up details, but is it wise for your…young lord…to show himself?"

My father didn't know how to speak about Jonathon. His daughter had been courted by a soul in a painting when the man's body had been at large. It was hardly proper. He'd have to meet Jonathon. No father could refuse a man like Lord Denbury.

"Lord Denbury moves with caution and care. He's more patient than I am," I said, chuckling. "I daresay you'll meet him soon. He plans to return for me."

"Well, patience is…commendable," Father murmured, as if trying to convince himself to like Jonathon. "But if he returns for you, he does so through *me*."

"Didn't you see his letter to you, Father? Sent with the diary?"

"I did, but anyone can write a letter. He needs to say things to my face that I can believe."

"Where is that diary? I'd like to have it back."

I blushed, thinking of how I'd described our first kiss and many others. Wondrous as they were, such things were private. I hoped to God my father had respected my wishes and only read the pertinent bits about the case. Otherwise he might meet Jonathon with a gun. But truly, we'd only kissed—and touched. There really wasn't much harm in that, was there? I wasn't ruined. I was wrenched from this reverie by my father's reply:

"Your diary is in the care of the New York Police Department."

I felt the color drain from my face. Police officers would *certainly* read the kissing bits…"What? But I'm—"

"You're fine, yes, but I didn't know that immediately. You could have left a note, you know," he accused. "I went right to the police department to report your disappearance."

Thinking of the telegraph in the Chicago station, I sipped my coffee and picked at a cucumber sandwich. "Yes, I could have…but it was a…difficult night—"

"I'm just glad you're safe. But all of us acted in the spirit of survival and instinct. You would not expect a father not to report his daughter missing."

Mrs. Northe sat and watched our exchange. Knowing her clairvoyant tendencies, I wanted her to share what was on her mind, but the faraway look on her face meant she wouldn't be forthcoming, only maddeningly mysterious. So I turned to her.

"It was Rachel you wired me about, wasn't it?" I asked. "I think she's in danger."

"Yes, I believe she is. When she came to call, inquiring after you, she was so surprised that I could sign that she quite opened up about her situation. I didn't like what she had to say about her employer."

"Who might that be?"

"Dr. Liam Preston."

I clapped my hands over my mouth in shock. Father looked at me in alarm. Mrs. Northe sighed. "I take it, by your reaction, that this is no coincidence."

"He…Preston was there!" I gasped. "In St. Paul. He was visiting Lord Denbury's friend, Samuel Neumann, another doctor, en route to learn from a family of doctors in Rochester. That's why we weren't comfortable staying.

Jonathon saw an aura crackling with fire around Preston—same as the demon's but to a lesser degree. And he recognized Preston from a visit he'd paid to Lord Denbury's clinic in London. He was asking for bodies. Jon—*Lord Denbury* sent him away empty handed. He thinks that's when he was first targeted, and while Samuel wasn't there at the time, Preston went for him now."

Mrs. Northe whistled low, shaking her head. "A resurrectionist added to the mix," she mused. "The plot thickens."

Father kept looking between us and finally burst. "What the devil is this nonsense all about, you two?" He leaned toward me, his fair skin pinking. "Ever since the business with that blasted painting, you've had some secret self, full of codes and ridiculous notions as if supernatural espionage was your new profession, and I won't stand for it!" He whirled suddenly on Mrs. Northe. "And, Evelyn, you do nothing but aid and abet. You're at the very heart of it. Natalie is right in questioning you…"

Evelyn? She was *Evelyn* now? Did she call him Gareth?

"Why Gareth, we've been over this. You heard Helen."

She was calling him Gareth. And Helen…did she mean my mother?

"Through a strange *deaf girl*," my father countered. "How on earth could I trust information from beyond the grave that you might be influencing?"

"Because she said things, through Rachel, that Rachel could not have known."

I stood, this news like a slap in the face. "Wait just one moment!" I cried. "You had a séance? You contacted Mother? *Rachel* did? Why didn't *you* say so?"

"We're saying so now," Mrs. Northe retorted. "After you left, this was the only way I could calm your father and not have him running off after you. He needed to understand that some things were beyond him. We didn't conspire to keep anything from you."

"I planned to tell you, Natalie," my father contributed. "You only just now walked through the door."

I sat, stung. Suddenly, I felt as my father must feel, kept ignorant and left out, and I hated it. "Well, what did Mother say? Lord knows I've asked her to talk to me! How could you do that without me?"

"I didn't think I needed your permission to talk to my dead wife," my father snapped. "You're hardly in a position to take offense, Natalie, after what you've put me through—"

"Your mother repeated what she said to me when you were solving Denbury's mystery, Natalie," Mrs. Northe replied calmly, diffusing the tone. "You're meant for battles she could never have fathomed. She has seen great things between life and death. You are meant to be a messenger and soldier. We must leave you to the circumstances presented to you and help you as best we can."

That sounded biblical, like I was some prophet or tragic martyr. I didn't want to be either, and I most certainly didn't want to be a "soldier." But what else could I say or do? And Father was right. I was in no position to be angry, considering that most fathers would, after my antics, send me away to some sort of ward for misbehaving girls.

"Is that why I'm psychic now, too?" I asked Mrs. Northe. "I dreamed about Rachel. I know she's in trouble. I've dreamed of a morgue, of dead bodies sitting up. Am I clairvoyant, now? Prophetic?"

"Dear God." Father put his head in his hand, rubbing the crease of his worried brow.

Mrs. Northe sipped tea before replying. "When your soul communed with Jonathon in the painting, it opened mental doors that could not have been opened otherwise. Jonathon, too, has gained a second sight since his incident. His ability to see auras will help him see danger directly. The paths of light are not leaving you defenseless against the walk of darkness."

"Evelyn, please," my father begged. "Can't she be spared all this? Can't you enlist your friends upstate, fellow spiritualists, in this cause instead?"

"It's too late," she replied simply. "Natalie is inextricably a part of the unfolding drama. Jonathon, too. As am I."

I closed my eyes briefly, fighting back tears, struggling to speak, struggling to come to terms. "Please do not...talk to Mother again without me," I managed, dabbing a handkerchief to my eyes.

I was still reeling about *Gareth* and *Evelyn*. Initially, flirtation between my father and Mrs. Northe had been novel. I'd never thought of my father as a possible suitor to anyone. But this was becoming something real that would change the dynamic forever, something that would at long last displace not only me, but my mother. I couldn't think about that now.

"Have you been in touch with Rachel since the séance?" I asked, my jaw still clenched.

"I went to look in on her at the hospital," Mrs. Northe replied. "But Preston's wing has gone dark and quiet, and she wasn't there. A matron at the door said Preston was traveling while his wing is under renovation. Rachel left a note for you. Hopefully her address is therein."

"We must go to her tomorrow."

My father stared back and forth at us as if he wondered what he'd let into the house.

I was exhausted and had no more energy left for this or any other conversation.

"It's good to be home," I said, kissing my baffled father on the head and Mrs. Northe on the cheek. "And it will be good to get a good night's sleep."

I took Rachel's note and went upstairs.

There, I began reading and wished I hadn't.

Chapter 7

My dear Natalie,

It's been too long. Don't scold me for hiding under rocks. I came to see you, and while I regret I missed you, what a pleasant surprise that there was a woman when I came to call who could speak in sign language! Mrs. Northe signed very lovely things about you and said you were on vacation out west. I hope you are having a lovely time and that this finds you well when you return.

I've thought of you often since I left Connecticut to tend Aunt Miriam in her illness. I still have all your notes from class. I read them to put me in a good mood.

I'm sorry I never wrote after I left. I got so caught up with Auntie. You remember her, don't you? From the Seder she hosted when she came to visit?

Do you speak at all? How is your condition? I kept expecting words to burst out of you. Like a bird from a cage. Not that I would be able to hear them. But I imagine reading your lips would be as amusing as your notes.

After Aunt Miriam died, it was like I died too. She was so full of fire. To see her waste away was shocking. It wasn't fair. I was angry at God for taking her. I guess I still am. I'm even more angry that her spirit didn't stay to keep me company. I guess it means she's happy and at rest. But I'm very lonely. I've written to my family in Germany, but they don't have any money to bring me home. I'll have to save for the trip.

I'm hoping that since you didn't run away from me when I said I heard the dead, you'll bear with me now. I need your advice.

I work for Dr. Preston in the basement of the German Hospital on Seventy-Seventh Street where Aunt Miriam was being treated. The moment I saw him, I heard a voice in my head say: "That man is my husband. He'd give anything in the world to know I am all right. To speak with me. It's his love for me that won't let me go…"

I took a patient's chart and wrote that message on a blank space. When Dr. Preston saw the words, he was shocked. He told me they could only be from his dead wife, Laura. He said he'd pay me if I spoke with her more and would tell him what she said.

I agreed. It was the only way I could think of to help support Aunt Miriam—even though I could never tell her about it. Suffragette and union organizer she may have been, but she did have her limits.

I never saw Laura. I don't see spirits. I feel them. I hear what they want me to hear. But Laura told Dr. Preston, through me, to let her go and that she would be all right. That she loved him. Everything you'd hope the dead would say.

Then he started bringing others into his office. He'd call me in while I was helping the maids in the hospital. In his office where wide windows let in bright light, some sorrowful face would look up, hoping I could share something from someone they had lost.

Sometimes I connected. I'd write out words or phrases. Objects or articles of clothing, trinkets or favorite jewelry helped make contact. I try to make sense of the scraps. But spirits are scattered echoes of us. It isn't like sending letters. I'm like a faulty telegraph cable. Now and then a choppy message comes through.

More often than not, though, I don't connect. I try to scrawl notes saying it means loved ones passed peacefully. Hardly a comfort to those who want "proof." But I don't know any more about what happens after death now than I did as a child, clinging to the beliefs of my people.

My séances have been moved into a small, gray basement room. Dr. Preston calls it my office, but it's more like a dungeon. I'm a door down from the morgue. Dr. Preston thinks if I'm closer to death, I'll be able to communicate better with it. Even on warm days, nothing can shake the chill.

Dr. Preston has started bringing in trinkets on his own,

possessions from those who died in his wing of the hospital. Once I touch the items, he puts them in a box and asks me to connect the spirit who owned them. He claims he's testing how materialistic a spirit is and that I'm helping his experiments on the soul. But I don't think a spirit should be encouraged by anything but seeking its rest. I'm afraid that by tying spirit to object, I'm participating in an unnatural part of the human relationship between the living and the dead.

What do you think, Natalie? Am I doing something wrong?

Dr. Preston was so passionate, so desperate. It's hard for me to say no to the living. But I wonder what the dead think of it all. All I can sense is sadness, which worries me.

Today a new box arrived. Again Dr. Preston asked me to connect a spirit with the item therein. But I don't know what it was. With lockets or other personal items, I have the piece in hand. Not a box to separate the connection. But Preston said it was extremely private and I'd been requested by family members not to touch anything directly. Yet no family members were present. Dr. Preston just had me make sure I asked for a name.

Even if I wanted to play Pandora with that box, it was locked. All I heard was a spirit's name. A name and lots of crying.

I try to pray out my troubles at the synagogue a few blocks away to lift my sorrows up. Like prophets did. But I'm scared. Light a candle for me, Natalie, like in the seder. I'm afraid I'm bad luck. When you receive this, if you could write or visit me, I'd be grateful.

Your friend,
Rachel

Of course, a nightmare followed that night.

Rachel appeared in that room where I'd first seen her, a small, dim room. Her "office." She sat at a round table, a leather-bound box before her. A red droplet pooled at one of the corners. The room was freezing cold, making my breath a cloud. Rachel didn't look at me at first. She was dazed, focused on the box, her hands limp on either side of it.

I took a step closer, and she turned to me in a jarring motion, her dark hair disheveled, her pale face gaunt. Her expression, which was usually so soft and amenable, was horrified, her dark eyes wide and bloodshot.

"Make it stop," she signed to me slowly, her hands shaking to form the words.

Then she put her hands on the lid of the box. And opened it.

Inside was a severed human hand.

Voices from unseen bodies started screaming. So did I.

A moment later my father was at the door, having groggily flung it wide without knocking. "Natalie, what on earth—"

The sight of my room and my father steadied me.

"Nightmare," I said.

Father rubbed his face, worried. "Mrs. Northe said you needed to go far from the city to clear yourself of the cloud of dark magic. Have you done so? Did you go far enough to break free? Or does the curse linger on in your dreams?"

These were not terms my father was used to. He hated such talk, so it was valiant of him to try and relate to me. "I…I can't say. But nightmares are nothing new, Father. I've always had them."

He came forward and kissed me on the head. "I wish you didn't," he soothed, and went back to the door. He turned. "Tomorrow, why don't you meet me at the end of my workday and we'll go visit your mother. What do you think?"

I felt a smile break over my face, and with it, the shadows of nightmare rolled away. "I'd love that."

"So would I. Please rest, darling. No matter what you've gotten wrapped up in, it's so good to have you home."

A stray tear fell from my eye. "It's good to be home."

Chapter 8

First thing in the morning, when I came down to the breakfast table for eggs, Father handed me an envelope marked "Cunard." That was a steamer line.

In the same instant that my heart thrilled at the prospect of an important note from Jonathon, it chilled. What if it was something terrible? Father stared at me, as if waiting for me to elaborate. I ran to my room, my heart thudding. I didn't want to open the envelope in front of Father. I was still trying to protect him, even though he was making every effort to keep pace with our strange events.

"News from your lord, is it?" he called after me, bewildered.

"I hope…" I called back from the top of the stair.

"I'm off to work," he said. "I assume Evelyn is entertaining you today?"

Evelyn. I was going to have to get used to that familiarity. "Yes," I called. "Have a lovely day. I'll meet you in your office this evening and we'll go to Woodlawn. I love you."

"I…love you too," he said, surprised that I was the first to say it.

I tore open the envelope. My relief was immediate when I could tell it was not news of doom or death. But it was an odd instruction.

TRANS-ATLANTIC TELEGRAPH COMPANY
Across the Veil. Booth's Theatre. Ask Veil about the last time he saw my family—if he remembers anything odd. —J

I thought a moment about what or who he meant. I realized he must mean Nat, his actor friend who'd been involved with the London clinic.

I'd have to ask Mrs. Northe to go with me to the show. I couldn't afford to be wary of her. She'd so swiftly become inextricably wrapped up in my life that I couldn't seem to operate without her. This chafed at my increasingly independent sensibilities. But I didn't understand operating in high society—or much of any society really. I was nowhere without the calm, capable guidance of Mrs. Northe, and I needed to accept that fact. It seemed I needed to accept her increasing presence in my *home* as well.

Father is a museum man, a man of static art and the occasional concert. He finds theater a bit silly. Not one for crowds unless they stare silently in appreciation of a canvas, so I couldn't ask him to go. And if he suspected any more foul play surrounding the Denbury name, I was afraid he'd forbid Jonathon to come anywhere near me.

Bessie announced that Mrs. Northe's carriage had pulled up. It was as if Mrs. Northe knew I needed her. Of course she knew.

I darted out and down the stairs, kissing Bessie once on the cheek, which seemed to surprise her. I was through taking the people in my life for granted.

Once I ducked in the carriage, I handed Mrs. Northe the letter from Rachel.

"Read it."

She did and paled. "Oh, my. I wonder what's in those boxes."

"If it's what was in my dream, I fear even more for her," I murmured. Mrs. Northe stared at me a moment, and thankfully didn't ask me to elaborate upon my nightmare.

We gave the driver Rachel's address on Seventy-Seventh Street. We rang and rang. No one answered. There was no activity in the curtains of her floor. No one was there. We then strode an avenue over to Preston's wing of the hospital to find it still shuttered. Mrs. Northe paused a moment outside. She closed her eyes.

"I sense no one within. Just…death."

"And Rachel?" I asked fearfully. "Can you sense if she's alive?"

"She is, but she's fled somewhere. Scared. That's all I can gather."

"I've been given an instruction," I told Mrs. Northe later that afternoon over tea. "Jonathon sent a telegraph. I must attend a performance here in the city. A show called *Across the Veil*. Do you know it?"

Mrs. Northe nodded. "Nathaniel Veil. I hear he's quite the talented young man. Popular with the young ladies, too," she said with a knowing look. "Take care."

"Well, he's a friend of Lord Denbury. An attractive man like Jonathon invites attractive company," I said, and had a sudden panic at the thought of him being mobbed by society ladies when he returned to England. "Jonathon thinks Mr. Veil may have seen his parents just before their death."

"Any further news from London?"

I shook my head.

"Have you a suitable gown? You'll get more out of Mr. Veil if you're at your beautiful best," she said with a smirk.

I thought of my one evening dress, the green one, the one Maggie and her friends had made fun of. It must have been the look on my face that made her drain her tea, pay the bill, and drag me back to the carriage.

"Well, then. Ladies' Mile, my dear. I never did get to take you shopping."

I grinned despite myself. Wary as she made me at times, she always pulled me back into her warmth, her spell impossible to break. "You're too kind, Mrs. Northe."

"I do try. Maybe one day you'll even call me Evelyn."

I looked at her a moment. Somehow, I just couldn't. I felt more comfortable thinking of her in a position of authority, and she was still too mysterious for me to call her by her first name, to accept that she was family.

Ladies' Mile.

On Fifth and Sixth avenues, the boulevards of castle-like stores are filled with unimaginable treasure. It was the only place a respectable woman can walk the street unescorted, as she is there upon the harmless business of beauty and fashion. Ladies' Mile is the one sphere in the city where women are allowed wholly to rule.

I'd passed this parade of palaces with trepidation, as I was a woman who could *almost* be welcome there. My clothes were fine enough not to be escorted from the buildings, but I'd be regarded in the same way I saw the finery: with aspiration. As if it was something I could hope for, nearly reach, but not quite grasp.

With Mrs. Northe by my side it was a different story.

The tailors and clerks knew her by name, and in a whirlwind of satin, organza, bombazine, taffeta, lace, and thousands of buttons and clasps, I was transformed time and again into a princess. I didn't say much through it all. I really *couldn't*, in fact.

Each store was staggering in its interior, as if they were palaces or opera houses.

The wide, yearning eyes of each seamstress and tailor, counter girl, and milliner—all of them my class and striving, surely wishing they too could have a fairy godmother like mine—were so overwhelming that they triggered that anxious clench in my throat that constricted my speech again. I managed a brief hello, enough that they didn't think me incapable, but Mrs. Northe did most of the talking. After all, she'd be doing the buying. I hoped Jonathon might offer her something in return for all this kindness; I was doing *his* bidding in this business, after all. I hated to owe anyone anything, and things like this only put me further in debt to Mrs. Northe.

It was, ironically, at A. T. Stewart's (no relation, I only wish) that Mrs. Northe and I finally settled on something, as if everything else had just been whetting our appetites, and I realized she'd been dissatisfied only so that she could save the best for last.

"Now, from what I know of Veil and his tastes, it has to be something dark. Dark and dramatic. What is your favorite color, Natalie?"

"Purple," I managed after a moment, needing to press past my comfort in quiet colors.

"Indeed, you'll look ravishing in a deep, dark plum. It should be trimmed darkly with onyx beads and starched black lace. You'll see why."

Jonathon had said something about how Nathaniel was

as fond as I was of Poe and dressed daily in mourning. This evening's costuming should fit his bill.

We found something breathtaking in a purple that looked nearly blood-black from some angles and then shimmering rich plum in other lights, the sheen of the taffeta making it like a jewel shining darkly in its cut angles. The dress was beaded in black, and satin ribbon trim gathered up the bustle at the rear. Trim gave elegant definition to each ruffle of the layered skirts, the taffeta brushing out around me a foot in each direction with a gathered train. Flattering to curves, the dress had a tapered, V-line bodice, a plunging neckline, and capped sleeves opening to a bell at mid-forearm. Just a bit of wrist was left exposed once netted lace gloves, each clasped by a black pearl, glided over my palms.

I stared at myself and didn't recognize the woman in the trifold mirrors. The fitting-room attendant, Fanny, truly seemed to enjoy her job, as if she were a sculptor creating a goddess. Indeed, once my corset was tightened and I was cinched, clasped, and buttoned into these many exquisite layers, I was scared to move and thought I'd best be as still as a sculpture.

Fanny had swept up my hair and clasped it with pins hidden beneath a beaded, ostrich-feather fascinator. She left a few errant curls around my face "for whimsy and seduction," she murmured with a grin as she lightly rouged my cheeks with powder that had a faint, glimmering hint of purple.

In this light, all my colors seemed heightened. The auburn of my hair seemed to glow with its faint red traces, and my green eyes were lit as if a candle were flickering behind thin peridot. All I could think was how I wished Jonathon could see me now so he would know for certain that I could rise to the title of Lady Denbury and fill the role.

Mrs. Natalie Whitby, Lady Denbury.

Oh, that does sound nice, doesn't it?

"Natalie, are you pleased?" Mrs. Northe said softly, as if she was reading my mind. Perhaps she was. I blushed and nodded vigorously. "We'll take this, Fanny. Nicely done."

Fanny clapped her hands. "Brava. You're fit to make some lord seek you as his lady."

"Oh, indeed, she quite plans to," Mrs. Northe said, chuckling.

When I was back in my chemise and petticoat, Fanny helped me into my own dress, a rag by comparison, a utilitarian dress I didn't need help with, but I accepted her help anyway with murmured thanks. I clutched my new black lace fan, an accessory that was a must during a New York summer and would replace my small, worn wooden one. I opened and shut it nervously a few times.

Once Fanny had gone to ring up the bill, I leaned into

Mrs. Northe, murmuring: "I wish Jonathon could see me in this. But I'm afraid I'll make a fool of myself before a star of the stage. You see…I don't always…present myself well when nervous."

"Natalie Stewart, you're the bravest young person I've ever met."

"When it's life and death, perhaps I have my moments. But in day-to-day life, in crowds, new encounters, I…falter."

"If in moments of *crisis* you are at your best, then you've a gift the rest of the world should envy. Think of meeting Veil, then, as life and death. If dire situations force your impetuous bravery, then you must think of anything involved with Lord Denbury as such. He needs you now, just like then."

I nodded. That would have to do.

On our way out, I noticed a tray full of sparkling baubles, hair-pins, and brooches. I paused.

"See something you like?"

I shook my head. "I was just thinking of Maggie. She'd like these. How is she?"

"Still in trouble. I didn't tell her mother everything about the ritual mess she'd made in the Metropolitan after dark, but enough to make Maggie regret it. She's quite under house arrest. You should go pay her a visit."

"I'd like to. I do want to be her friend."

Mrs. Northe sighed. "I'm afraid you're better to her than

I am, and I'm her aunt. Thank you for having the patience with her that I no longer have. It would be good of you to go. Her calling hours are Tuesday and Thursday afternoons."

"I'll do so this week."

Mrs. Northe and I picked out a hair-pin and brooch set I could take as a present.

A few hours later, I met Father in his office. He immediately left his paperwork and escorted me to the door. He seemed to be done taking my presence for granted too. Usually he would have made me wait.

We rode the Lexington Avenue Elevated rail north as far as we could, then a trolley into the Bronx until the vast necropolis of Woodlawn Cemetery—a garden-style cemetery founded seventeen years ago, in the year of my birth—spread out before us.

We strolled toward the Gothic stone pillars and iron gates. Familiar ornate tombs loomed in the verdant distance.

"Tell me again how you and Mother met."

My father eyed me. "Again? Haven't I told you this a thousand times?"

"It's important."

He smiled, the green eyes I'd inherited from him twinkling. "It was at the Cooper Union. A speech."

"But not just *any* speech," I added.

Here began Father's tale, which I'd never tire of hearing:

"Abraham Lincoln's speech, the one that would make him president. But I didn't know about that then. I was only vaguely interested in politics. All I wanted was to open a museum. I was told potential investors for all sorts of noble causes frequented the Union, so I was sure to bring my friend Weiss, who knew everyone who was anyone, along to help me navigate the crowd.

"I was admittedly riveted by the odd-looking, tall man whose voice was reedy, almost a joke of himself, but no one laughed when Lincoln built to his conclusion. Everyone held their breath. But for me, that great man was outshone by a woman who stood near the front of the dais: tall, elegant, and utterly radiant. Weiss saw the object of my stare and chuckled: "*Viel Gluck…*Lots of luck, friend."" I asked Weiss who she was.

""*Germania* in all her glory,"" he said, ""as painted by Philipp Veit in the heart of Germany's democratic revolution. Currently she's giving the Lutheran Society hell. She'd like them to ordain women.""

"I laughed. I could see from across a room of breathless people that she was full of fire and life. Lincoln would go on to be president, and I knew my life would never be the same for having seen Helen Heidel. Thankfully for us, she cared about art as much as any cause. Once Lincoln was done stunning the crowd, Weiss introduced me to her and presented my cause. And by grace alone and a good bit

of planning the Metropolitan, she came to care for me."
Father's tale ended as we reached the gates.

*And then she died in the street. Rescuing me, at the age of
four, from an oncoming carriage.*

That was the part none of us said. But I thought about
it every day.

The familiar bent, old woman near the open, wrought-iron
gate looked up at us with a stunning smile that transformed
her wrinkled face. She wore a drooping, tattered shawl, and
at her side was a baby pram overflowing with cut flowers.

I knew what to look for: black-eyed Susans, golden daisy-
like flowers with coal-brown centers. These were Mother's
favorite. Father used to call her his Black-Eyed Helen for her
dark eyes and bright personality. Laying these bright flowers
down on a smooth gray stone was my earliest memory.

I pointed to the lone bright sprigs that were being
drowned out by tumbling roses.

"They're wildflowers, of course," my father explained,
gesturing to the flowers as we crossed through the gate
toward the stone mausoleums marching ahead of us,
sloping rows of small Gothic and Romanesque houses in
a silent city of death, shaded by lush trees and shrubbery.
"But a part of your mother was always a bit wild, as if she
walked barefoot in the field like a goddess of spring when
merely crossing busy Madison Avenue. All auburn hair
and dark eyes," my father said gently, touching one of the

dark hearts of the black-eyed Susans, "yet with such bright and golden light around her." He ran a finger along the bright yellow-golden petals.

I'd heard this, or some variant of it, a hundred times. I'll never tire of it. Father said these words like it was the first time he'd ever said them. A private liturgy, a poetic ritual on behalf of a woman he loved more than I could have understood as a child. But I was beginning to understand now.

We wound our way through lanes marked with the names of trees, past great monuments and small, some nestled cozily into the ground, others towering obelisks pointing to the sky. And angels. Beautiful angels. Looking up and seeing angels: that was another formative memory.

Around a gentle bend we found the Stewart plot, a rectangular space allotted with granite stones yet to be carved, space enough for Father and me. Only one name was there: HELEN, BELOVED WIFE AND MOTHER.

I was always the one to lay the flowers. We used to do this weekly when I was home, but we had fallen away from it since I was done with school. I resolved not to neglect her so again.

Father wandered off. There were times when he didn't quite know what to do with me, but more often than not, he sensed my mood and when I wanted privacy. Our time spent in silence for so many years had developed its own language.

I spent countless moments just looking at her name and

the inscription, as I'd done a thousand times. As if that stone was a Rosetta Stone to her life and death and could explain why she was taken from me so soon.

As usual, I begged for a sign. I begged for her to speak to me, for her spirit to kiss my forehead. But nothing.

"Mother, if you brought me into the strange life I'm now leading, or at least if you condone it, please don't stay silent when I need you."

The rustle of the trees was the only answer. The sun was setting. My father had his moment at the graveside, and once I linked my arm into his, it was time to go.

"It's good," I said quietly, "to resume our routine."

Father nodded. "But things will change. You're changing. I'm changing."

It was true. There was no denying that eventually our family dynamic would change. If Mrs. Northe became my new mother. If Jonathon actually did ask for my hand… But Father didn't say anything further. And I was glad. One upheaval at a time.

After a small dinner of soup and bread, I excused myself to my room.

"I've got to get my beauty sleep," I said with a smile to Father and Bessie.

"Oh? And why is that?" Bessie queried.

"Because tomorrow Mrs. Northe puts me in a fine dress, and I go to the *theater*."

Chapter 9

Booth's Theater at Sixth Avenue and Twenty-Third Street was grand as one would expect. It had been the prominent theater since it opened eleven years prior. With a granite exterior in the Renaissance style, it seated nearly two thousand people.

Tall posters outside the grand entrance shouted ACROSS THE VEIL! The poster featured an imperious, dramatic, shadowed figure, a raven upon his shoulder, eyes blazing and the outlines of women swooning around his feet as his cloak billowed against a dark and stormy night. I was impressed that Veil commanded a theater that had housed the foremost theatrical talent of our day, albeit for a brief run.

Golden filigree and sculpting adorned each box and level, while glittering chandeliers and sconces reflected the gaslight and cast only flattering shadows about the house. The rolling murmur of the crowd was like a lulling tide. The rustling of fine fabrics and gossiping whispers hidden behind lace and feather fans reminded me that this was a place where society was made and broken, much like a ball, where everyone was displayed. Particularly us.

I should have known Mrs. Northe would have a prominent box, and that gazes would inevitably turn our way when our usher opened the box door, pulled back the curtain, and gestured for us to step into the warm velvet interior and to our seats.

From a lifetime of being ignored as a mute, I was the one used to watching, not being watched. It was unnerving. I knew so little about Mrs. Northe, really. Who her friends were, what her late husband, an industrialist, had actually done to make a good deal of money, or what void I filled in her life.

"You're wondering about me," Mrs. Northe said. I bit my lip. "It's all right. Our goings-on have had little to do with outside society. You see me waving, and you know no one I know. My late husband made his fortune in coal," she began. "A dirty business in more ways than one. Philanthropy became my passion to offset the ruthless companies. Peter tried very hard to be a good man and run a good business, but it wasn't perfect. He never interfered in my charity, nor my spiritual affairs. I loved him very much. He was taken from me too soon."

She glanced around the auditorium, blinking back tears. "I'm not exactly sure I've recovered from Peter's death, even after eight years. All my gifts were useless to save him. I suffered that frustration alone." She looked away, her body tense, emotions held in like a tightening corset. "To these people, I'm merely a wealthy patron of the arts who is rumored to hold an occasional séance. My dear friends are few and far flung, some upstate, the rest in Chicago."

"Your gifts…were they with you since childhood?"

"At least in part. But everything sharpened the day I watched a ship sail in with Civil War wounded and dead. I saw the ghost of my beloved cousin, fainted right into the river, and nearly died. In that space between life and death I understood that I had a purpose: to use my gifts for love and peace while so much hateful darkness seized the world. I understood then that there will always be a war over souls, and I chose in that moment to live and to fight for the light."

I shuddered at the word "war." I hadn't bargained on being a solider in that battle, but I'd been drafted anyway.

"As to why I remain involved with you, Natalie," she continued, "Fate brought you to me when your father wished to buy Denbury's portrait. The moment we met, my gifts told me our fates were entwined. You came at just the right time. I was terribly lonely and bored, my gifts atrophied.

"None of these people," she waved her hand about the box seats and glittering jewels, "are brave, bold, or terribly interesting. Nor are they my friends. Nor are my talents useful in their shallow worlds. Wealth buys you visibility but not true friends, not happiness. Remember that. I think Lord Denbury knows this well, but in this striving, greedy city, don't you forget it. You are meant for so much more than an average, petty life."

I sat stunned, taking in everything she'd said. I hadn't expected her to open up so, but I was glad she had. Before I could query further, the orchestra in the pit struck a melancholy chord. A slow dirge of a tune began, similar to Bach's infamous organ Toccata, yet original and dramatic, mournful and glorious. As the music swelled, the gallery gates were opened and an intriguing crowd pressed forward.

Into an open, standing-room gallery at the front of the theater filed a group of men and women entirely in black, as if they'd all just come from a funeral. Yet their faces were full of excitement and expectation, as if waiting for a god to descend. Some clasped hands, and some waved from one side of the gallery to the other, as if they all knew one another. Many glanced shyly at the ground, and in each body—I could interpret the language of each one's body as if they were speaking—there was a trembling vulnerability conquered only by the radiant excitement on their faces when they stared toward the footlights, which cast a glow upon the red curtain.

The program stated only: "Assembled works of Great and Melancholy Literature, resonant to Body and Spirit, and Transcendent of Mortal Coil. Music inspired by Dark themes from Bach and Chopin."

"When he first appeared on the theatrical circuit," Mrs. Northe said, "a friend in Baltimore raved about him, saying I'd appreciate his sensibilities. Though he never embraces spiritualism directly, the notion of body, spirit, and transcendence of mortal coil are parallel."

"And he has quite a fascinating following." I nodded toward the crowd below.

"Everyone needs a muse," Mrs. Northe said appreciatively, drinking in the crowd, examining them, perhaps using her gifts for insight. "Especially the melancholy. We live in a Gothic age. It's refreshing to see a crowd who acknowledges it, those who cannot ignore pain and darkness yet come together in celebration, a living memento mori…"

There came a sung note, and everything went still and dark.

Girls in the black-clad crowd swooned, leaning on beaux at their side or holding hands with their friends. If I wasn't mistaken, many of the boys swooned too.

Out stepped Nathaniel Veil. He was tall, black haired, onyx eyed, and clad in a fine black dress suit, his presence wild. If Jonathon had the clear breeding of an English lord, Nathaniel Veil seemed as though he could have been raised by a mythological god in some forbidden forest before being taught how to be a gentleman.

He sang, and I recognized the lyrics as from Shakespeare's *Twelfth Night* because of the chorus: "For the rain it raineth every day…"

Veil's arrangement was keening, the strings supporting his vocals as if he wasn't just one lone man in black but his own chorus. Somehow he was singing for the world and to each one of us, balancing grandeur and intimacy.

The song led into poetry, Poe's "The Raven." The curtain rose, revealing a castle, and Veil stepped into a red-drenched chamber the narrator would leave "nevermore." The scene was a Gothic novel come to life, and for the next hour, we were treated to a cavalcade of characters and music, from the literary adventures and outrageous trials of Otronto and Udolpho, to the verse of *Hamlet* and more from my personal favorite, Poe.

A celebration of sadness and mystery, morbid and macabre, ghosts and haunting, somehow the play was spectacularly *alive*. With slight changes of wardrobe, a cloak or hat added or removed, Veil transformed fluidly between characters. All of them, despite their darkness, struggled on toward a faint light at the end of a long tunnel, toward hope. Toward life. And Veil's magnetic presence never let us forget how very alive he was as he discussed crossing the veil itself.

After the curtain call and encore, a rousing rendition of Poe's "Annabel Lee" (so fitting to end with Poe's final completed poem), I sat in the darkness of the box for a moment, watching as the rest of the house adjusted to the brightening house lights. The gas jets lifted their flames to a warm yellow height, and I felt like those in the fore seemed to, that I was being roused from a trance. Those swaying bodies in black below all looked to be in the same pleasant stupor.

"That was incredible," I said. Mrs. Northe nodded and we remained seated in silence a while longer before I steeled my courage for my task.

"How does one get…backstage?" I asked.

"Leave it to me."

Skirts rustling, we exited into the dress circle where other murmurings of fine fabric were layered with delighted whispers (or horrified murmurs, depending on if the ladies liked the show). Regardless, no one was unaffected. One either loved or hated it. One had to be willing to let go and release themselves to the adventure. Much like the recent course of my life.

We descended past stately statuary and draped fabrics of velvet and brocade, down to the orchestra level and beyond into an alcove where a tall man stood miserable guard at a stage entrance. A throng of young women in black stood a quiet vigil. Their stillness was far more disconcerting than if they'd been loudly clamoring for Veil.

"Hello, Mr. Bell," Mrs. Northe said sweetly. "I've a young lady that needs to see Mr. Veil."

"Don't they all," Bell drawled.

Unruffled, Mrs. Northe squared her shoulders, saying, "She's a visitor on behalf of Lord Denbury. And you, Mr. Bell, know better than to insult an emissary of British aristocracy."

Mr. Bell raised an eyebrow and we were let by, to the pouting, angry murmurs of the pit crowd.

"Really? Did I just get *hissed* at?" I whispered. Mrs. Northe laughed.

Past a phalanx of black curtains in the wings, a shaft of gaslight fell upon a doorway. A paper raven had been tacked at eye level and the painted script on it declared: VEIL.

"I'll leave you to it," Mrs. Northe said, turning to walk away.

"You're going to leave me alone with him?" I gasped. I didn't want the quiet throng outside in the stalls to kill me. "Won't that appear—"

"Oh, come now, he's a dear friend of your beloved. You've put yourself in far more compromising positions than this. You'll get more out of the man on your own than with my being a chaperone."

"That's your instinct, is it?" I said warily.

"I'll make sure no one besmirches your reputation, though no one would know any better. It's good that you were never introduced into society, my dear. Invisibility has its privileges." She walked away.

It wasn't that I feared Veil. I was overwhelmed and I didn't want to make a fool of myself, afraid language might escape me. "I'm here for Jonathon," I murmured, and knocked on the door.

"Ah, Bell, you've let someone by?" came a deep, accented voice from within, a bit less affected than it had been on the stage and similar to Jonathon's, high class or at least pretending to be. "She'd best be young and pretty."

I opened the door. "I suppose you'll have to judge for yourself, Mr. Veil," I replied as I entered and closed the door behind me. The room was covered in capes and hats. Black feathers dusted the floor from several prop ravens and a few skulls sat on a shelf, watching us with hollow sockets.

"Well, *hello* there," he said appreciatively. "Indeed. You're not bad. But you're not one of my Association. That must make you the lovely Miss Stewart, Jonathon's girl. Do call me Nathaniel. I was warned you'd be coming," he said, grinning and showcasing the fangs from his *Camille* bit that he'd retained for the rest of his show.

"I am indeed Miss Stewart. The lovely part is up to you."

Nathaniel laughed, putting fingers to his mouth. With one snap, the fangs were gone. Part of me was sad to see the illusion fade.

"You play a vampire, but do you believe in them?" I asked. "In all the characters and creatures you portray?"

Nathaniel considered this as he placed his teeth into a jar of fake incisors. "Vampires surely exist, in one way or another. Something that preys on human life? I've seen that well enough. Fantasy is the only way we can understand reality." There was a darkness to his tone. A familiar one. "The world is full of devils and thieves, Miss Stewart. To make the darkness playful is the only way to survive it. We must externalize that which might kill us otherwise."

I nodded. "Jonathon described you as unapologetically melancholy. I find it refreshing. I've terrible nightmares. They don't make for pleasant conversation. But life isn't always pleasant, is it?"

Nathaniel shook his head, gauging me with an intensity that surpassed custom. It was thrilling and off-putting all at once. "Funny. Jonathon didn't say I couldn't stand close to you. I'd have thought he knew me better." He took a step closer. I could feel heat coming off his powerful form. Perhaps Jonathon only kept company with men who were as he was: distinct, bold, and impossible to ignore.

"Is this what you say to all those young women there in the gallery, swaying in black?"

"My Association."

I raised an eyebrow. He explained: "We are united in melancholy, nothing more. We revel in it, turning our black hearts outward to find joy. We cannot remain in shadow's ecstasy always, so we must make a game of it.

Would you like to join us? I'm not usually forthcoming with strangers. But, alas, you've disarmed me."

Beaming, he produced a card. In bold, elegant script the card declared membership to "Her Majesty's Association for Melancholy Bastards."

I couldn't help but chuckle. Turning over the card, I saw that it read:

President: Hamlet

Vice President: Edgar A. Poe

Social Chair: Mary Shelley

Secretary: Ophelia

Treasurer: Manfred, Lord of Otranto

Grinning, I glanced up from the card to see Nathaniel looking rather pleased with himself. "Brilliant," I agreed.

"Would you like to join?"

I gave him a wary look. "Is there a membership ritual?"

"I'll forgo the bloodletting for you," he said and laughed when I looked wary, gesturing that I should keep the card. "Show this at the theater door whenever I play, and they'll let you into the pit. We're self-selecting. We don't want anyone making fun or starting trouble. It's why there's a dress code—grand dark aesthetic aside—it shows you want to play in the spirit of community and camaraderie."

The way his art defined yet didn't overwhelm him was

wonderful. He didn't take himself too seriously, which made me take him utterly so. But standing too close to him was a bit dangerous. He was so powerful and alluring that I understood the swooning crowds on a more personal level.

"Some are born with darkness," Nathaniel stated. "Some have darkness thrust upon them." He turned to his mirrors to wipe a bit of kohl from his eyes. "I hear you and Jonathon were put through quite the trial. He wasn't born with darkness, so it was thrust upon him. You?"

"Thrust upon me and always pressing in. You?"

"Born with it," he stated airily. "And when you're born with melancholy you learn how to live with it or else you die of it. Simple as that."

I knew it wasn't as simple as that. My disability proved that rising above challenges, no matter what kind, took discipline and ritual. Veil had figured out his ritual, and once learned, the discipline seemed simple.

As much as I enjoyed our unexpectedly intimate line of conversation, I was recalled to my task. "Mr. Veil, Jonathon is looking into his parents' death. Do you remember anything odd about the weekend you last saw one another?"

He thought a moment. Moving to his shelf of skulls, he picked one up and pressed it to his forehead as if gleaning some insight. "Hmm...His parents came to my show." Nathaniel tapped the skull to his own. "*Think*...Someone approached them, now that I think of it. Jonathon couldn't have seen them. Our stage manager was feeling poorly, so Jonathon played the good doctor and examined him backstage. But there was a man, odd looking—"

"In the eyes?" I finished, dread in my stomach like a rock. Jonathon's parents hadn't died in a tragic accident at all; they had been targeted by the Society. The whole Denbury clan. "I don't suppose he was French?"

"Yes!" Nathaniel returned the skull to its brethren. "Yes, some Frenchman and his odd consort. They were discussing art with the Whitbys, a commission. Why?"

I paled. "You see, it wasn't that Jonathon was taken hostage, Mr. Veil. He was imprisoned."

"Imprisoned?"

"Yes. In a…very odd way."

"Define very odd."

"Well, if you must know…his soul was ripped from his body and trapped in a painting."

Nathaniel blinked. "A painting?"

"His own portrait. I know it sounds mad—"

"No, it's just…the Whitbys were talking about a portrait with that Frenchman…" Nathaniel sighed. "Denbury and I met back at our favorite lounge. I didn't think to mention it, as his parents moved in circles I didn't know. I couldn't have known. A painting? What the hell—"

"It's all right. No one would believe anything that's happened to us."

"Try me."

"It's a long story Jonathon will relate when we're all relaxed, safe, and toasting your magnificent production together. Then you can tell me the story of how you met. Jonathon mentioned you in connection with his clinic, but you're—"

"Not a doctor. Hardly. But I've…responsibilities to my Association. That, too, is a long story. Dear God, I miss that chap."

"Me too…" I murmured.

Nathaniel looked pained. "I should not have mentioned it. I feel terrible, but I hardly remember anything after a show." His eyes glittered at me. "Don't worry, I'll remember *you*. Tell me, how can we help our dear friend now? I may have failed him before, but I shan't again—"

"That's kind of you, Mr. Veil, but information is all that will help now. Spare him kind thoughts and traveling mercies. I'm worried sick for him. There's a group targeting good people. He's overseas all alone, sniffing them out."

"Ah, don't you worry for Denbury. He's too clever by half. The sensible members of his family schooled him fiercely. He's grown more resourceful than all of them combined. He's got a wicked mind for medical magic that utterly eludes me, with a bit of detective in him. You must allow him to solve his mysteries."

I felt a surge of pride for Jonathon and was pleased by

how much I liked his friends. His very *handsome* friends. Goodness. I'm sure I blushed the *entire* time.

"I'm engaged until the end of the month," Nathaniel said. "I do hope this won't be the last I'll see of you."

"It won't be long until Jonathon returns to New York. I'm sure he'd love to see you, as he mentioned you with a brother's fondness."

Nathaniel beamed, and I ached suddenly for a friend who could light up like that for me. Being in love was one thing. Having best, bosom friends was another, and people were meant to have both in their lives. I missed mine from Connecticut. Nathaniel snatched my hand, brought it to his lips, and kissed it dramatically.

"Behave," I cautioned. He dropped my hand reluctantly.

"Ah, yes. Denbury did say he'd kill me if I pressed my luck. Give the old man my regards, and if there's anything I can do to help—"

"We'll be in touch. Thank you, Mr. Veil. We will, I'm sure, need all the friends we can spare…" I trailed off. Speaking of friends, did I dare mention Samuel? "Oh…one more thing."

"Yes?"

"This…group, the Master's Society, is behind strange, supernatural things. Not only was Jonathon targeted, but Samuel Neumann, too."

Nathaniel gasped. "Is Sam all right?"

"Frankly, I don't know. Please help keep an eye on him.

Jonathon is…constrained by his circumstances. And since you were involved at that clinic, watch yourself too."

Nathaniel bit his lip. "I can't think this could be related, but two strange men approached me after the show when I first came to New York. One was blond and ridiculously dressed, like he wanted to look the dandy but failed. The other was small and mousy and said a lot of large words. He approached me and pitched a 'miracle serum.' Showed me the chemical breakdown of it. He claimed it would wipe all melancholies away, replacing sadness with ecstasy, and he thought my Association would be a good *market*. Now I've seen enough damage from opium, laudanum, and the like that I don't believe in any such miracles, and I didn't like the feel of him."

"What was his name?"

"The blond didn't say a word. The mousy one was Dr. Stevens."

Good. Not Preston. But we knew Preston wasn't the only doctor involved. This sounded like another "department" of the Society.

"Yes," I said carefully. "You were right to be leery. Don't trust any doctors. Well, not any…unconventional ones, that is. Note who approaches you. And if anyone asks about these goings-on, you know nothing and we didn't speak."

Nathaniel stared at me, a bit bewildered and frightened. There was nothing else to say. With a little curtsy, I ducked out of the dressing room and managed to find a different way out through shadowed backstage corridors rather than having to face that quiet mourners' guild.

On the ride back in the carriage, Mrs. Northe eyed me. "Well?"

"The portrait was arranged with Jonathon's parents. I presume the Frenchman, the artist, was already demonically possessed. The theater was a rendezvous to discuss the deal. It's harder and harder to believe their deaths were accidents. Veil was approached by a creepy doctor with a 'cure for melancholy.'"

"Sounds like it could be related."

"Thankfully Veil didn't trust him, but I doubt it's the end of that query. And yes, Veil behaved. Flirtation is his nature, but he's a friend to Jonathon."

Mrs. Northe smiled. "When does Jonathon return?"

"I don't know. I'm desperate for a letter to know he's all right and what he's found out."

Dropped at my front door, I turned and looked up at Mrs. Northe as I descended from the carriage.

"I'm sorry if what I said when I first came home was ungrateful. I'm just scared. Strange things follow you and me, and the circle is growing. I just don't want my father wrapped up in it. He's all I have."

"You've a larger family now—me, Jonathon—"

"Father's all I've had all my life. All I know I can count

on. He needs to be protected from the dark things I've seen, not brought into them."

"You can't protect everyone, Natalie."

"I'd like to try," I said. "So please be careful with him. Thank you for this evening, for the dress, for knowing your way about things," I said, and before I could say any more, I turned and walked up my stoop, my cheeks flushing with a realization.

I didn't want Mrs. Northe to replace me. I didn't want her to become more important to Father than me. I was the center of his world, even if he didn't always know what to do with me. But Mrs. Northe was perfect and charming in nearly every way. How could she not become the whole of someone's life? He'd said himself that he was changing and I was changing. There was truth in my fear of bringing supernatural woe to my father's attention. But it was also about my father's attention in general.

I took a few deep breaths upon my stoop, listening to the evening sounds of the city, which mixed into a soft whir. Looking down, I admired my gorgeous gown. And then I looked down the street past the brownstone row houses and across avenues to see the corner of Central Park. In the gaslit distance, the Metropolitan stood shrouded in shadows of parkland, remaining as full of mystery and grandeur as when it was dreamed up by New York philanthropists.

I was elegant and so was my city. I felt *so* alive and so was my city. Jonathon would be here soon to share it with me. There was nothing to fear.

"My, my." My father examined me at the door. Bessie dragged me inside and into the light so she could turn me around and admire all the gathers, beads, and bustling. "And how was the show?" Father asked. "I saw the posters. Were you one of those swooning women straining to clutch at Veil's cloak?"

"One could hardly swoon and catch him from the height of Mrs. Northe's box, Father," I replied pointedly. Bessie chuckled.

"But was it any good?" she asked.

"Brilliant," I replied, perhaps a bit too eagerly. Father smirked, and his nose went into a book. As I kissed him on the head, he gave me a wary eye.

"And when does that lord of yours arrive? When must I keep an *extra* special eye on you?"

"I don't know yet. Mrs. Northe will collect him, as he'll stay in her home. You'll meet him soon after. He doesn't want to vex you, believe me," I assured him, and I went to my room to admire my dress in the mirror again before there were any further questions.

Something of my mind must have been in the mood for testing the waters that night. For guess who stood at the end of my mind's darkened hallway in my most recent dream?

Nathaniel Veil was lit only by dim gaslight from indeterminate sources, casting contrast on his sharp features and making his silhouette just like his dramatic poster. His wide hand was stretched out to me, like some mesmerist drawing me in. I was somehow helpless to resist, and I fell into the folds of his black robes. He dove upon my neck with searing kisses and a teasing nibble as if he were one of the vampires from his show. It was admittedly thrilling.

But then Jonathon was there. And he did not like this scene one bit. He stood behind me in the hall, bright blue eyes flashing with fury.

"Veil, unhand her," he said coldly. "Natalie, why are you cruel?"

Nathaniel whirled my body around so that I could face the sound, and there was Jonathon, just as tall and striking, but less wild and unpredictable than his friend. He was hurt and angry.

Nathaniel did not let go, instead kissing the back of my neck gently and drawing my hair aside. My hair was down, which had to mean I was in my night-dress. And so I stared helplessly at Jonathon while I could not help but shudder at the sensation.

"Cruel," he repeated. "I'm in *London*. You know, I can have plenty of attention too, whenever I like."

At that, the hall suddenly flickered to life, one flaming lamp after the next in an inexorable line. The corridor now filled with pretty ladies, and the burning wicks against mirrored sconces cast illuminated glittering jewels like stars in a gaslit sky. Each finely bedecked female stared at Jonathon hungrily.

My mouth dropped open. "Is that a threat, Lord Denbury?"

"Just keep your dreaming focused, Natalie. I can't take any more betrayals."

"As if I'd betray you—"

"But she's under my spell, old chap," Nathaniel finished. "Can you begrudge a spirit like hers a bit of curiosity? It isn't like you haven't kissed other girls before."

"Not since meeting her," Jonathon insisted, breaking free from a long-limbed girl in a sapphire ball-gown who had wrapped her arms around him and staring down Veil. "And you're not really here, Veil. It's just the two of us, Natalie." He pinned me with his gaze. "It's just us and whatever your mind creates. So stop it. I'm having enough trouble sleeping without seeing another man have his way with you."

I closed my eyes. I tried to break free, to move toward the beautiful blue-eyed man in the hall that I knew I loved. "I choose you," I said to Jonathon, praying he'd believe me, and stumbled forward as if pushed, a hand—no, a claw—raking down my back and scoring me with a sharp pain. I cried out, falling not forward into Jonathon's arms but straight up in my bed.

I'd managed not to wake Father this time, for which I was grateful. I wrestled myself back to sleep. I had plans to visit Maggie tomorrow, and it would do no good to go looking like hell. I needed to be at my very best. Dealing with Margaret Hathorn might be its own careful game.

Chapter 10

To my surprise, I found I was nearly as nervous about paying a visit to Maggie as I was about dealing with curses and double-crossing intrigues. Chiefly because I wasn't sure what sort of reception I would get, and I never really knew where I stood with her.

"Hello? And you are?" the maid asked at the door.

"Miss Stewart. Miss Hathorn knows me."

"I'll announce you to the mistress," the maid said, bobbing her head. She closed the door a moment. I fiddled with the small silken pouch in my hand. At least I came bearing gifts. The maid opened the door and led me through the lavish entrance hall to the open doors of an even more elaborate parlor.

The residence was just as fine as Mrs. Northe's home, but I didn't like it. It was ostentatious in a way Mrs. Northe's home was not, trying very hard to impress. While Mrs. Northe's home was elegantly classic, the Hathorn residence was on the cutting edge of so many fashions that nothing matched, but I'm sure it was all *very* expensive.

Mrs. Hathorn was a bit confused as the maid led me into the parlor. "I know I know your name, Miss Stewart, but—"

"Hello, Natalie," came a wary voice from the top of the grand staircase. Maggie was looking very lovely, her dark hair pinned up at the sides but left down in the back, as I used to wear mine as a girl, giving her a youthful look even though her day dress was sumptuous in layered satin stripes. Her eyes were dark and wide, sizing me up.

"Ah, yes, the Metropolitan, that's it. Mr. Stewart," Mrs. Hathorn said, finally placing me. The Stewarts didn't rank high on her social list so it took her a moment.

"Yes, the *Metropolitan*," Maggie repeated carefully.

Last I'd seen Maggie, she was standing before Jonathon's portrait in the museum, chanting in his exhibition room at midnight and looking like a ridiculous gypsy. She had laid out a chalk pentagram on the floor, not even knowing the right way to draw it so that it wasn't a sign of the devil.

Clearly, we were both thinking of that moment during the strained silence. Just as I had no idea why Maggie had been there, neither did she understand why I was. We had to move toward some semblance of the truth.

"Claire," Maggie called to the maid finally.

"Yes, mum."

"Bring us lemonade on the balcony. Come, Natalie." Maggie was so used to ordering people around that it came effortlessly. She gestured for me to join her on the landing, so I climbed the grand staircase.

The balcony looked out over a painstakingly manicured lawn with landscaped flowers in bloom. It was admittedly impressive. There were fewer and fewer grand mansions these days along midtown avenues. Blocks were giving over to town houses and row houses and fine shops, but mansions like this still clung to Millionaires' Mile, where a higher concentration of wealth resided than anywhere else in our country, maybe even the world.

"How lovely," I breathed. Maggie started.

"Ah, yes, that's right, you can speak. I'd forgotten about it amid the…madness when last I saw you. Where did you go after that night? It was awfully suspicious that you were out of town visiting a relative."

Was that the alibi Mrs. Northe had given? I thought a moment. "I had to get out of the city. That night proved…traumatic."

"How so?"

"Here, I brought you a present." Distraction was always such a lovely way to change the subject.

"Ooh!" Maggie squeaked. She opened the drawstring pouch and pulled out the pin and brooch. They sparkled in the sunlight. Maggie held them up to admire the glitter. Claire brought us lemonade. I thanked her, and she smiled at me.

"These are very nice. Where did you get them?

"Stewart's," I replied.

"Ah. Shame you're not—"

"Related, yes. I know."

"I suppose Auntie took you shopping then," she said, a bite to her tone. Of course. It wasn't as though I had money to get them on my own, and the fact that her aunt had been out with me and not her was an additional slight. I looked into my lemonade, shamed.

"I'm sorry." Maggie sighed. "I'm still angry at Aunt Evelyn. And you. I don't understand why you kept things from me. Why you still keep things from me. Maybe there are things I know that you don't. Did you ever think that?"

"Maggie, I want to be your friend," I said earnestly. "I never wanted to keep anything from you. But things got very…complicated, and it wasn't just my safety at stake, but the safety of others."

"Lord Denbury. I don't think he's dead, Natalie," she breathed.

"No, I'm not sure he is either. But whatever happened to him, it's a mystery."

"What do you know about it?" Maggie breathed. I sighed. I had to throw her a bone and debated how to do so.

"Why were you there that night?" she pressed. "I was trying a spell to bring him to life before me. Were you there to do the same?"

"No." I took a deep breath. "I was there as bait."

"What?"

"The painting was tied to unsavory types who'd seized the Denbury estate. One of the criminals had a particular...penchant for young ladies. So I stood as bait."

"Have you met him? Denbury?"

"No, just a solicitor in touch with my father. Denbury, if alive at all, remains to be seen."

"Your father risked his own daughter as bait?"

"No, I volunteered. Insisted, really, and since it was Mrs. Northe's painting, she agreed, provided Mr. Smith stood guard."

"Because you wanted to meet him too," Maggie said, a hint of conspiratorial glee in her tone. I looked at her. "Admit it." There was a mischievous sparkle in her eye. And with that, she was a girl who could be my friend.

I laughed. "All right. Yes. I wanted to meet him."

"Finally, some truth—"

"I thought if I was bait, he'd at least want to meet a girl who risked her safety to help him. I mean, no girl is immune to that man's looks."

"That's for certain," she sighed dreamily.

Oh, if you only knew, Margaret Hathorn, if you only knew. I blushed, thinking of his kisses and caresses.

"I still dream of him," Maggie whispered. "Scandalous dreams."

I opened my mouth as if to agree, to giggle and blush and conspire with her further, so glad to have the icy gulf between us bridged, but I really couldn't share the contents of my dreams with Maggie; they were too complicated by nightmares. Jonathon had indeed been in my dream the night before, but it was hardly a dream I was proud of or could share.

No, I could never really tell her the truth. She could never be the sort of confidante Mrs. Northe was, and for that I doubted Maggie could ever forgive me.

"So what happened?" Maggie prompted. "In the museum room."

"Someone came. He tried to attack me, then got arrested."

"The crazy man, that awful broker—" Maggie clapped her hands over her mouth.

"One of his people."

"Oh, Natalie, that was very brave," she said and meant it.

"Thank you."

"And he has yet to reveal himself? After all that? After his painting is…"

I eyed her. "Is what?"

"The painting is gone, Natalie. Don't tell Mum or Auntie, but I sneaked out to the Metropolitan the next day. I saw workers throw out the pieces." She bit her lip, as if she was about to say something more. "If you hear anything. Anything from him, promise to tell me."

"All right…" I replied hesitantly. "If I can."

"Natalie, you must." There was an odd urgency to her tone. The clock down the hall struck half past three. "Ah, I must get ready for my drawing lesson. I'm hoping to study in Paris. Wouldn't that be heavenly?"

I nodded. I'd like to see Paris. I wondered what it would be like to live with every opportunity available. Well, every opportunity available to a woman.

As she saw me to the door, she thanked me for the baubles. "Do come again, Natalie. It was good to see you."

I nodded and agreed. Most likely, Maggie would always say oblivious things that rubbed my middle-class status in my face, but she had her bright sides. I needed to at least try to have a normal relationship with someone not supernaturally affected. It was a shame she was so fascinated by the supernatural; she should be careful what she wished for.

She was far too preoccupied with Lord Denbury for my comfort, but at what point did I tell her he was alive? At what point would they inevitably run into one another?

Chapter 11

The next morning Father handed me a letter. The postmark was from Connecticut, the penmanship familiar. Rachel. He kissed my cheek, and just as I was about to tear open the envelope, he asked, "Are you coming with me to the museum today? Or since there's no longer a haunted painting to tend, do you have no use for the Metropolitan and its acquisitions?".

I'd nearly forgotten about my post on the acquisitions committee. It wasn't really a job; it was the appearance of one. But I missed the museum and wanted to at least appear useful, so I agreed. My dress was suitable for day and business, so I merely ran for my sketchbook, tucked the letter in its pages, and walked out into the lazy summer heat.

New York City in late July and August moved at a slower pace than the rest of the year. Father's associates nodded at me in their conference room. I perused the papers on the long table, and while Father was procuring a cool pitcher of water for us to weather the warm rooms, his associates were only too happy to ignore me, as usual.

There were sketches for consideration from artists I could care less about. I recognized one name, that of a French symbolist I'd seen on postcards in Jonathon's study when we'd been sharing our interests. There was an opportunity for the Metropolitan to gain a Sphinx, or more specifically, *Oedipus and the Sphinx* by Gustave Moreau. It was a provocative painting of the mythical, riddling creature climbing up Oedipus's beautiful body.

"Oh, you *must* buy the Moreau," I said finally. "It's classic with its Greek themes, and yet it's modern. You'd please two sets of patrons. Besides, I love the symbolists, don't you?"

Everyone turned to stare at me. During this long silence my father returned with water.

"Gareth…" Mr. Moore said slowly. "Since when does she speak?"

My father looked around at them all for a moment and replied airily. "She has for a while. You just haven't noticed, you oblivious lot—"

They all broke into loud denial, grumbling and refuting with scowling faces and wobbling jowls. I laughed. "Gentlemen, my voice was only recently recovered. By spending a great deal of time here at your wonderful institution. In celebration of my successful treatment, what say you agree to the Moreau?"

"Oh, yes, do take the Moreau," Father said. "It's classic and modern at the same time."

I laughed again. "I said the exact same thing."

"Chip off the old block, I'd say," said dear, oblivious Mr. Nillis with a grandfatherly smile.

"I believe my duty is done for the day. Father, if you need me I'll be sketching in the sculpture wing."

I took my glass and made my way to a bench in the sculpture wing, where I was surrounded by ideal specimens of beauty. I thought of Jonathon. Not long ago he'd been a work of art. I refused to let the horror of what had happened to him reflect poorly on art or museums. I would not let devils tear down one of my great sanctuaries. Although only founded a decade prior, this museum was a treasure.

But in a basement room it had been a prison. I couldn't help myself. I wandered down to the small, auxiliary exhibition room where the portrait of Lord Denbury had hung. The door was locked. I still felt a cool chill creep up my spine on the warm day.

I returned to the Greek gods. There, as I sketched, Rachel's letter slipped out from the pages. Part of me dreaded to open it, but I couldn't deny that she needed help.

My dear Natalie,

I've fled to the Asylum. I didn't know if you were home yet, and I was too scared to go to the authorities. I don't know what to do. Dr. Preston left for Minnesota two weeks ago, but after that he sent his "associate"—a gaudy, cold man who does nothing but leer and smirk—with a new sequence of boxes of varying sizes that I must connect to spirits.

The boxes, Natalie. I managed to open one. With a hairpin.

Inside was a severed human hand.

I'm scared. The spirits around the hospital just cry and shriek, creating a constant mental ward in my mind. I don't understand what Dr. Preston wants, but it can't be to help anyone or to reach Laura anymore. This is unnatural. Mrs. Northe promised I could trust you both. If you've any advice, I'd gladly heed it. I'm one step from madness.

Sincerely,
Rachel

I put a hand to my chest, as if pressure would stop it from pounding so hard it felt as though it would leap from my chest. I'd foreseen this.

"God?" I asked, looking up in prayer. "Whatever is going on here, please don't throw us into the water if we can't swim. Don't give my friends and me something we can't manage."

I couldn't understand why this was so terrifying and personal. Walking home slowly, lost in thought, I tried to appreciate the pleasant day filled with light, full of New

Yorkers enjoying the glorious park at the heart of our city. My eye caught something.

A glistening spiderweb had been spun between two tree branches at the end of my block. At the center of the impressive web sat the weaver, a spider no larger than my thumbnail. I felt in that moment that if there was any explanation to be had, then the spider's web was it. A web had been cast around Jonathon, and somehow we'd been caught up in it. Rachel too, though I didn't see the connection.

Oh, but of course. Young and talented, Preston had said. Her talents as a medium had ensnared her. Her knowing me was mere coincidence, though I'm not sure I can believe in coincidence these days. Thank goodness she knew me; otherwise she'd have no one. And Jonathon. Within his painted prison he'd dimly seen countless people pass him by before the fateful light about me set me apart and made him change the portrait to get my attention. Thank goodness he had found me.

You remain at the center of mystery, Mrs. Northe had written. I glanced at the spider at the heart of her web. Was that me? I had accused Mrs. Northe of being a magnet for the supernatural. Maybe I wasn't being totally honest with myself. I didn't want to be the spider.

Mrs. Northe met us for dinner at our home. Quite a different experience from dining at her mansion. But she seemed just as at ease in our modest dwelling as in her lavish one.

"I received a letter from Rachel," I said to her. "She went to Connecticut, to the Asylum, terrified. It was as I feared."

"With the boxes?" Mrs. Northe grimaced.

"Yes. What was in them. I was right. A hand. So now what do I do for Rachel?"

"The question is," Mrs. Northe continued, "what's being *done* with those body parts and the spirits trailing them?" We shuddered collectively.

"Body parts?" My father choked.

I continued with: "It can't be good."

"Hand this over to the authorities at once," my father stated, the color gone from his face. This sort of talk was too much for him, but he was trying to take more of an active part in the goings-on of our lives, for the sake of both Mrs. Northe and me. But he strained.

"The authorities wouldn't know the first thing about how to reverse a curse or contact a spirit, Gareth!" Mrs. Northe scoffed as if that were perfectly obvious. "Denbury's body and soul would be dead and destroyed by now if we'd contacted them. Rachel is in a similarly delicate place. If she's tied spirits to body parts, they're being used for something. We must find out what. Confrontation with Dr. Preston is inevitable. I don't understand his aims, but I've my suspicions. However, I don't see the larger picture. Hopefully Denbury can enlighten us from England."

"What do I tell Rachel?" I asked.

"Write and ask her to come and stay with me. She must *untie* those sad ghosts. She's the only one who can. Only those directly involved in the action of the magic can affect it. Just like you and Jonathon were the only ones able to reverse his curse."

A thought occurred to me, something that had been nagging at me in my world full of loose ends. Did I dare tell her about the rune that had appeared on my skin? I needed to translate it, to see if there was a message imprinted on my skin or just random aftereffects of the magical portals I'd traveled through to get to Jonathon.

"What happened to the painting? The shreds?"

"I went to the museum first thing and instructed that workmen should dispose of the shreds," Mrs. Northe replied. "I demanded that they be incinerated, though I cannot be sure if the workmen complied to the letter. I didn't want to appear directly involved, lest Sergeant Patt might find me any more interesting than he already did."

I nodded. Father scowled. Bessie, who had kept entirely silent and had made it clear she wanted nothing to do with this talk, entered with a snifter of brandy and slid it toward him.

Soon Jonathon would be here and everything would be better—at least, when he wasn't expected to be evil. Rachel would return, and we could put her abuses to rest and give her—and those spirits—well-earned rest. But what hope do we have of coming out unscathed? I remain the fulcrum of a dangerous scale.

Father didn't say another word the rest of the day, reminding me why there was silence in my house for so long. I wrote to Rachel as instructed and lost myself in an adventure novel to take my mind off the waiting.

The next few days passed in a blurred haze of summer heat, museum meetings, meals with Father, and reading. And writing. I wasn't sure if I'd ever get my first diary back, so I tried to keep up accounts from then and now as best I could.

Part of me felt as though I was frozen, that my soul had separated to visit with Jonathon's when he was still trapped in the painting, and here my body was, hovering. Waiting. I yearned to be with Jonathon where we could work together to solve all that was keeping us apart. But part of me dreaded his letters, his return, for that would also mean new facets of his intrigue, and I doubted either of us would rejoice in his findings across the pond.

Instead I threw myself into enjoying every moment at the museum, dining with Mrs. Northe and with Father, and watching them grow ever closer and trying not to feel jealous of it.

At night, the dreams were consistent for a while. The long corridor, as usual. But at the end of that hall was a beckoning dark silhouette, as if something was waiting for me or knew I would eventually come home to its shadows.

There were constant whispers and murmurs, but I couldn't make out the words. Just when I began to feel like the shadows wanted to hurt me, I heard Mother's Whisper, that very specific Whisper that had once made me believe that death was not always the end. And when I heard her Whisper above the rest, I knew I was safe and could sleep soundly. But would she always be there to protect me? And where was Jonathon in my dreams? Had we lost our connection? Perhaps the soul had limits when another's was so far away.

Chapter 12

To: The loveliest girl in all of New York

From: Her paramour stranded in a mess of demons' making in London

My dearest Natalie,

By the time you receive this, I'll already have thrown myself on the swiftest ship back and will see you soon. London is grayer than ever. Everything here is dreary and downright odd. And cold. I'm very cold even though it's summer.

I've taken detailed notes. While I'm not the diarist you are, I hope I do my tale justice.

Mrs. Northe's solicitor friend, Mr. Knowles, is a man of letters and law, and a lifesaver. I owe him much. The moment I walked into his fine office in North London, he gave me a hearty handshake and a stiff bourbon. A sharp man with graying hair slicked back, he sat across a great mahogany desk, with glasses low over wide gray eyes above a long nose. His office was fastidiously organized.

"Lord Denbury," Knowles began, "while I never met your family, I know all of you were highly regarded. I deeply regret the tragedies that have befallen you. I assure you, your being here remains secret."

Mrs. Northe had told him every last mad detail.

"All the documents I've gathered pertaining to your affairs are in a file in your quarters. I've good friends at the deeds offices. Always make friends with clerks, I've learned. Peruse the documents at your leisure, though, I warn you, they're not pleasant."

He then bade me to come back in the morning and gave me keys to rooms he'd procured for me across the street. "Though I am sure you would like to get back to your family's town home, let's not make you—or any property of yours—obvious, shall we?"

He led me out and down the front stairs, gestured toward my rooms, and disappeared under a wrought-iron arch into an interior courtyard and was lost to the night.

The street was lit sporadically by gas lamps. Not a soul walked along it. It was not too far from great King's Cross station, and there were rumblings in the distance. It was a comfort to see discernable life moving in the city. Even if I was alone on the street, I was not alone in the world. I did search the shadows for anyone following, but there was no one there. No light, no aura, no movement in the shadows. Only the sound of trains. It made me think of our time alone in those cars, and I ached to be next to you again.

I've yet to see your signature green-and-violet light elsewhere, Natalie. You remain unparalleled, while a white light flashed around Knowles, similar to what I see flicker periodically around Mrs. Northe.

As I stepped into my rooms where no one greeted me, the lamps were trimmed low. I drew the shades on all the windows. Tea and a tray of sliced meat and cheese were laid on a table by a large armchair. The wide fireplace across the room would normally be unnecessary in late summer, but I was chilled to the bone. I took to the whole spread and lit a fire.

Across the room on a writing desk sat a green folder: my evening's task.

I wouldn't step foot onto the Greenwich estate this trip if I could help it. It had been a prison once, and I'd not be locked onto its grounds again, painted or real. I wasn't ready to again take up my title, not with servants likely to shriek and faint upon seeing me. I'd had enough of being a fright, and all I'd see down those halls were the ghosts of my parents: Father in his favorite armchair and Mother fussing about with the meticulous energy I inherited. I missed them too much to see the home we'd all lost.

That the first document on the pile was a deed was both a relief and an insult. The Denbury estate had been sold at auction. A freshly wealthy merchant, his wife, and their two children had taken up residence in my home.

Monies went to "the Society," according to the letter, which was on fine stationery designated by a coat of arms of no family I recognized. The center escutcheon was not divided into quarters but was a single golden crown, with red dragons rampant on either side. Red and gold: the colors that crackled around my foe when his magic was strongest. I swore I even saw a shimmer of those sparks flutter across the page. Perhaps that was just a trick of my angry eye, but regardless, clearly the Society was my enemy.

Tomorrow I'll confront them and write you immediately thereafter. I send this so it will make this evening's final post, and I've booked my return ticket. So be comforted that by the time this reaches you, I'll already be close on its heels in Atlantic waters.

I've more documents to read, so I leave you with a kiss and my love.

Yours,

Jonathon

P.S. It would seem I'm still connected to your dreams, darling, at least in part. I do recall you dreamed of Nathaniel. I'm glad you chose me, but really, Natalie, I mean it. Don't be cruel.

Chapter 13

Drowning in anxiety, I felt as if the day passed on pins and needles. I had no way of knowing what had happened to Jonathon in that viper's nest. I knew steamers traveled to and from New York and England daily carrying mail along with passengers, so there was a chance that if he had written the next day, that post would reach me soon. But with so many miles between, there was no guarantee it would arrive at all. I tried to write, to draw, to mend, but I kept throwing things aside and pacing.

I would've gone to the museum and worked with the acquisitions team, but they were off at a board meeting I hadn't been invited to. I took up the journal Mrs. Northe had given me and saw the markings I'd inscribed. I needed to tell her about them.

My restlessness found its way to her doorstep. I unburdened all my anxieties in one babbling rush. I opened the journal to show the runes I'd glimpsed upon my arm. "They could be hallucinations," I offered hopefully.

"Or it's likely lingering magic," she replied. "You came back too soon."

"I didn't really have a choice," I protested.

"That was merely a statement, not an indictment. Come, let's decipher." She led me into her library, where books were immaculately kept in glass cases from floor to ceiling. She shook an elegant silver set of tiny keys down her thin wrist and into her palm, fingered the correct key without looking at it, unlocked a glass case, pulled out a volume in Swedish full of her translations, and opened it to a runic alphabet. I turned my journal to the page where I'd taken down the marks from my sighting.

"They appeared as if they were carved into my arm," I explained. "There was a burning pain, and then they were gone."

"Did you do anything? To break the hold?"

"I…think I renounced it. Like in the liturgy, when you deny evil."

"'I renounce thee.' Yes, good. That's good. From the characters, it would seem that the markings read: 'I am.'"

"I am?"

"Well. At least it's self-actualized magic." She chuckled. I blinked at her. "Sorry. It isn't funny. It's also an incomplete message."

"Lovely," I muttered.

"Don't let dark energy keep hold of you. Do as many

positive things as you can. Spend time with that wonderful father of yours," she exclaimed. I couldn't help but notice how her face lit up at the mention of my father. Before I could inquire further on that count, she continued: "Now, Natalie, I need you to be prepared. My dearest friend is ailing in Chicago, and I must go to her side. I have the crushing premonition that I'm meant to go west."

I panicked. "You can't go. Not until Jonathon—"

"I'm not saying it will be tomorrow. But soon, and I want you to be prepared. These are to my house and library." She handed me a set of keys. I stared at them.

"You've placed an awful lot of trust in me," I said quietly.

"And until you prove unworthy of that trust, you have it," she replied. "When Lord Denbury returns, he will be staying here. If for some reason I am indisposed, I'd like you to let him in and introduce him to the staff. Rachel too. She should stay here, not near the hospital. Now, there's someone I want you to meet. I'm not about to leave this city without making sure you have a spiritual guardian on your side."

I knew better than to do anything but follow her. We had strolled a few blocks uptown before she volunteered where we were going.

"Reverend Blessing is a supply pastor who serves several congregations in the city. He's also become somewhat of an exorcist," she said matter-of-factly.

"Ah, yes, of course," I murmured. "Catholic?"

"No, Episcopalian like me."

Really, I wasn't sure what many denominations meant. I didn't know what Presbyterian meant either. As a Lutheran, I recognized that the denomination's name was an obvious derivation from the name of Martin Luther. Regardless, here I was, a Lutheran, beside an Episcopalian and off to see an exorcist.

"An exorcist," I breathed. Not that it was any stranger than what we'd already encountered. "Could he have gotten the demon out of Jonathon's body?"

"Perhaps in part, but then making sure Jonathon re-inhabited *himself* and trapping the demon to keep him from inhabiting others, that was a task for you and the counter-curse. Your situation was new territory. We may be in for any number of things. Hauntings, possessions, poltergeists, you need to be ready for anything."

"His name is Blessing," I said with a smile. "*Really*?"

I fell quite silent and didn't dare question his name when Reverend Blessing opened the door.

He was tall, broad-shouldered, and imposing in a fine, dark suit with a crisp, white cleric's collar, his skin gleaming brown-golden. As soon as he saw Mrs. Northe, his stern look turned into a wide smile. I don't know why I should have been surprised at first glance that the priest was a man of color, but then again, Mrs. Northe was a woman of many friends. Besides, the church claimed it was a place for all peoples, and the Episcopalians seemed to have at least attempted a modicum of equality. I wondered if they'd ever let a woman in the pulpit.

A fond chuckle erupted in the reverend's throat. "Mrs. Northe, to what do I owe this sudden honor, and who have you brought with you?"

"Gail in the diocese office told me these were your calling hours, and while I'm sorry to disturb you, I'm never sorry to see you." She embraced him briefly. At this, Blessing took a step back. Mrs. Northe turned to me.

"This is Miss Natalie Stewart. She's been through quite a lot."

I was too shocked by the two of them embracing to pay much attention to my introduction. New York may long have been a free state, but prejudices still run deep. In another state, that embrace could have gotten the reverend killed. Then again, Mrs. Northe was never one for convention. I didn't have time to assess further for I felt a small, wet something on my hand and I drew back with a start.

Two heads poked curiously out from the reverend's suit coat, one on either side. They were two tall and elegant dogs, greyhounds by the look of them, one beige and one a gorgeous gray, nearly blue. They sniffed the air and sized us up, but did not bark. What I'd felt on my hand was a nose. Blessing chuckled again.

"Ah, pardon my fearless guard-dogs, Bunny," he put a hand on the beige creature, "and Blue," then on the gray-blue one. "Shall we show our guests in?" He guided the lean creatures back. "We can't stand long in the doorway lest they tear out of the house and down the sidewalk. They're racing dogs, you know, not the best fit for the city, but I'm fostering for the moment. Don't worry. They're as friendly as can be."

It was true. The dogs wagged tails and sniffed around us but did not jump up. Instead they circled us closely, lean bodies shaking with excitement. Bunny managed to lean her head up into my hand, as if the sole purpose of a hand was to pet her. I laughed and scratched her between the ears.

"Amazing, resilient creatures, dogs," Blessing stated. "They were built to love humans. When they sense kindness from you, they will return it tenfold. If only humans were the same."

As we filed into the entrance foyer of polished wood and religious iconography, I heard other barking from the rear of the house. Were there more dogs? And what was that from the other room? The squawk of a bird? I saw a cat dart across a banister. Then another one.

The reverend laughed. "Welcome to the Blessing zoo." It was quite fine and clean for a zoo, and I wondered what sort of menagerie the rest of the house held. "Stewart," he added, gesturing for us to sit in his parlor, which continued the theme of crosses and saints. "How do I know that name?"

"Gareth Stewart is in acquisitions at the Metropolitan Museum of Art," Mrs. Northe offered.

"No…was your mother—"

"Dead," I murmured.

"Ah. Yes," Blessing said quietly, bowing his head a moment. "Helen Stewart. Taken from us too soon. I met your mother once. She offered to translate our tracts and give lectures to German congregations. Our cause spread like sweet wildfire, I'm proud to say."

I must have looked a bit stunned or confused, for Mrs. Northe explained: "Reverend Blessing worked closely with Mr. Bergh and his American Society for the Prevention of Cruelty to Animals. It's thanks to their efforts that there are any laws at all about child and animal abuse."

"I don't meet many people who knew Mother." I said, blushing, trying to explain my surprise. "Though it seems she was infamous. Father fully supported her causes but couldn't bear to take them up or associate with her circles after her death. It was too painful. He saw her everywhere." I stared down at my hands. "I wish I did. I wish I could listen to the city and hear her echo."

"She was a force of nature. A force for good in many causes," Blessing said. "When she died, there was a void in every project she touched."

I looked up into Blessing's warm dark eyes and resolved to take up some of Mother's noble causes myself, once all of Jonathon's affairs were sorted out. I could learn to be a force of nature. For good.

"Are these rescue dogs?" I asked, watching as Blessing's large, dark hand scratched fondly behind Bunny's ears.

"Yes," he replied. Bunny closed her eyes, blissful. "We managed to get them out of a coursing run where a horde of dogs was being mistreated. I volunteered to house them here until a new family could be found... and then I grew fond. Animals are such pure souls that they're hard for me not to get attached to. I take the liberation of every innocent soul very seriously, human or animal." Blue repositioned herself to stare at me, as if sizing me up or judging my character. "Blue here wants to know, as I do, what we can do to help, Mrs. Northe. What's the trouble?"

"Well, it's more that I'm being preventative, Reverend. I want to make sure you're someone Miss Stewart can turn to. I've been her...spiritual consultant on a manner of dark things that befell her and her suitor. But I may be called away to a friend's deathbed. We have two dear friends who we believe are in danger...and not the sort that normal channels of authority would believe. If I'm out of town, I can't leave her to fight her battles entirely on her own."

"What sort of battles?" Blessing asked calmly, as if they two had dealt with supernatural goings-on before.

"Well, we've seen a strange manner of possession by dark rituals and séances gone wrong. I've a sinking suspicion we haven't seen the end of it. So while I'll be leaving Natalie here in charge, I don't want her to be without recourse."

My mouth fell open. "Who said anything about my being in charge? I don't want to be in charge!" I sputtered awkwardly. Blue turned then to stare at Mrs. Northe, as if she was following the conversation and expected a retort.

"I just want to be prepared," Mrs. Northe said honestly.

"I am at your service, Miss Stewart, in whatever ways you need." As if to prove his point, Blue put her head on my knee. My anxiety vanished in the face of this lovely creature. I thought of Jonathon having hidden stray, starving dogs in his room. My heart ached for him.

"Thank you, Reverend Blessing. If nothing else, I think it might do my…suitor's heart good just to see these ladies," I said, smiling at the dogs. "I hope we won't need to call on any of your other talents. No offense, but I hope this all doesn't come to an exorcism."

"You and me both."

"I confess, I'm surprised. I thought only Catholics did exorcisms. As a Lutheran, I've never heard the rite spoken of."

Blessing shrugged. "Well, when someone gets asked to banish spirits, appease ancestors, cleanse houses, and perform exorcisms and all manner of spiritual interventions from up in Harlem to down in the Five Points, the church has found it useful to have a man like me around. And I come from New Orleans. Now talk about a haunted city and a lot of different beliefs." He whistled. "It was a good training ground for this mess of a city. Of course, here I need my wits about me for *every* sort of battle, spiritual or social. You never know what you'll encounter. My family down in New Orleans is all Catholic, but while I knew I was called to be a man of the cloth, I just couldn't manage the idea of a life without a wife and children. I always saw that in my future."

"And how is that coming along, Reverend?" Mrs. Northe queried with a smile. "Any prospective leading ladies?"

He shook his head. "Haven't found the right blessing to make a Blessing out of. And you? Shall you always remain a widow?"

Mrs. Northe shrugged nonchalantly while I knew better. But she didn't put either of us on the spot about her potential place in our family, and for that I was thankful. She rose. I followed suit. "Well, Natalie, let's allow the reverend his hours for others. Thank you as always for your time."

"Always. And Miss Stewart," Blessing stared me down. "Keep your faith. It seems to have gotten you this far."

"Yes, sir, it has," I said earnestly.

"Promise you'll call on me if you or yours are in distress," he said.

"I promise," I said, feeling my anxiety calm. I needed to feel I had blessings on my side. Now I did, literally.

The dogs escorted us out, and I felt a small lick on my hand at the door. Blue was looking up at me, and it almost seemed as though she smiled, her mouth hanging open slightly from her long snout.

"Girls, no." Blessing steadied them, long fingers looped around their collars as they saw the great racetrack of a New York City street and their long legs strained to leap forward. "I promise you a long run in the park. After my calling hours," he said. With a chuckle, we waved good-bye.

Mrs. Northe and I walked in silence for a long while.

"Why didn't you ever meet my mother?" I asked finally. "You're a philanthropist, fond of *causes*. Wouldn't your paths have crossed?"

Mrs. Northe set her jaw and offered an apologetic grimace. "Wealth segregates, too, my dear. I once moved in an exclusive, limited echelon. After Peter died, I gladly changed that routine but too late to have met your mother. We'd surely have been dear friends in life. Not just acquaintances in death."

The reminder that Mrs. Northe heard more directly from my mother than I did drove a knife's point further. And here she stood poised to take Mother's place...

"It isn't that I wouldn't trust or enlist Reverend Blessing's help," I began, suddenly eager to change the subject. "But you can't leave town. You have to hear what Jonathon has to report, and I'm very worried about Rachel."

"One day at a time, my dear. It's all we can do." She took my hand. "If I must go, you'll be fine. You, Denbury, Rachel, and Blessing, that's a team I'd trust with whatever may come."

"What do we do next?"

"Preston. It all hinges on Preston."

"In St. Paul, he mentioned other doctors in other cities. What if what he's up to is being replicated elsewhere?"

"All the more reason for me to check in with my associates in Chicago."

I sighed. Without Jonathon or Rachel to help navigate the lay of the land, I felt helpless.

I met Father at the Metropolitan and we all dined together pleasantly, but the small and meaningless talk of the day's events passed around my head like birds flitting about, with nothing really landing. Mrs. Northe mentioned she'd taken me to visit a man of the cloth, one of her spiritual confidantes, but left out any talk of exorcisms.

While trying to solve the mystery of Jonathon's curse, I remembered how much I disliked the waiting between finding the pieces of the puzzle.

My dream that night was hazy, with few details. All I recall is that a collected, chanting whisper grew in volume, a common theme in my dreams since we'd banished Jonathon's demon.

I was again in the darkened hallway of my mind, and this time the corridor was lit by red candles dripping scarlet wax, like the kind used in state seals and other rites. The corridor was blackened, as if entirely burned. Wax pooled into misshapen heaps below the iron holders that kept the tallow in place, like mineral deposits that grew into spikes in caves over time. The other end of the corridor was in shadow, but I could vaguely make out a silhouette whispering to me seductively—a low, rich male voice set apart from the monotone chorus of chants in Latin or some other ancient tongue.

It was beckoning for me, the silhouette in a suit. That was Jonathon calling for me, wasn't it?

Waking, I reassured myself with that fact until I found a letter on our entryway table downstairs. Concern for my dreams was supplanted by news about Jonathon's confrontation with those who had attempted his murder.

Chapter 14

My dear Natalie,

As promised, I tell the tale of a terrible Society. The only fact that can comfort us both is that by the time you read this, I'll be on a ship back to see you.

I wasted no time in confronting my enemies. I was up at first light, pacing the flat. I nearly seized the hot water out of the maid's hands. Bolstered by my favorite brew of Earl Grey, I waited until a reasonable hour before entering Knowles's office.

"Tell me about 'the Society,' whatever you know."

Knowles sighed. "I inquired after your estate to the family now living there. The merchant family appears quite separate from the affairs that displaced you. They paid a mad sum of money for the property, and I believe that was the Society's sole intent: a fundraiser of sorts. The agent, by the family's admission, was a bit odd, and they were uncomfortable about the run of bad luck that surrounded your family name. I'm sorry, Lord Denbury. I'm about to tell you things that will enrage you."

He lifted the snifter of bourbon, but I took more tea instead. "Go on."

"Your crest was removed everywhere from the estate, replaced with monograms. The family has no coat of arms with which to replace it. What I found in perusing the sale papers was the occasional seal."

He pointed to the paper, to the "crest" of the Society.

"The exact agent brokering the sale was never referred to by name, only the Society, with this seal. I had to appear entirely casual and not give a whiff of Scotland Yard, so that's as far as I could take things. I wonder if you shouldn't pay a visit to the one address you see there, Earl's Court."

I knew I would have to go as the demon, of course. Would they sense that some distant arm across the Atlantic had been severed? As long as I didn't look them directly in the eye, they couldn't *see* any difference, so long as I was a good actor…But would they sense it?

But not only demons were at work. The Society would have to be made mostly of mere mortals, so how could they know? Mrs. Northe promised that the demise of the painting would not be broadcast even to those who worked in the Metropolitan Museum. It was our secret victory. And couldn't I explain any inconsistencies away, at least enough to glean some insight?

I could've used your presence to bolster me as you used to do in the painting, brightening my day and restoring my sanity. I wasn't eager to take on that beast's manner, but I couldn't say no.

"The play's the thing," I muttered, and we were off. Much as Hamlet set a trap with his little play to draw out Claudius, I hoped to do the same with mortals who served demons. "Let's go. I don't think the demon is the sort to leave a calling card. If no one is home, I'll leave a message with whatever staff I might find."

If I didn't try immediately, I'd lose momentum, nerve, and anger. Anger at all that had been taken from me. I could care less about the property; it was my loved ones I missed. Anger would keep me sharp and smart.

I'm not sure what I expected, but the bustling heart of a new Earl's Court development was not the outpost of the insidious that I had anticipated. Perhaps it was better to hide nefarious activities here rather than in a darkened mansion on a howling moorland. Instead, evil had offices. A corporation. I got a chill up my spine walking up the stoop.

As I rang for the uppermost floor, a beady-eyed man in a footman's uniform opened the door. He looked me up and down, scowling.

"Society business," I said casually. Still scowling, he pointed up a sweeping staircase. I suppose that was a welcome in. He strode on ahead of me, boots loud on the wooden stairs. The dark, expensive, and elaborately carved wood everywhere made the place look like a rococo cave.

"Majesty's busy, though. You know, all his *transactions*," the doorman said in a rough cockney voice that sounded like his throat had been cut and sewn back together. "I'll have to announce you. And you are?"

"Denbury," I said. A dim flicker of recognition passed over the man's face. He nodded and knocked on an unmarked door with a particular rap—four knocks, a pause, and then one more. Soon the door swung open as if on its own and the doorman slipped in, closing it in my face.

The Society seemed to exclusively maintain the top floor of this fine, three-story edifice. The windows bore crests and proud British symbols in stained glass, and I noticed that Society members would be able to see everything around and below them. I guess they liked looking down on things.

The door swung open again, and with a grunt from the doorman, I was motioned into a dim flat with high ceilings and exquisite furnishings fit for a king. Perhaps "Majesty" was one himself from some time or another. Everything smelled musty and old, even though the building was of the very finest new row construction.

Across the vast room, drapery cascaded down from the ceiling, making a sort of ceremonial corner steeped in shadow, and from this shadow came a voice—thin, reedy, and disapproving: "Why are you back? You were to remain in New York as we prepare the colonial offices!"

"Your Majesty." I genuflected. "My apologies. Crenfall

went batty. They locked him up for my deeds, which is just as well. I must let the rabble in the press die down."

"Your deeds?"

Did this man not know? Wasn't the demon who'd overtaken my identity the type to have bragged about his bloody conquests? I decided to chuckle and give one of those looks that had made us both shudder when we'd seen the demon use it. I edged half into one of the shadows.

"I got a little…carried away with local women, you know. But I don't want it to detract from our greater goals. So I'm on holiday."

"Ah, yes. Well…you are a creature of your own nature. And we did tell you to seek to increase your powers by any means necessary. I expect a full report. We need to learn from your rituals and institutionalize them among the Majesties, the three of us."

I waved a noncommittal hand. "If your kind can understand them…"

"We are *disciples* of your rituals," the Majesty said, wounded the demon should think otherwise.

The last thing on Earth I wanted to do was recount what had been done in my visage. I thought of the carving of flesh, of all the terrible things we had seen, and I held back a shudder.

It was the greatest injustice that this person, this cretin, was talking to me as if dipping ink in the devil's well were a simple business transaction. As if no one had died torturously.

But I recognized the nonchalance of the upper classes when it came to the lives of those below them: toys, labor, annoyances, servants. I'd seen that mentality break hearts and create conditions tantamount to murder. My mother had tried to offset this mentality, and she'd done a damn good job of it. A pang of sentiment hit me hard. I hadn't had time to grieve her.

But this was not the time. I had a part to play, and I had to respond. I tried to imitate the mannerisms the demon had taken on. It was the *strangest* thing to imitate someone who had done an affected, false imitation of me. But I could never forget how that demon took and mocked me. I waved my hand in the air, pacing in and out of the dramatic shadows of the room as they fell strangely across gaudy Louis XIV-style furniture.

"I'll share with you what of my ways may translate to you mortals, but remember I am *beyond* you, the laws of my existence and yours are different—"

"Yes, yes," my host interrupted defensively, "you're a demon from the shadow-lands between life and death, a once-human soul that, so darkened in its earthly rounds, can no longer claim mortal derivation. You know, it's *tedious*, really. You may have come to Monsignor in his dream, but do not think for a moment that we collectively bow to you. We are not your tools. You are *ours*."

I folded my arms. "I know you bow to no one but

yourselves," I retorted, my tone just as biting as his. "It's what attracted me to Monsignor in the first place. But I am here only upon *my* whim and *my* pleasure."

A wave of distrust and fear rippled off this "Majesty," making the air sour. I saw a faint shimmer of red and gold light flicker over him, the indicators that had illuminated the demon. My enemy laid bare, this Majesty might make good on his threats, but he was not at ease with the demon. I hoped I could use that to advantage.

"Of course," the Majesty relented quietly. "But I beg you to remember that you exist for one purpose: to increase the shadows that claimed you. The Master's Society works toward a common goal: growing shadows across the most powerful lands so that we may restore the civilized world to the proper heights of aristocratic rule. Once that is attained, you have free rein over the gutter and can slake your every thirst."

"I assume the Denbury estate is in good hands? Not to question your judgment, but I really wouldn't have put Crenfall in charge of anything. He's a disaster."

"He had his uses. He yearned to serve, in hopes we would give him a place in our kingdom, but cracked under the strain. The estate was sold handsomely to a merchant family." He said the words "merchant family" with such disdain you'd think they were curse words. "Once the morbid curiosity surrounding the Denbury deaths settles down, we'll relocate

English operations there, and the rest will move to our new New York branch."

Before I could inquire further about that location, the Majesty continued. "How that young Denbury was talked about," he said with a sneer. "You'd think a finer youth had never been born. How besotted society ladies were by his piercing looks and disinterest in anything but his noble causes. The whole family. Gone. So *tragic*." He hissed. "Serves them right. Ungrateful wretches. That pretty little visage of yours should have been *mine*." I didn't have any idea what he meant, but I desperately wanted to throttle him.

"But that's all ancient history. Locals have been happy to gossip about the new estate tenants. And they'll be just as happy to gossip when the Denbury grounds are seized again at the proper time. But by then so much will be happening that no one will be able to keep up with one family's intrigue…"

I let this sink in, breathing deeply to keep my calm. "I like being popular and this body has its charms, but anonymity has its advantages."

"That's why we had to ship you off to New York, young man. That body of yours was just too beloved here. It would attract too much attention, whereas in New York, Lord Denbury serves as a pretty face with clear breeding and an accent to make all those aspirational American girls his playthings."

You can imagine how difficult this was to listen to without betraying my feelings. But you know what that's like, Natalie, having had your various parts to play in my drama. Still, it's a wonder I didn't draw my pistol and shoot the man dead right there. But then I'd have learned nothing. This was more useful and revelatory than I'd imagined. Justice in due time.

"Truly, though, how long *do* you plan to keep that body?" the Majesty scoffed.

"I rather like this one. Don't you go rushing me."

"You're missing your ring."

I glanced down at my hands. I tried to recall: had this body worn a ring? Did the demon now transferred and trapped in the painting wear it? Did it have some magical property?

"Came off amid one of my…tumbles," I explained. "I regret that. Lovely piece. But I did get rather carried away with them. My conquests."

His body partly in the light, I could see him shiver in anticipation. "Oh, you *must* share your ritual secrets, if not with the others, than with me, I *beg* you. Have you taken the time to visit your grave?" he asked cheerfully.

I shook my head. "Any reason why I should have?" I recovered from this question. Maybe there was a rite or ritual the Majesty had been expecting graveside. "I mean, the man had his uses. Hell of a painter. But did it all go to plan, without trouble?"

"My, yes. A decomposed body with the right details does the trick, just as you suggested. And the police, with all their useless municipalities…" He laughed. "I daresay a man could run about *ripping* people apart, night after night, and they'd not be able to catch him. It makes me want to try, just to see how much one could get away with."

"Isn't that what drew you into this?" I posited, pressing my luck and trying to get my mind around these people. "Isn't that why you called upon the likes of me? Isn't it one of the occupations of the leisure class? To see what you could get away with?"

"Oh, you mustn't get caught up in our games and think it's all about the experimentation. Our aim remains the grand restoration of power where mankind intended it." He leaned back, and I could see a corner of his face in the light.

An unattractive face with a balding pate and pockmarked cheeks. He appeared dull and sallow, yet his eyes were dark and sharp, and clearly his tone was meant to reassert his authority. He continued with his sense of mission:

"During one of your…tumbles, don't lose sight of the main goal of seizure. We want as many deeds and purse strings as possible. You may be called out from those shadow-lands as our colleague, but you are here under Society rule, and we mustn't have chaos. Not yet. Chaos comes far later on our schedule."

I bowed my head to him in acquiescence.

"And so," the Majesty said proudly, "with the soul-rending we've managed on you and the good doctor in New York working on reanimation and another on pharmacology, we've the tools of our operation in the process of implementation. In order to overturn the world, we must have fear on our side. Well, and opiates for the fearless. But our creations will wield a staff of fear that will clear our way like Moses once parted water," he said, chuckling.

Fear. Opiates. I thought of how I'd been kidnapped and tricked in an opium den. I kept my roiling anger well hid. A good doctor keeps his diagnosis veiled behind an impassive face. My visit had served as much of a purpose as it could.

"Back to New York, then, Majesty?"

"Back to New York with you. Check in on Dr. Preston. German Hospital, one of those benevolent places that treats whoever comes," he grumbled with distaste. "I suppose he has to work *somewhere*. His trial should be operational soon. Tell me everything. Send a secure address to this one, and we'll correspond from there. Remain clear of the telegraph wires; letters will do. Don't let me lose track of you again in any of your little games. Don't get attached to anyone or anything but the cause."

"Give me tasks, and I will see to them," I replied, "but give me leave and space. Do not have me followed or hovered over. Crenfall was miserable company, and I'll not tolerate the like. If you don't let me be a lone wolf, I will kill you in your sleep." I used the quiet pitch the demon used. It worked. Fear flickered across the man's ugly face.

"Agreed. Beyond your duties, your time is as you'd like it

to be, provided you compromise no one but yourself. Enjoy the body provided you."

"Oh, I shall. Good then." And with that I bowed my head, going for the door. "Ta!"

A grunt of amusement was all the good-bye the Majesty gave.

I maintained a jaunty walk down the three floors and around the corner to where Knowles had shifted the carriage. I hopped in and nearly collapsed against the leather cushion, my knees suddenly weak. Sitting inside with a hat tipped low over his long face, Knowles gave me a moment to sit up and regain steady breathing before he asked, "Any luck?"

"Oh, indeed, Mr. Knowles. More than I bargained for."

So there you have it, Natalie. I'm sent off again to New York.

I need a day to collect my resources. Only a fool would keep all his assets within his estate and obvious family holdings. So I send you this account and am off to collect some treasures and the bulk of my personal holdings.

Did I mention it's strangely cold in London? Perhaps I still walk the valley of shadow. I'll send word of my exact arrival time. Until then, dream well of me, and I promise to do the same.

Yours,

Jonathon

I shook so hard while reading the letter that my arms ached.

When he meets me in New York, will we have to look constantly over our shoulders, even though he demanded he not be trailed? I'd hoped that getting his affairs in order would mean we'd be free to exist as any normal, courting young couple might do, without fear of death, spells, or evil institutions hanging over them. But the moment I met Preston, I knew it wasn't so simple. The Society was the spider, and its web was large.

As I looked into the vanity, my reflection back was deathly pale. This new part Jonathon had to play was yet one more obstacle between us, one more matter to be resolved before we could be together. "Don't get attached to anything," had been the warning. The demon had no sweetheart, no fiancée, no woman he courted.

He only had victims.

Chapter 15

My door open, I was sitting and reading, hoping Dickens could get my mind off everything, when Bessie came into my room. "You've a visitor, Natalie. Miss Horowitz."

"Rachel!"

I tore down the stairs to see a dark-haired girl who had grown taller and even more waifish than I remembered, as if she'd become one with the spirits who spoke to her. She didn't turn at the sound of me on the stair, but she did jump as I threw my arms around her from behind.

I sat down beside her, and she took one look at me, her lovely face drawn, dark circles under her eyes, and tears flowed down her cheeks. She fell into my arms and wept there a while.

Stroking her hair, I just let her cry, small sounds and sniffles muffled by the handkerchief she put to her mouth. After a long moment, she pulled back.

"I'm sorry," she signed to me.

"For what?" I signed back. "For reaching out to me?

Everyone else would have thought you were crazy." I finished signing. She looked at me sheepishly. Then I grinned. Her face broke into a wide smile. "Guess what?" I signed. She raised her eyebrows in response. "I am speaking now," I said aloud, making sure she was watching my lips. "It's a long story, but I regained my voice. Just like you always thought I would."

This pleased her, and she clasped my hands in hers.

"Should I sign or speak?" I signed. She shrugged. I continued to sign. "Mrs. Northe wants you to stay with her. Not your house. For safety."

"No trouble?" Rachel signed. I shook my head. She shifted to pin me with a gaze that said she was desperate to be believed as she signed, "I promise I'm stronger than this. I will do the right thing. I'm just tired—"

"I know," I said and squeezed her white-gloved hand. I'd worked so hard to break this girl out of her shell in school, but I couldn't blame her now if she wanted nothing more than to retreat back into it.

Father entered with some light lunch he'd procured for us both. Living so near to the Metropolitan, we had lunch together at home if I wasn't with him at the acquisitions board, which had yet to give me any real responsibilities. Considering my more pressing duties, that was for the best.

Father welcomed Rachel like another daughter. Then I remembered they'd all had quite an experience, communing with my mother in a séance. Without me. I shoved that sting aside.

Rachel held out a note to my father. It read: "I'm so sorry for bringing any trouble upon your house. I'll try to make it up to you."

My father blinked back tears. He looked at her directly so she could more easily read his lips. "You gave me a chance to talk to Helen one last time. And that gift can never be repaid." He cleared his throat, kissed Rachel on the forehead, and walked out the door to work. Tears were in my eyes too, before I knew it.

"About that," I said, rubbing my face. "I want to know everything that was said. I've been desperate to talk to Mother. I wish I could've been there."

"She's always watching over you," Rachel signed.

Damn. There went the tears again. "Well, she could at least give me a sign of it."

"She does. Sometimes you're not paying attention."

I opened my mouth to protest but then shut it. I'd have to pay attention. "I want to know everything about what's been going on, Rachel, but let's get you to Mrs. Northe." I took Jonathon's letter with me.

Mrs. Northe was as welcoming as ever, looking fresh and summery in a lavender silk dress with a white lace modesty panel. There were no undue pleasantries. It wasn't as though we were beginning as strangers, and by the look of Rachel, haggard and weary, she couldn't have kept up the pretense of anything other than emergency. I handed Mrs. Northe Jonathon's letter.

"Read it, please. I don't know the strength or member-ship of the Master's Society, but it's something to work with. My poor, brave Jonathon."

"Mary, will you give Rachel a tour and show her to her rooms?" Mrs. Northe asked, taking the letter and reading it immediately.

Mary nodded and took Rachel by the arm. Just as I had done, Rachel looked around in amazement at the finery of the Fifth Avenue town house that was in the same city and yet a world away from the manner in which she and I lived.

Once Rachel felt safe and strong enough, we tried to find out how things had gone terribly wrong. It took a while to get the account out of her, about Preston's darkening days and the progression of the boxes tethering spirits to objects. Or, later, *parts*.

"What are the parts being used for?" Mrs. Northe asked. Rachel shook her head and shrugged. She signed that she had tried to get answers out of the spirits, but all she could glean was that they were angry, that they weren't meant to be alive anymore, that they wanted her to let them go or to put them back where they belonged. That the natural order of things was being overturned.

"Preston's chief interest seemed to be in reversing death," I mentioned. "*Reanimation*, the Majesty said."

Rachel's pale, hollowed face turned pleading. "Please. Not evil," she signed. "He didn't start evil. Laura—"

"We understand," Mrs. Northe said. "Hardly anyone drawn to dark depths begins that way."

I thought of Samuel, and I was scared for him. If we could get him to New York, perhaps we could all help break the allure...

"The spirits," Rachel signed. "They don't stop. They have so much to say, so much wrong, but it's all jumbled. I don't know what I'm hearing, or who. A floodgate. It's all just a sea of pain."

And then she sank in her chair exhausted, her head dropping. I wondered if the spirits had been allowing her any sleep. Likely not. If they had no rest, neither would she.

"Well, then." Mrs. Northe looked at me. "We need her to untie those spirits, but she has to be able to survive trying to reach them, to have the presence of mind to separate one voice from the pack. Poor girl," she murmured. "Those with gifts so easily become targets. That Society likes to prey upon the most vulnerable and cut to the quick those who would fight against them." The words hit me strongly, making sense out of what might have appeared to be a random pattern.

Mrs. Northe gazed at Rachel a moment and then took

her up in her arms, showing a surprising strength. "Natalie, do me a favor. Gather my skirts and hand them to me." She shifted Rachel's weight, a large, tall child in her arms, and held out an open hand. I gathered the doubled layers of fine silk, handed them up to Mrs. Northe, and pressed the folds into her open palm while her forearm was tucked under Rachel's legs.

"One of these days, women will be able to wear clothing that allows them to move properly and do something productive," she muttered.

"Oh, but it's such a beautiful dress," I said longingly. Mrs. Northe laughed.

"And that is what we must do in these coming days, my dove. Hold tight to the positive."

Chapter 16

My dearest Natalie,

This will likely reach you just before I see you again, but I had to tell you an odd thing that happened to me after I met with the Majesty.

Walking in Bloomsbury on business, I turned down a narrow street between Romanesque buildings. A severe woman—tightly buttoned in gray, with brown hair pulled taut beneath a hat—exclaimed as I came around the corner.

She blurted out as if she couldn't help herself, "Good God, young man, you must be freezing!"

"Headmistress," chided a tall man all in black. More severe than she, if that were even possible, he swept out from behind her and past me like some swooping raven, black hair and black frock coat billowing, looking behind me as if I were being followed by a parade or something.

"One moment, Professor. That's too much for one boy to handle. Look at all of it," she said, gesturing around me.

"Excuse me? All of what?" I asked.

She turned, piercing me with gray-blue eyes. "Pardon me if this seems rude and presumptuous, but you're very haunted. Recent brush with death?"

I stared at her, then back at the man who, with a sour expression, was nonchalantly waving things off around me as if I were surrounded by flies. Or worse.

"Yes," I replied slowly. What else could I say?

"That explains it," she replied. "And why you're wearing a scarf in summer. They do give off quite a chill."

"What does?" I asked.

"Ghosts." She clapped her hands in an authoritarian way and spoke sharply to the retinue of spirits that had evidently been following me. "Go on! Off with you. He's the picture of health, no thanks to you." She looked at me, behind me, then at me again. "There. All better. I shouldn't be saying this to you, but I've a suspicion you've seen and heard stranger things than this."

"Thank you...I think? And you are?"

"Oh," the woman chuckled drily. "Don't you worry about who we are. If darkness follows you, turn your face away. Don't feed the shadows. You're a doctor." She tapped her temple, her eyes glittering though she never smiled. "I can tell. I've a sense about you. We need doctors, young man, of all kinds. My friends and I are doctors of sorts, in the way we're called to be. Death didn't claim you, so you've work to do. So go on and heal the wounds of this world, my boy. We can never have too many healers."

She reached out to touch me on the cheek as if I were a long-lost son but thought better of it. Turning back toward the mouth of the alley, she headed toward the man all in black who awaited her with his arms folded, looking bored and impatient. He held out an arm for her and she took it, falling into intense conversation as they turned the corner toward the heart of Bloomsbury with no further thought of me or glance back.

I was a lot warmer. I felt amazingly better. I rolled my scarf up and tucked it in my briefcase.

What else can I make of this odd meeting but that it was a sign? A sign that there are others in the world who are drawn, like us, toward inexplicable callings. If there's a Master's Society, then we must form our own society of peers in resistance. Perhaps London is that much safer with people like those two. Now New York needs people like us. I'm filled with purpose and cured of my chills.

Rallied by the encounter, life surges in my veins, and I'm more determined than ever to expose the entire insidious operation before more damage is done. I shall honor the strange good deeds done to me by strangers down a Bloomsbury alley.

In visiting family deposit boxes, I retrieved funds and a few treasures. I've enclosed a cameo pendant from my mother. It isn't doing her any good now, certainly, and I know she'd have liked you. Loved you. So please take it.

I'll see you very soon. In a dream? I'd like to see you in a nightdress, unless you're being modest. Which I respect, I do. Utterly. Even if modesty isn't any fun.

Yours,
Jonathon

I laughed, as if the pall that had been lifted from Jonathon by those odd good Samaritans was lifted from me too. I undid the twine and thin paper to reveal a gorgeous white cameo on an onyx surface, surrounded by a glittering pewter filigree and hung on a silk ribbon. The girl in the cameo was nymph-like, with flowers in her hair, a faerie queen for our strange fairy tale. Gazing in the mirror, I held it up to my neck, then put it on and waltzed about the room. I'd need Mrs. Northe or someone to give me a waltzing lesson before Jonathon and I could attend a ball together.

I slept well, at first. But the hazy dream of moving shadows came into sharp focus, likely somewhere around 3 a.m., when all my dreams seem to reach their zenith.

Jonathon and I stood many paces apart, the usual corridor of my dreamworld windy and noisy as with the clatter of steel and rail, or the blowing of a terrible storm. His boat was coming across the ocean toward me, so a certain rocking lull came into our hallway. Light came into the corridor as if from windows, but it blinked in and out as though we were standing between passing trains on either side, or in and out of undulating shadow constantly in transit.

"I'll see you soon," he called to me, the black waves of his hair buffeted by the wind. I ached to run my hands through the locks.

He looked me up and down, and I noticed that I was only in my summer nightgown, a more revealing one. "Ah, thank you for the nightdress," he said, grinning rakishly. "I'll come for you soon."

I stepped forward, reaching for him.

Love in its first bloom, all the poets said, was full of aching and impatience. So then was I. And so then was he.

But something changed.

The flickering lights went dark, and a single dim light from one far-off window cast my love into stark contrast and deep shadow.

It was not love that had him approaching me with the look I remembered from the demon. His eyes held that odd reflective quality of the demon's. "I'm coming for you," he growled. The noisy, echoing corridor was filled again with those dread whispers.

And he swiped a hand at me, ripping the neckline of my gown.

"You think they won't know what you've done? They'll know. My strength grows. I will kill you, Arilda, after all."

Arilda.

The name I'd taken when I tricked the demon. He had been targeting young women with the names of saints. It gave him some kind of added power. And it seemed he still remembered mine.

And then the reflective eyes were gone, and Jonathon stood before me as I knew him to be. But he stared at me as if in pity and turned to walk away.

"Jonathon…" I called after him.

"*Cruel*," he spat.

He reached into the darkness, opening a door beyond the charred study. He slammed the door behind him, and I was left alone again with only murmuring darkness and the sting of jagged fingernail scratches upon my collarbone.

I awoke and was alarmed to find that there were indeed scratches where I'd felt them in my dreams. While my bond with Jonathon was stronger for the supernatural experiences we shared, perhaps something of the demon was still an echo somewhere inside? Was Jonathon fully rid of him? Whatever conduit brought my premonitions, did it let in something ugly too? How could I filter the good from the bad?

I fingered the scratch and tried not to cry. As with the runes on my arm, I felt violated. When a person sleeps, he or she is vulnerable, and nothing should *ever* attack a vulnerable being. No unwarranted or unwelcome, uncomfortable attention should ever be tolerated.

Pushing back my nightgown sleeves, I cried out to find more runes upon my arm, the same red thin markings, as if carved with a delicate pen-knife. I denied them, shaking my head, my hair falling from its bun. "I renounce thee," I said, and they began to fade. I marked them diligently.

Later that morning, I caught a downtown trolley car to Mrs. Northe's so I could check on Rachel and translate the runes.

Mrs. Northe noticed me rubbing my arm as I entered the parlor and surmised the problem. Rachel was nowhere to be seen. "Nightmares manifest again?" Mrs. Northe asked.

"In more ways than one. If I'm not careful, could my own dreams kill me?"

"No. But something of that demon must be living in your subconscious. Feeding upon your nightmares."

"Growing stronger?" I choked.

"Only if you let it," she replied. I would have to enlist Jonathon to help me fight off the shadows as he used to do in my dreams. Something within me wasn't allowing him to be the hero as he once was. She led me into her library, and we sat again with the book of runes.

"I am co—" the letters roughly translated. Still incomplete. Mrs. Northe plucked a small, clear bottle of colorless fluid from a shelf of religious icons. She tapped a few drops upon my wrist and crossed my wrist with her long fingertips. Any lingering irritation completely faded.

"And that is?" I asked, gesturing to the bottle as she returned it to the cabinet from which it had come.

"Holy water, of course," she replied.

Before either of us could wonder further about the message, a rough sound came from upstairs. Rachel had some capacity for sound but it was untried. We both rushed upstairs and found her lying on her bed, eyes closed but moving rapidly beneath their lids. We tried to rouse her but to no avail.

"She's been like this now for a while," Mrs. Northe explained. "I can only think that she's receiving information, that she's in a sort of trance. Spirits have hold of her and are keeping her in this stasis. I've tried to break through, but she's resisting."

It was like her body was comatose. I thought of Elsa and my stomach sank, wondering about Samuel and what would become of them both.

Looking tired, Mary stood outside the hall in the open doorway.

"Yes, Mary?"

She entered and handed Mrs. Northe an envelope. Mrs. Northe quickly scanned the contents, then handed me the letter.

THE TRANS-ATLANTIC TELEGRAPH COMPANY

Almost at port. Arrive at noon.

Jonathon. I ducked my head into the hall where a gorgeous grandfather clock stood sentry. "It's eleven thirty!" I cried.

"Well, you'd better take my carriage and go then!" Mrs. Northe called.

"What, without you?" I said in the doorway, watching Mrs. Northe place a cool cloth over Rachel's forehead. My mouth hung open, a sudden blush blooming furious upon my cheeks, which only made her laugh.

"I remember being in love, Natalie dear. And I trust your virtue until I've reason to believe otherwise, so do take care of yourself."

"Th-thank you," I sputtered. I was more in debt to this woman than I could imagine. An uncomfortable thought. But Jonathon and I had become so used to doing things on our own for survival that it was hard to adjust back into the reality of chaperones and permissions.

Thrilled as I was for our reunion, the question remained: Was he forever entwined with the demon? What if in the next dream he did more than scratch me?

I need to stand strong for us both, to separate fact from fiction and realize dreams are not reality. Clues exist there, but what occurs face to face in the honest light of day is what matters. But the runes on my arm. Those were in the light of day. I wasn't sure if the idea that I might be losing my mind was a comfort or an additional inconvenience.

I took a seat on a Cunard pier bench downtown near the Battery, the scene incredible and dizzying. The screech of gulls, the bells of numerous ships, and the calling of various vendors made the waterfront a festive carnival. Great, long, floating behemoths of steel and bright paint set off on any number of potentially life-changing journeys.

I sat with a thrum in my heart, watching the parade of passing ladies, gentleman, and children, all with anticipation on their faces. Do they, like me, wait to reunite with someone special? Or do they await a boat to take them to an exciting destination where someone expects them, awaits them, longs for them? A pier or a train station is a thrilling place of aching and impatience, eternally in its first bloom of love.

In my mind, this was what I *hoped* would happen when Jonathon stepped off the gangplank:

I *hoped* we'd fall into each other's arms and into an embrace that couldn't be troubled by the impropriety of kissing passionately on a dock. That's what piers, docks, and train platforms were for. The playful, jovial couple I imagined we could be would act as if all anxieties were forgotten.

No. Instead, *this* was what really happened:

I stared at him as he exited the ship and came down the roped plank and onto the pier. His eyes sought the crowd and pierced me. *Oh*, he cut a handsome figure: black mourning jacket and crisp white cravat, wide-brimmed hat in hand, those eviscerating bright eyes brightening still at the sight of me, a delicious grin spreading across his face.

But despite this welcome, gorgeous sight, all I could think of was the moment in the corridor when he tore at me. My flesh still bore the scratches, and they once again throbbed in pain. How could a dream actually wound me? I looked him in the eye, knowing if I saw any of that tell-tale reflective quality the demon had worn.

"Natalie," he said, approaching me, reaching out for me. Something on my face stilled him. He furrowed his brow. "What. Why are you looking at me that way?"

"You hurt me…" I blurted. It wasn't the first thing I'd wanted to say. I'd wanted to kiss him.

He stared at me. "I beg your pardon?"

"The last dream, the loud corridor. You changed. You ripped at my gown. Look—"

I pulled the lace neckline of my bodice aside so he could see the marks. He hissed and reached out his fingers as if to touch them but then withdrew.

"Natalie, if you dreamed that, it wasn't me. We didn't share that. I remember seeing you," he lowered his voice, "in your nightdress, but you faded abruptly. I know I didn't…wound you…" He stared at the marks in horror.

"Then someone else has your face in my dreams?"

He set his jaw, bright eyes flashing. "Someone else *wore* this face, Natalie. You know that as well as I! And I hope you'd know me better than to think any part of *me* would ever hurt you, awake or asleep," he snapped, turning away.

I heard him begin to speak jovially, as if to someone else, staging how he thought our conversation should've begun. "Oh, Jonathon," he said, affecting his neutral American accent, "welcome back. I've *missed* you. How *brave* you were!"

He shook his head and replied to himself. "Oh, Natalie, it's been an awful business, playing the demon, alone. Thank God I have you—" He glared back at me as he began walking away. "*That's* what I hoped I could count on."

I watched him exit the Cunard gate, my throat dry and my cheeks burning with anxious embarrassment. I hurried to catch up.

We wove silently through the throng of passengers. On the street he stopped to gain his bearings. I gestured toward a line of carriages awaiting those who could afford them. We were provided for by our own "Northe" star, our guardian angel to whom we were increasingly beholden. I nodded to the driver as Jonathon helped me into the carriage. "I'm s-sorry," I stammered as I took my seat, "I…"

"You can't be responsible for your dreams?" he interrupted, climbing in after me and closing the cab door. "You *can*, Natalie. You can be the master of them. I've seen you banish demons. 'I renounce thee,' you'd say to what frightened you. But these days you let other men in and you wake up wounded. Where's the brave girl who crossed a world to get to me? Won't she believe in me? Won't she fight the demon off?" He was as stung as he was angry. "Instead you assume I hurt you and not your own mind? You think higher of your nightmares than me?"

"Jonathon, please." I did not expect such a vehement reaction.

He set his jaw. "I had a right terrible time in London, Natalie. I could use a friend. Some kindness and cheer. I'm tired of being frightened, so the last thing on earth I want to see is that sentiment reflected in *your* eyes. Dreaming of my friends is one thing. Being scared of the man you once claimed you love, for no founded reason, is another."

"I know, of course..." But still, the marks. "How could the marks be my *mind* alone? Do I not have reason to be scared?"

"You do, Natalie. For that, I'm scared for you too. Perhaps we didn't spend time enough away from the source of the dark magic."

"It seems I didn't. But if it's lying in wait for me, where? What do I do?"

"We banish it as before." He looked at me. "Together." He tried to smile.

Not knowing what else to do, I threw my arms around him. Couldn't we talk deliciously of flirtations? He tensed as I touched him. That only made me squeeze him harder, not wanting to be denied. "I should've just kissed you madly there on the dock."

"I'd have *much* preferred that," he muttered. I thought about obliging us both, but I wanted the tension to fade first.

"I was worried *sick* for you—" I murmured.

"It was the only thing to do. The Majesty couldn't have known the results of your amazing reversal. He couldn't know I was myself again, not the demon. Their confidence is their weakness. They don't think of the faithful or those who might prevail against their magic as threats. They assume their darkness trumps all."

"Jonathon, you were valiant and brave, but please don't become confident as their…double agent. They were happy to rip you apart once. They wouldn't hesitate—"

"I daresay they wouldn't. But I plan on keeping them at a distance."

"Even as they move 'operations' to this city?"

"Ah, yes, well…*Here* I have you. My secret weapon."

"Do not endanger your ward," I said, eyeing him.

"My ward? Ah, yes, Miss Rose, my ward."

"You have to admit that's a *delicious* plot, Lord Denbury."

"Oh? Delicious?" He leaned over me and his lips were against my temple, sending hot, tea-scented breath upon my cheek. "Tell me, what does the handsome young lord do about his pretty ward very nearly his age?"

"*Torments* her," I murmured, lifting my lips to his ear.

"Does he? How does he torment her?" he countered in mine.

"I don't know. You'll have to tell me," I whispered, and my body thrilled from the tips of my ears to my toes, delighting in the game.

"Ah. Well, then." He pulled away and spoke very seriously, his eyes somber. "I suppose it's time I told you that I've a fiancée back in London."

There was a terrible moment as I stared at him. Was he serious? He looked serious. I didn't know anything about how the aristocracy worked, and he was still in so many ways a stranger. It was completely plausible that his family had him betrothed since birth. I was suddenly dizzy, falling back toward the carriage door.

Jonathon caught my shoulder. "Oh…is that not the kind of torment you mean?" He grinned.

I hit him hard on the arm. "Don't *do* that. I'm still reeling from that dream with all those society ladies draped all about you."

"Oh, and Nathaniel had his arms about you, *kissing your neck*, and I'm supposed to just *ignore* that?"

"That was just his flirtation manifesting in a dream."

"Don't be a hypocrite, Natalie. What makes you jealous

will make a man *crazy*. I'm sensible and level headed, but don't test me. Play fair."

"Yes, my lord," I said, kissing his cheek, delighting in his title.

"My *ward*," he said, chuckling. We fell into an awkward silence.

"Can we...can *I* begin again?" I asked timidly, clasping his hand in mine. "Jonathon, my love, welcome back to New York. I've missed you terribly."

He looked at me, and I saw the haunted face I remembered from the painting. Yes, he was cured of the curse, but so much had been taken from his life and his reality had been shattered, a burden I could not reverse. He allowed his steeled armor to fall.

His delectable lips curved slightly. "Better. Come, torment your guardian, my pretty young ward..."

I leaned in and kissed him, finally. Slowly, deliciously, and thoroughly. I hoped my kiss explained how much I cared. "*Much* better," he breathed, and his arms locked around me tight and strong. The reality of him was so sure, so solid and true. How could I have ever doubted him? Absence can indeed twist perception. So can the wrong sort of dreams. But this. This was the truth. A truth I'd gained my voice for and risked my life to save.

As we clattered up Lexington, we finally drew back to

catch our breath. Then came questions. "So, other than flirting with you," Jonathon began, "what did Nat say?"

As I relayed the details, Jonathon looked around for something to punch and instead pounded his fist against his knee. "Murdered. My parents were murdered."

All I could do was take his hand in the long, tense silence. There was nothing I could say to bring them back or undo the horror done to him. "When all of this is said and done, Jonathon, they'll not have died in vain. I'll do anything I can to make sure that's true."

"See. Now *that's* my brave girl." He kissed my forehead.

"I told Nathaniel about Samuel. Since you might not be in a position, with your double identity, to help him, maybe Nathaniel could."

"Good."

"One more thing. Nathaniel was approached by someone, a chemist, about a drug that could eliminate melancholy. Seems he was interested in targeting Nathaniel's Association."

"More Society business? Another of the three departments, pharmacology? That might be the next phase of experiments. But I still don't know what Preston's really doing. I couldn't outright ask since I'm sure the demon knew well enough."

"That's where Rachel comes in. Preston is her employer. He has been asking her to do strange things, the most recent of which was to tie spirits of the dead to segmented body parts. Something, I might add, I foresaw in a dream."

"Dear God. Then what? What's being done with the parts?"

"You're going to have to ask Preston. He's likely returned. Ask to see the work, per your instructions from the Society."

"Well, then, that's the first task for both of us."

"Me too?" I gulped.

"He's already met Miss Rose. You may hear or pick up on something I cannot. Besides, I feel I'm at my best when you're at my side."

I smiled. This was the core of true love: when someone brought out the best, bravest, and strongest parts of you and stood with their best self beside you.

We stole another kiss for as long as we could before the carriage slowed. I pinned up a few locks of hair that had come undone and we smoothed our clothing.

"Hello, *dear* boy!" Mrs. Northe exclaimed, embracing him at the door. "Welcome back."

"Thank you, Mrs. Northe. It is good to be back again with you both."

There was genuine warmth between them, and I prayed that my father might welcome him with similarly open arms, but that seemed unlikely. Mrs. Northe doted on Jonathon like a prodigal son for a while, striking that enigmatic balance between mother and friend, making you think she was the most valuable woman in the world to you. And she was. But being so in debt made me nervous.

"Is Rachel all right?" I asked.

"Still resting. More peacefully this time. Perhaps the spirits are preoccupied."

We relayed our thoughts about what Preston may have in store. Mrs. Northe listened carefully but said nothing. Jonathon didn't waste a whit of time.

"We must be off to Dr. Preston, as directed."

I nodded. "Yes, Jonathon, it's true, that must be done… and…"

"And?"

"And you must meet my father," I said.

"Ah, yes. Of course. Come on then, Miss Rose, we've an investigation to begin."

And with that, brave Lord Denbury was out the door, seemingly suddenly more nervous about meeting my father than confronting a mad doctor. It wasn't as if Father was intimidating, but I suppose fathers of girls men loved always had that sort of power, the power of one simple word in answer to the question: *May I court your daughter?*

What if he said no?

Chapter 17

We walked up the many blocks to the German Hospital on Seventy-Seventh Street. It had begun to rain. We didn't have umbrellas, so we just got damp. Fitting, the rain, because it was gloomy and hazy. Not warm but not cool, a distinct discomfort in the moist air.

The building itself was imposing and multistoried. Tall, narrow windows lined the building, and its looming turreted rooftop, squared with wrought-iron fencing at the top, made me feel like I was looking at the House of Usher before it fell apart, ripped asunder in madness and death brought to life. A perfect home for a resurrectionist…

The exterior of the rear wing where Preston admitted patients looked entirely vacant. There were no lamps lit, no curtains or windows open. Everything was shut and shaded. As we approached, we saw a sign lettered "Closed for renovation" in unsteady script.

"Whatever it is, it's downstairs. Near the morgue."

"How do you know?"

"Dreams."

Jonathon tried the door. It was locked. He stepped back, but a sound drew our focus again to the lock. The curtain of the door was open, revealing an empty hallway beyond. No one was at the door, yet the lock audibly unlocked.

We walked in. The wing was empty. Save for one man.

A man in a bright suit sat in a bay window across from rows of empty beds. He looked like a large, garish puppet. He was pale and so was his hair. One long leg was propped up on the window seat, another lolling down. He was dressed like a seventeenth-century courtier, though mismatched with modern shoes and pants instead of breeches.

"What d'ye want?" came a cockney accent booming across the empty wing. I remembered what Nathaniel said about the men who'd approached him. I think this man was one of them. I pulled on the left side of my collar, a signal, but I felt assured Jonathon was already well on his guard.

"And you are?" Denbury asked calmly.

"Roth. And *you* are?"

"Denbury. Does the name ring a bell?"

Roth scrunched up his pale face in thought. "One of the demon's pretty boys, aren't ye?"

Jonathon bristled, but in a way that befit the role. "If by that, you mean I *am* the demon that is *collecting* pretty things, then yes."

"Like that dolly-mop there?" Roth sniffed at me.

"Yes. Miss Rose is a part of my collection. She can't speak or hear. But she's nice to look at."

"That's convenient," Roth said, his tone carrying a distinct undercurrent I didn't like.

"That's what I thought," Jonathon purred.

Indeed. That's almost exactly what the demon had said when it met me. That no one would know if I resisted him. It took everything inside me not to cross that room and slap Roth in the face. Or claw out his eyes. I turned an indifferent face to Jonathon but I'm sure he knew how uncomfortable I was, that he was playing his part a little *too* well.

"Why are ye here?" Roth growled.

"I have instructions from the London office. The Majesty said to check in on Preston."

"On the work? It isn't done. Had to clear the wing to work in peace. But there's not enough of 'em yet to make her go." Roth detached himself from the window and strolled up to us. "Takes a lot of death to make a life, it seems."

I wasn't exactly sure what he meant by that. While I told myself I didn't want to know, a part of me really did. My curious dark side was unwilling to leave well enough alone.

Roth stood before us, the shadow of the hospital shades drawn in such a way that only the lower part of his face was lit, the rest of his large head in shadow. I had to look up to take him in with that cruel mouth and an ugly scar down the corner of his lip that gave him a permanent frown. His eyes reflected strangely in the darkness. Like a dog. My already chilled blood now froze. This was a possessed body.

I pulled at the left side of my collar again in what I hoped appeared to be a nervous gesture. I noticed Jonathon did not look Roth straight in the eye but did glance at me.

"Regardless of the progress of the work, I have to tell the Majesty something, so you'd best show me to Preston. Don't deny me. The Society doesn't like it when their hierarchy is undermined," Jonathon threatened.

"Oh, gettin' all high and mighty, are we, brother? What makes you more important than me?"

"*Breeding*," Jonathon said, wielding class like a hammer, careful to distinguish his upper-class accent over Roth's cockney tones.

Roth snorted. "I know the Society's all for preserving the aristocracy, but really, brother, it won't matter when it all begins to unravel. *We'll* win in the end."

"And when we do, Mr. Roth, there will still be hierarchy. Take care. I am not your brother."

Roth clicked his tongue. There was a terrible, tense silence. "Dr. Preston is right this way, Lord Denbury, *sir*," Roth said with exaggerated deference. His eyes flashed at me.

I wasn't sure at first if it was wise of Jonathon to play class in the way that he did, one that might engender resentment, but really it was brilliant. Establishing him as a more valued and important player to the Society was its own safety measure.

Preston's office door was open, and the doctor sat in a rumpled yellow suit with a strange contraption attached to a dead mouse. Looking up, he scowled. "It's you."

"Oh, please, don't stand on ceremony, Dr. Preston," Jonathon chided, grabbing my hand and leading me into the office.

Preston glanced at me. "What's she doing here?"

"She's my pet. My favorite accessory. For now."

"Yes, you and your transient pleasures," Preston said with disdain. "You know, demons could learn a thing or two from humans about loyalty and love."

Jonathon snorted. "Oh, teach me, Doctor, *do*."

"You had the mind of a doctor once," Preston said, his voice still quiet, as he stared at the mouse. He pressed a button attached to a wire and a tiny, dead paw twitched. "That body of yours was a prodigy."

"Yes, and I still retain some of his knowledge. Useful. Especially knowing what parts of the body will bleed out the fastest from a puncture wound."

I forced myself to look away, scared I'd look up and see the demon in Jonathon again. Preston glanced up, then back to his notes. I wandered to the bookshelves, hoping curiosity, as supposedly deaf and mute, wouldn't be seen as threatening.

"Are you here to threaten me?" Preston asked.

"Not at all, just checking in on your work, per the Majesty's instructions."

"It isn't finished."

"So that lackey outside tells me. May I see the progress?"

Preston looked up at Jonathon with beady, bloodshot eyes. "No, you may not."

"So what, then, would you have me tell the Majesty?"

"That it is ninety percent complete, with residual spiritual matter pending."

I examined the bookshelves, surprised to see Preston had compiled a great deal of fiction alongside medical texts, alchemy, occult matters, and botany. I wasn't sure what plants had to do with dead bodies, but there was always room to be surprised these days. As for the fiction, perhaps Preston was looking for inspiration.

On a shelf I noticed a small, glass-topped box that held a pendant inside. Thin and delicate, it was a six-pointed star inlaid with pearl. It looked familiar, though I couldn't place why. But a sudden instinct said it was important, and I slid the small box up the cuff of my sleeve.

"I could exhibit the work within the next few weeks," Preston assured Jonathon. "It depends on the state of the medium. She's become…less reliable. I may have to replace her."

Rachel, surely.

"My suggestion is to keep your staff as is," Jonathon replied. "We don't recruit indiscriminately. It behooves the Society to keep those informed about your work to a limited number."

"I can't be pushed toward productivity and constrained at the same time," Preston said, exasperated. "Please leave. I have work to do."

"Noted. You'll see me again."

"I'm sure," Preston muttered. "Can you see yourself out?"

Jonathon nodded and led me out by grabbing my arm.

"We're going to have a look downstairs," Jonathon stated. I tensed. I didn't want to go down there if it was just the two of us.

Roth stepped in the way of the staircase that led below.

"No," he replied simply but firmly. "In time."

"Soon, or else," Jonathon replied and turned on his heel. Roth said nothing further. He just watched us as we exited, Jonathon leading me as if I were his hostage.

Once we'd taken a few winding blocks and were far enough away, Jonathon shuddered all over and loosed a cry of disgust, as if he could shed the bitter taste of his darker half like an insect shaken off his fine clothes. "Good God, I hope I won't have to do this much longer."

"What's frightening, Jonathon, is you're very good at it. You even had me convinced you were him again." I closed my eyes, trying not to think of the attack, trying not to succumb to the panic the memory triggered.

Jonathon stopped me and took hold of my arms. I froze. "Please. Natalie. Don't be frightened of me. Not here, not now—"

"I'm not sure that's fair, Jonathon. The demon almost killed me. It's hard not to remember—"

"Almost killed us both. But we're stronger than it was. Bear with me. Please. Trust. I need your trust. Otherwise I can't play the part well."

I nodded. "Just…hold me a moment. So I remember what *you* feel like." He gladly obliged, folding me tenderly in his arms, kissing my hair. "That's better."

"Yes, it is."

We couldn't shake the chill, even in the summer, as we walked downtown.

"Jonathon," I said. "Roth. I think that's the same man that paid a visit to Nathaniel with another doctor. 'Big, pale, with garish suits can only describe so many. I assume that doctor who visited Nathaniel was from the pharmacology department of the three branches, miracle elixir and all."

Jonathon took a deep breath. "The ever-widening web."

"Preston?" Mrs. Northe asked, taking one look at our

faces as we walked in her door. I wonder if she felt the chill we brought with us.

"Going batty, if you ask me." He turned to Mrs. Northe, continuing, "And a bit paranoid. His guard, sent by the Society, is actually a possessed body, we believe. Preston has shut down his wing. The building was *unnaturally* cold. In England I was taught what that temperature means."

"That the building is full of spirits," Mrs. Northe commented.

"Can you see them?" Jonathon asked. "Spirits? It would seem some people can. I didn't see any ghosts, but good Samaritans in London shooed away an entourage I didn't even know I had. I was a lot warmer afterward."

"You and I have both had brushes with death, Lord Denbury. That tends to bring them out," Mrs. Northe stated, handing us tea we hoped would mitigate our lingering shivers. "While I've only seen an occasional ghost, and only at certain times, I do feel them around me more often than not."

"Ah, our haunted life," Jonathon sighed, taking a seat at Mrs. Northe's lacquered writing desk at the corner of the room. "We weren't allowed downstairs, where Natalie presumes the work is being held, and I wasn't inclined to pick a fight. Not today. May I use your stationery, Mrs. Northe?"

"Of course."

He set to work on a note, pulling out a piece of paper plucked from his breast pocket that bore a red and yellow seal. He glared at the paper as he began to write.

"Your expected correspondence with evil, I presume?" I asked.

"I wish it were otherwise," he replied.

I shuddered. Letters should be for love and fondness, not for matters like this. Faint, hollow traces ringed his eyes. That old haunted look. I remember it well from the days within the painting. Perhaps playing the part was just as draining as being split body from soul.

A small movement out of the corner of my eye turned me to the door. Rachel had her hand on the pocket doors, steadying herself, and when her eyes fell upon me she smiled weakly.

I jumped up and brought her to the sofa to sit beside me. "Feeling better?" I signed.

"Comes and goes," she signed.

Jonathon looked up, put down his pen, stood, and bowed.

"Miss Horowitz, I presume?" he asked me, coming closer.

I nodded. "She can read lips, so make sure she's focused on you and don't mumble."

Jonathon knelt before her, reaching out and asking for her hand. She gave it. "Jonathon Whitby, Lord Denbury, at your service." He kissed Rachel's hand. "Any friend of Natalie's is a friend of mine."

Rachel smiled, her wan face suddenly transforming into something healthier.

"Now, Miss Horowitz, I am a doctor, and I hear you've been plagued with spirits."

Rachel nodded.

"I don't know how to cure *that*, but it doesn't appear you've been eating well. No appetite?"

Rachel shook her head.

"But if you drank something, could you keep it down?"

Rachel nodded.

"Do you like juice?"

Rachel nodded again.

"Mrs. Northe, may I have access to your kitchen? And also to your medicine cabinet? I'd like to prepare a concoction for Miss Horowitz to get her strength up."

"All my supplies are at your disposal. Make me a list of anything I lack, and Mary will get it for you straightaway."

"Excellent," Jonathon said. "We need to get her strength back for the coming days." He bowed his head to Rachel and exited.

"I like him," she signed to me with a wide smile. "Is he yours?"

I blushed.

"Yes, he's very taken," Mrs. Northe signed.

Rachel blushed. "I forgot you could sign, too." Rachel bit her lip.

"I learned to sign when Peter lost his ability to speak. The last year of his life," Mrs. Northe added. "We brought a tutor in to teach us both. It was so much better than just wasting away in silence," she said, blinking back a tear. Yet another detail about Mrs. Northe I feel I should have known but didn't. She rarely spoke about herself, but whenever she did open up, I couldn't help caring for her more.

"Oh, Rachel," I said, plucking the pendant from where it had been tucked safe in my sleeve. "You mentioned that you often contacted spirits through tokens, something meaningful. Does this look familiar?"

Rachel clapped her hands to her mouth, then seized the pendant and held it to her breast.

"Oh," I said, realizing why it had seemed familiar. "It's yours." I remembered it from school. Everyone had asked about it, and Rachel had gotten tired of signing out explanations of what the Star of David was, so she'd taken to wearing it beneath her dresses.

Watching the exchange, Mrs. Northe came over beside us and squeezed my shoulder. "Oh, Natalie, that was very wise of you to find this."

I blinked and smiled. "It was?"

"Yes. Just as Rachel has been tethering spirits to objects, I think that she has been tethered to this work herself, tethered to loyalty to Preston, through this meaningful token. Returning it to her gives her soul more freedom. Talismans are very powerful in this particular brand of Society magic. While the spirits will not readily let her go, you may just have broken Preston's hold."

I smiled, proud of myself and my instincts, and moved to clasp the pendant where it belonged. Rachel kissed the star and pressed it tightly against her chest.

Jonathon returned with a glass of orange juice with thick syrup at the bottom. Honey, probably, and some white grit I assumed must be additives Jonathon deemed important.

"Miss Horowitz, please do a doctor the great favor of drinking this." He handed the glass to Rachel, who looked at me as if for permission.

I signed to Rachel that she could trust him.

She nodded and drank, looking up at Jonathon with shy thanks. Maybe it was my wishful thinking, but she soon began to regain some color to her cheeks and lips.

"Lord Denbury," Mrs. Northe began with a sly smile. "I know you've had a trying visit already today, but you *do* know there is another visit yet to pay. A very important one."

Jonathon paled.

"Yes. Of course. Let me put on a fresh suit. I want to look my best." He turned to me. "Then I shall come to call."

Chapter 18

Mrs. Northe had her driver send me home while Jonathon prepared for the visit.

"Lord Denbury has returned and he would like to come calling," I announced to my father the moment I walked in the door. "He can come, can't he?"

"Of course. Knowing you, you'd find a way to see him anyway, even if I forbid it," my father said as he made his way to his small study. "I have to have some idea of who I'm dealing with." He closed the door.

Bessie moved about the parlor, straightening up every surface with a fastidious eye. "Don't mind him. That's how fathers are at the prospect of losing their daughter. Especially an only child. But Natalie, love, you're *talking*. You're being courted by a *British lord*. I don't care what kind of witchcraft happened to cause it, looks like God's work to me," she said, moving to our kitchen to make sure there was plenty of tea.

"It's been God's work indeed, I promise," I said, following her and helping to prepare small tea sandwiches. "We couldn't have fought a devil without faith founded on light and love, not darkness and fear. I want you to know the sort of man he is, what sort of woman I want to be. We may have gone about things unconventionally—"

"I trust you. I know how it is to do things unconventionally. Lord, my whole family did. So long as the Man Upstairs guides that convention," she said, pointing to heaven, "your methods are all right with me."

I readied Father's dinner and took it to him, sure to place a kiss on his cheek as I set the silver tray upon his desk as was our custom. We'd long ago done away with family dinners on account of my lack of speech. Breakfast was the meal we ate together, and being a bunch of readers, writers, and artists, evening was time for work, reading, daydreaming. Perhaps this custom might change now, but then we knew everything was changing.

"I just…want you to be happy and taken care of," he said quietly. I turned at the door.

"I *am* happy and taken care of, by you. And I will be by him, I promise."

Jonathon Whitby, Lord Denbury, charmed everyone he met, so how could he not charm my father?

Father hardly cuts an imposing figure; he's tall but slight. But he's an academic who has his moments of intensity, and he stared down Jonathon with all of it when he opened the door.

Jonathon was dressed to make any girl swoon. He'd taken extra care to impress in a fine, new suit coat, something charcoal and magnificent, with a navy waistcoat and light blue cravat that emboldened the already piercing quality of his blue eyes. His black hair was combed neatly, and his kid gloves met my father's bare hand. Jonathon was the first to extend his palm for a firm shake.

"Hello, Mr. Stewart. It's an honor to meet you. Jonathon Whitby, Lord Denbury, at your service." He nodded to me, bowing. "Miss Stewart."

"Lord Denbury," I curtsied. My, how *formal*. But surely my father had read that Jonathon and I used to rendezvous by my falling through a painting and into his arms.

"Indeed, do come in." Father gestured, and we ascended the stairs to our top floor. Bessie opened the door and bowed her head. I could see her holding back a wild grin that almost made me laugh.

"My lord," she said.

"Oh, please, miss, no titles with me. I do hope all of you will call me Jonathon."

"There's been plenty of familiarity here already," my father cautioned. "Lord Denbury, this is a friend of Natalie's mother and the all-around saint of our house, Mrs. Cartwright."

"Mrs. Cartwright, a pleasure."

"The pleasure is ours, Lord Denbury," Bessie exclaimed.

"You're a miracle indeed to get our Natalie talking again. That sure is a blessing."

"She certainly is," Jonathon replied. He moved to take my hand, it being such a natural gesture between us, but then he thought better of it.

Inwardly I said a prayer to my mother to bless us here, now, in her house.

Mother never had been gone from our house, not in my mind, not in anyone's. I gestured for us to move to the sitting room, where Bessie had gone to the trouble of polishing the fine silver candlesticks and making the place glow with glittering light. I gave her a look of thanks I hoped she understood. She beamed.

I let the men take what chairs they were comfortable in, leaving me the divan, where I arranged my skirts carefully as I sat. I'm sure my father had never seen me so poised in all my life.

"Natalie has informed me, Lord Denbury, that you've been dealing with your affairs in England after your…unfortunate circumstances. I am deeply sorry for the loss of your family. Having endured loss myself, I certainly empathize."

My father was trying to be easy and warm, but I could see his strain. He hadn't any practice with my being courted, and now he knew our situation was serious and sudden.

"Thank you, sir. It seems our Greenwich estate was seized, but with due diligence I am sure in time it will be returned to me. Our London apartments remain unscathed, but I was in the country only long enough to transfer investments, secure further holdings, and rescue a few treasures."

I fondled the cameo about my neck, one such treasure. I hadn't given a thought to his London property, though I suppose every aristocrat has multiple properties. I was glad he was not entirely without a home in his home country. It was smart of him to move through London as he had done—safely, quietly. And telling my father about secure provisions certainly wasn't a bad move on the wooing-the-father scale.

"Do you intend to stay in New York, then?" my father asked pointedly.

"My parents intended to buy a townhouse here, in Greenwich Village, in honor of our Greenwich estate. I plan to make good on their intentions. If you or any of your Metropolitan fellows has a recommendation of a good broker, I'd be grateful. I'm a bit leery of unsolicited solicitors."

I chuckled at this. Father just kept watching.

"But in the meantime," Jonathon continued, "Mrs. Northe has extended the courtesy of her guest rooms."

"So I should take care how much time my daughter spends at Mrs. Northe's residence, then?" Father asked sharply. "She's visited nearly every day since they met."

"Mrs. Northe has been here, too, of late, hasn't she, Mr.

Stewart?" Bessie said as she entered the room with our small, wheeled tea service, which I hadn't seen used in years. "One big happy family these days, all of us." She winked at me.

"Oh, is that Earl Grey?" Jonathon said delightedly, taking the cup with his most charming smile.

"Natalie told me it was your favorite."

"You are indeed a saint, Mrs. Cartwright."

Bessie beamed again. Not a woman to keep thoughts a mystery, her face was an open book. Still, my father would not be distracted from his point.

"I'm not questioning whether we all enjoy Mrs. Northe's company or not. That has been quite established. I am wondering about her ability to chaperone."

"Oh, she watches us like a hawk," Jonathon supplied quickly. A bit too quickly.

"I'm sure," my father drawled.

"Speaking of Mrs. Northe, she has invited us over for late cordials and dessert," Jonathon shifted the focus artfully. "Her friend just returned from Germany inspired to make apple torte for everyone she's ever known. She delivered a whole pan this evening, and Mrs. Northe says it's a crime to eat it alone."

Father's eyes misted over. "That was Helen's favorite," he murmured.

Mother, was that you blessing us? my heart asked. Stunned, I glanced upward as if I might see her ghostly, shining face looking down on me and smiling. That wouldn't have been a haunting; it would have been a prayer answered. Instead I stared at her daguerreotype upon the mantel, lovely and fierce, her hair a bit wild, betraying her gregarious spirit.

"Well, then, we must oblige," my father said, rising. "I'd offer you some of my store of a man's luxuries, but I promised Mrs. Northe that I'll help her with the late Mr. Northe's bounteous supply. I daresay Mr. Northe had better taste and stores than I."

He clapped Jonathon on the back and was the first to leave the room. Jonathon whirled to me as if looking for my approval.

"Brilliant," I offered, stealing a swift peck upon the lips when I was sure no one was looking, and hurried out after Father.

"It's a nice night. We should walk the distance," my father stated.

It wasn't exactly *nice* outside; it was too warm and too humid. But Father didn't want to subject Jonathon to the small buggy we stored at the carriage house down the street. Early on, my father had had to navigate our social position amid the wealthy patrons of the Metropolitan. He knew what to show off and what to avoid.

Regardless, he was a man who liked to walk everywhere in the city he possibly could. So, it would appear, did Jonathon.

"I'd much prefer it," Jonathon added.

Something about being out of the house loosened everyone up. Or it could have been the sight of the grand Metropolitan itself as we crossed over to Fifth Avenue. Then another thing that my father had in common with the upper classes naturally came out: a healthy knowledge of and unparalleled passion for art. Jonathon mined that common vein.

"Tell me what you think, if you would, Mr. Stewart, about the role of the symbolists in the current aesthetic? Will they influence your collection at all?"

"I love the symbolists," I blurted excitedly. "I just recommended a Moreau."

"Brilliant," Jonathon breathed.

It took every ounce of my power not to snatch up Jonathon's hand in mine as we walked past the impressive redbrick and granite structure of the Metropolitan, gaslit and alluring in the twilight. I wondered how the museum would look when the expansion was approved and financed, giving it a luminous, white beaux-arts facade that would take up twice the space along the avenue. It would look so different that I wondered if it would be less romantic. But at the moment I couldn't think of anything more romantic than walking the city street at twilight with my English lord talking about the French symbolists.

"I like how they're a distinct breed from the

impressionists," Father began. "It's hard to say who will be the most lasting painter among them all. There's interesting literature and poetry around the symbolist circles, that's true, although that Baudelaire—"

"Right creepy, that one, if you don't mind me saying so," Jonathon muttered. Charles Baudelaire had been used in the mystery of Jonathon's curse, so he had an understandable bias. My father cleared his throat, embarrassed.

"Oh, yes, right, the painting and all. I'm sorry, didn't mean to bring up—"

"No," Jonathon assured him, "one case of art used for evil hardly turns me against it."

The two fell into a vigorous discussion about the role of a literary movement alongside a painting movement, and before long they were walking lockstep, their theories on justice and social issues coming into play. Even their points and counterpoints were laced with underlying visions of hope, education, and, above all, equality between the sexes. I knew in this moment that my father was won. Jonathon would treat me as a partner, not just a pretty face or doting wife who would do only her husband's whim.

I hadn't realized until that moment that none of my father's nerves had anything to do with the title or the unconventional way in which Jonathon and I had met. My father didn't want me to lose what sense of self, resourcefulness, and relative freedom he'd tried to give me in a world that still sought to bind women into extremely limiting stays.

I couldn't even bother to chime in. Having been a listener for so long, I wasn't confident enough to interrupt. For the moment, I was overjoyed to watch them forge a tentative alliance.

Mrs. Northe flung wide the door at our approach, crying, "Friends! Come save me lest I explode from another bite of apple torte!"

As we gathered in the entrance hall, I glimpsed an unexpected face through the open pocket doors of the parlor. Maggie was being hurried off by Mary, who had her things in tow and was begging her to consider the hour.

Maggie didn't see us at first; she was too busy protesting. Her dress was finer than usual, and there was an enormous, glittering bauble about her neck. Mary tried in vain to place a golden-beaded shawl about Maggie's shoulders, which showcased far more skin than she ought to outside of a special occasion. She was, as usual, whining to her aunt about why she had to go home when the fun was just beginning. There were dark circles under her eyes as if she hadn't been sleeping.

"As I say every time it broaches nine o' clock," Mrs. Northe droned, "your mother will have my head—"

Maggie looked up, and the moment she saw me, she froze. I'm not sure what I'd been expecting; our last encounter was pleasant and friendly. She flung her arms around me and kissed both cheeks. Then she noticed the man at my side.

"Hello, who's this? Oh. *Oh, my.* Oh, my…you're from the painting, you *are* the painting. Oh, my God, Natalie, it's Lord Denbury!" The rising pitch of her voice was like the shrieking of birds or a mythological harpy. The acoustics of the high-arched ceiling of the entrance foyer amplified her cry. My father and Jonathon both winced.

"Hello, miss. I've been told I resemble that chap," Jonathon said sportingly, bowing his head in greeting.

"But how…how are you here? You *are* alive! It worked! You've come! You've come *home!*" she cried.

We all stared at her as if she were mad. Sudden tears of joy rolled down her cheeks, and she threw her arms around him.

"I beg your pardon?" Jonathon said, laughing nervously and extricating himself from her unexpected embrace.

"It has to be you." She breathed. "You're *unmistakable.*"

"Margaret, this man is in danger," Mrs. Northe said in one of those cold tones that would not be questioned. "Whoever you think he is, keep your mouth shut or people will die. This young man is simply my guest, a visitor from England. Nothing more will be said. Is that *entirely* clear, Margaret Hathorn?"

Maggie winced and nodded. "But, what are you doing

with *her*?" she asked Jonathon, gesturing to me. Her words weren't a slight as much as she seemed confused, as if Jonathon had shown up at the wrong home. "Oh, because of Mr. Stewart, the Metropolitan, I suppose, but…"

"The Stewarts are my friends," Jonathon supplied, trying to tread carefully.

"But they're not of your station," Maggie said matter-of-factly.

That's when Mrs. Northe forcibly walked her out the door. "*Enough*. My driver is taking you home."

"Auntie, why are you so mean to me?" Maggie asked softly at the door, showing a sudden, genuine vulnerability that I'm not sure I'd ever heard out of her.

"For your own good."

"I'm not sure that's true…" Maggie's sad voice trailed off down the walk.

"What was that about?" my father asked slowly, once she had gone.

Mrs. Northe sighed. "I tried to get her out before you came, but she always wants to stay later and later, as if by approaching the witching hour she might watch me turn into a bat or something," she muttered. "I'm very sorry, Lord Denbury, but it would have been hard to hide you from my niece indefinitely."

Jonathon chuckled, but he seemed as uneasy as I was.

"Maggie always professed she was in love with your

portrait," I explained. "The night I freed you I found her at the museum. It seems she's—"

"Deluded," Jonathon snickered.

"Not necessarily," I replied, looking pointedly at Mrs. Northe. "She just doesn't know the truth. Maybe if we told her, she wouldn't have to resort to her own flights of ridiculous fancy rather than ours."

"I don't really want her in on our secrets, Natalie," Jonathon said. "I actually think she could be trouble if we're not careful."

I didn't know whose side to be on or what to say. Maggie didn't make me comfortable either. She seemed the sort who, if she knew you had secrets, cared all the more to find them out.

"Never a dull moment when it comes to you and those around you, Evelyn. I will say that." My father broke the tension and headed directly toward Mr. Northe's study full of manly treasures. He gestured for Jonathon. "Come, Lord Denbury, I must have your take on Cezanne and the cubists. But one needs a cigar for such talk!"

Jonathon looked at me hopefully, and my father's desire for further company had to be a good thing. I squeezed his hand and nodded him off.

I joined Mrs. Northe, who was examining some correspondence at an ornately inlaid parlor writing desk.

"Those two seem to be getting on famously." Mrs. Northe smiled.

"It took a moment," I replied, positioning myself delicately upon a brocade fainting couch. "I hope it holds."

"Art makes fast friends."

"It certainly does," I agreed. Jonathon's portrait had brought us all together. "I'm worried—"

"About Maggie, and so am I. I can't get a read on her." Mrs. Northe tapped her temple. "Psychically, I mean. I can't get into her mind. She's addled. Her mother wants her focused on the upcoming Season, and for once I'm trying to encourage frivolity and gossip. Maggie simply won't accept that spiritualism is an augment to my faith.

"She thinks I must operate on some entirely different system, on spells and incantation, talismans and powders. I lifted up a cross saying *that* is my talisman, and she set it aside as if it wasn't glamorous enough. She wants something flashy and controversial to have her friends screaming about at balls. Mere Christianity isn't scandalous enough."

"Her reaction to Jonathon was…intense."

"To say the least."

"Do I dare let on that he and I are…" I ran my fingers over the raised embroidery of the cushion nervously. "What are we, even?"

"Courting. Soon to be engaged, surely, by the way everyone's acting. It isn't as though the two of you can simply exist as friends. I wish lovers weren't hurried into wedlock the moment they blossom from child into adult, but such is the way of our age."

"Maggie's confusion about why he was with *us*..." My nerves had me picking at the golden embroidery before I stopped myself from doing damage. Instead I picked at the frayed hem of my petticoat, wishing I looked more the part of Lady Denbury.

"Oh, I heard it."

"Is that what everyone will think? I'm not cut out for high-society cruelty," I said, blinking back a sudden, unexpected tear. Fearing I'd rip my hem entirely, I helped myself at the tea service to occupy my hands. "I'm only just now getting used to *conversation*. I'll never speak a word if I'm in her world's pit of vipers, hissing gossiping snakes."

Maggie's careless words drove open a crevasse of faltering confidence. Was I only at ease around friends of my own "kind" and class? Maybe I'd fit in with Nathaniel's Association, those who were proudly unconventional.

For all Maggie's claims of interest, I doubt she'd really want to be haunted like me. She wanted good parlor tricks, something sensational. I doubt she'd last one moment in one of my nightmares. But she wanted Lord Denbury and thought she had some weird claim to him. That silly and misguided spell she'd tried to cast at the Metropolitan must've done her head in. Jealousy and worry bloomed like a fanged flower within me.

"While Jonathon is a guest here, please keep an eye on Maggie—"

"Natalie, there's nothing more tedious than a rivalry," she laughed, ignoring my vehemence. I set my jaw, wanting to be taken seriously. Mrs. Northe eyed me before sliding a letter into an envelope. "I think you can handle your right to Lord Denbury on your own."

"What do you think they're talking about in there?" I asked, glancing toward the other wing of the house where the late Mr. Northe's vast, leather-filled, masculine den sat as a foreign threshold beyond a green velvet curtain and a large oak door.

"Art," Mrs. Northe replied. "Not your future. Not yet. The boy's going to be nervous. He's got a lot on his mind. I know you're lovesick, but don't rush things. Especially not while he's functioning as our double agent."

My stomach twisted at the idea of him beholden to the Society indefinitely. "Don't encourage him to get any more involved than he has to," I cautioned. "I don't want him to be a pawn. Not any of us. Not me, not Jonathon, not Rachel."

We all had become Society pawns in one way or another with Mrs. Northe outside of it all, watching, invested, but not directly involved. Yet still moving us like chess pieces. Something about my tone had Mrs. Northe stare directly at me.

"Of course. You don't think you're some sort of game to me, do you?"

"Just…make sure we don't become one."

I sat with my tea and she sat with her letters for a while before Jonathon and my father came through the open pocket doors, smelling of pipe tobacco and a trace of bourbon, all finer, richer, and more subtle scents than what the professors and academics brought into my father's modest study.

"Say good night, Natalie," Father said. "I daresay we'll all see each other soon." Jonathon caught my hand and kissed it. He then turned and shook my father's hand again vigorously. "Your family, Mr. Stewart, has my loyalty, and your museum has my patronage. Thank you for your friendship," he stated. He bowed, and I watched him disappear up Mrs. Northe's grand staircase to the guest rooms. Father turned away looking pleased. Jonathon had given me a wink and a kiss upon the air when no one was looking.

Mrs. Northe had her driver take us round to our home. Father didn't say much, other than, "He's a good man, Denbury. Smart. Did you know he opened a clinic in London with his friends? That's good. A sense of civil service. I like that. Your mother would like that…I just worry about all the darkness. The spells. The madness that man brought upon you."

"It wasn't—"

"His fault, I know. But I can't possibly give your hand until I know you're well and truly safe."

And with that, the comfortable silence that had so dominated our house since Helen Stewart's death when I was four again descended. But at least the ice has been broken, however uneasily.

Chapter 19

When a carriage arrived the next morning after my father left for the museum, with instructions to bring me to Mrs. Northe, I was surprised to find Maggie waiting for me. Mrs. Northe sat across her parlor looking tired and irritated.

"Natalie, I'm sorry. I must be off to Chicago by the next train. My friend is dying, and I *must* see her alive once more. But Margaret simply will not believe that we're not hiding something from her. There's nothing *magical* about that man, Margaret."

"That man is Lord Denbury. Stop pretending he isn't. I've memorized that face. I was at the museum late the night Natalie was there, and the next day his portrait was—" She stopped herself from saying something else and instead said: "*Gone.* You think you know what happened, but you *don't*. It isn't fair. I did the rituals. *I* brought him to life. Why are you hiding him from me?" She turned to me, anguished. "Why do you steal everything from me, Natalie? You steal my aunt. You steal my beau. Why?"

My mouth dropped open in shocked and indignant amazement.

"Is that what this is? You think *you* brought him to life?" Mrs. Northe asked.

I clenched my fists, wanting more than anything to tell her the truth: That *I* had been chosen to cross worlds to save him. *I* risked my life on chance, deduction, and faith. That *I* pursued clues into dangerous New York neighborhoods where people had died, that *I* had been wounded and stared down devils. That *I* reversed the deadly curse. But what would she know of any of that? How would that help?

Just then, a confident stride could be heard down the entrance hall and Jonathon's handsome face came around the corner. He saw us three ladies, perched and tense. I hadn't even bothered to take a seat.

His jovial expression turned sheepish. "Oh, hello. Forgive me, ladies. Good morning. Hello, Miss Stewart. Hello, Miss...Hathorn..."

He seemed *awfully* nervous when he looked at Maggie.

"Hello, Jonathon," she said, biting her lip and blushing like a schoolgirl, dropping his familiar name when I'm sure there had been no permission granted to use it.

He went white as a sheet. Recovering, he looked first at Mrs. Northe and then at me. "Right. I'll be...in the study if anyone needs me."

I wanted to run after him, to ask about his behavior. But just then, there was a cry from upstairs. Rachel.

As I ran upstairs, I could hear Mrs. Northe showing Maggie the door. "Margaret. Please go. You've caused enough headaches this morning."

"Mother will hear of this. How you deny me—"

"Please *do* sic your mother on me," Mrs. Northe replied wearily. "I'd prefer that to your endless refusal to see me for anything other than what I can do for you."

Rachel was convulsing upon her bed. I took up her thin body in my arms, touching her face, seeing if I could rouse her.

Eerily she shot up, and a sound came out of her mouth that sounded like a name. Her shaking hands signed a phrase.

"My name is Elsa. Please tell my love to let me go," she signed. "All the spirits. All must be let go."

I sat back as if shoved back in alarm. "Mrs. Northe," I called. She was at the door.

"What is it?"

"Samuel's comatose fiancée! Elsa. I think she's dead. Or otherwise she's communicating from her comatose state into Rachel. But whatever Preston is doing for the sake of Laura, it must be happening in St. Paul, too. It's Samuel. We have to help him. I don't know what to do. What do we do? We can't do anything from here!" I was losing the battle against panic.

"I will see my friend in Chicago, gather help, and take

a train to Dr. Neumann. I will set that girl to rest. I will take care of it. But *you* must gather Reverend Blessing and find Preston's work, together, with Rachel. *You* must set the spirits to rest that are plaguing her. Take that basement by force if you have to."

"By force? But none of us——"

"I told Mr. Smith you may need his assistance. He's in the carriage house."

Mr. Smith. Bodyguard, driver, intelligence officer, hired hand, a man of many eerie talents and no words. He was someone you wanted on your side, not the enemy's. Thankfully, he seemed ever loyal to Mrs. Northe.

"I knew I'd have to put you in charge, Natalie. I don't want to leave you, but if I don't go to my friend, it could be catastrophic. I can't explain why, just trust me. I'll be more help there than I will be here. I wouldn't go if I didn't think you all could handle yourselves. There's no time to waste. We don't know what's about to wake up in that hospital, and Rachel can't sustain the trauma much longer. Be well." She kissed me on the forehead, then Rachel, and was out the door. "Say good-bye to Jonathon for me. I'm already late for the train."

I moved to walk out the door. Instead, Rachel grabbed me by the hand and sat up.

"End it." She signed. "Make it stop."

"We're going to," I promised, and I tried to ease her

back upon the bed. She refused, sitting stiffly, eyes wide like an animal being hunted.

Wearied and scared, I went to find Jonathon.

He was not alone in the den. Maggie hadn't gone out after all. Instead, she was atop him. Pinning him, really, her knee upon the arm of the leather chair where he sat pressed back, his hands like claws on the armrests.

She was *kissing* him. Was he kissing her back? The sound of the door didn't disrupt them, but whatever sound came out of my mouth did. I tried to recover speech. "I…beg your pardon!"

Jonathon pushed Maggie aside, jumping out of the chair as if it were a tub of scalding water. "Natalie, she just threw herself at me."

Maggie whirled to me and back to him. "Why should you excuse yourself to *her*? Why won't you recognize me for who I am? After all I've done for you and what we've shared?"

I folded my arms. My voice wouldn't work. I could feel perspiration on my upper lip. I felt nauseous. Truly? Now was the time for my speech to flee? When I was an injured, shamed party, discovering my beloved kissing another? What did she mean?

"We've shared nothing, Natalie," Jonathon said. "Last night she sneaked behind the house to the little garden, using a pebble to strike my window. I was hoping it was you—"

"No, don't you understand?" Maggie asked with that

same earnest, wounded confusion. "We needed privacy, a balcony scene like Romeo and Juliet, to consecrate the rite. Why do you continue to deny me?"

I stared at her, just as confused. She'd lost her mind. Jonathon was alluring and charming, no doubt, but his effect upon women wasn't *insanity*.

"Taking off your cloak to reveal yourself, Miss Hathorn," Jonathon said, exasperated, "in far less clothes than was proper, is hardly the way to introduce yourself to a man, unless you're a—"

"Are you about to impugn my honor, Lord Denbury?" Maggie murmured through clenched teeth.

"No more than you've done yourself. Stop this game. I don't understand it."

Tears suddenly poured down Maggie's face. "You ungrateful wretch. This is the thanks I receive for saving you? This is how I'm repaid for bringing you out of the painting?" Her agony made her voice tremble.

"Wait a minute." Jonathon shook his head, reacting with the same incredulity that Mrs. Northe had a moment prior. "You think you…saved me?"

"Yes!" Maggie said, similarly exasperated. "I've done nothing but say incantations, pray to you, and dream of you. I've done so much. Haven't you seen any of it?"

"No…" Jonathon said, looking at her blankly. "We're truly at a loss here, Miss Hathorn."

"Maggie," I said, "if this is about the markings on the floor of the Metropolitan—"

"No, it's more than that!" She waved a hand, batting me away. "Far more! Stop interfering, Natalie. This is between Jonathon and me."

"No, actually, it isn't," Jonathon said slowly, gently, as if he were talking to a child. "You must be mistaken. I was…never in a painting at all. My death was a ruse. It's a very long story, Miss Hathorn. I'm sorry for anything that you've been misled to believe."

She shook her head, and the tears continued. "No…No, you're mine. They promised you'd be mine."

"Who?" I asked, feeling dread creep up my spine.

"None of your business," Maggie said, turning away. "You won't understand, Natalie."

"*Try me*," I hissed.

"Stop! For *once* this isn't about *you*!" she cried, burying her face in a handkerchief a moment before she looked up again, staring at Jonathon like a wounded animal bearing its fangs. "You're lying, Lord Denbury, and I'll find a way to prove it. Lying and ungrateful!"

Storming out the door, she slammed it behind her with a great wooden thud.

Jonathon turned to me, eyes wide. "That girl is stark, raving mad. Please believe me. She threw herself at me, and for a moment, I was honestly too shocked to move."

I stared at him, wanting to believe him. Yet I had walked in on him not shoving her away, but kissing her. True, she had pinned him beneath her, but still…

"Please, Natalie. What happened to her? I saw a flash of red and gold crackle around her. Perhaps somehow, with her being around the painting, residual magic is on her as well. And she, hardly as strong as you, is more easily affected."

It seemed as plausible an explanation as any for her odd behavior. "I don't know. But let's be very clear," I said, taking his hand and leading him to the door. "*I'm* the only one allowed to kiss you."

"That's bloody right you are," he breathed, wrapping his arm around me.

"Come, we don't have time for this. Rachel just told us something very important."

"Is that girl gone, Mary?" Jonathon asked in the hall. "Please God, tell me she's gone."

"In a huff, that's for sure," Mary said, wearier by the moment. "Mrs. Northe is gone too. She sends her love, Lord Denbury."

"Gone?" Jonathon cried. "She can't leave. This place is a madhouse." I ushered him into the entrance hall. "Why on earth would she leave at such a critical—"

"Because her friend is dying. Her friend with important information. You know I don't question Mrs. Northe's important information. And she's also going, Jonathon, because of Elsa," I replied. He stilled.

"What?"

"Rachel has been receiving information from spirits, all in a jumbled rush. She's been quite knocked out by it. She just woke with a message from Elsa, either transmitted through her comatose state or because she's dead and her spirit has a message. Something's wrong in St. Paul. Elsa is begging to be let go, as are all the spirits Preston has been asking Rachel to collect. And Mrs. Northe has dire business in Chicago."

"We've got to get to Samuel."

"She promises to go farther west to take care of Samuel. You know that woman has more resources than she'd ever let on. It's up to us to take care of Preston."

Jonathon ran a hand over his face. "Good God." He entered the parlor, looked at me, then greeted Rachel. "Do you ever get the feeling we've become the grim reaper's clerks?" he asked.

Rachel nodded. "All the time," she signed.

Something overtook Rachel again. She swooned on the divan. Jonathon placed a steadying hand on her shoulder. I shook Rachel gently, as I had before.

"What are they saying?" I asked calmly, squeezing Rachel's hands, clutching her by the arms, and forcing her to look at me.

"So many tears," she signed, tears falling down her own cheeks, which had again gone gray pale. "They're calling.

For me. All of them. They don't understand. *They're* not alive, so how could *it* be alive?"

"What's she saying?" Jonathon asked quietly. I translated.

"What's...*it*?" he asked as if he really didn't want to know.

Nearly as quickly as she had fainted, Rachel jumped to her feet with a gasping breath. It was dizzying, the shift between her receiving information and then coming out of an alarming-looking trance to an utter, sharp lucidity.

"I must go," she signed. "Whatever is in the basement, I must end it. Today is the day it will wake. It must not wake. It must not live."

As I translated, Jonathon and I shuddered but straightened ourselves.

"Yes. But we're going with you," I said as she looked up at me.

"You don't have to," she signed, and I grabbed her hands.

"Yes. We do," I insisted. "The Master's Society used Preston and you, and has hurt all of us."

"Come, let's get to the root of their dirty business," Jonathon stated, putting on his black wide-brimmed hat by the door. A hunting hat. Fitting. I saw a small flash of light shimmer over him, as it did when he came to my aid or affected positive change. Perhaps he wasn't the only one who saw the truth of a good soul in ways beyond the body alone.

"Mrs. Northe left me in charge," I said sheepishly, wondering if Jonathon would chafe at this. "So…"

"So, lead on, captain." Jonathon saluted me with a grin.

I let out a kept breath and put my hands firmly together in a gesture of strength, but really it was to keep them from shaking. Since I didn't have the luxury of time to question being leader, my mind went to the same state I'd been in while pursuing clues to save Jonathon's life. There were simply things to be done. There was only time for action. It was actually far better than the anxiety of waiting.

"First off," I stated, "we alert Mr. Smith."

"And he is?"

"A man I wouldn't want to cross. At our service, courtesy of Mrs. Northe. He's in the carriage house awaiting our orders." I turned to Rachel. "Are you sure you're ready? Strong enough?"

"If we don't do something soon, they will kill me," she signed.

"We won't let them kill you," I assured her.

"We promise," Jonathon added.

The three of us strode to the carriage house where I found a lean, tall man in a pinstriped suit and a bowler, with a scar on one cheek that sloped slightly upward from the dark stubble of his chin. He was brushing one of Mrs. Northe's mares.

"Mr. Smith."

He set down his brush, came forward, and tipped his hat. I introduced Jonathon and Rachel. He tipped his hat again. "The German Hospital on Seventy-Seventh Street," I said. "There's a doctor named Preston and a guard of his, a large, pale Brit who will likely prove more powerful than he seems. They'll try to keep us from entering the basement. There's something down there I doubt any of us want to see, but we have no choice. We must get into that basement and stop whatever is being done there."

Mr. Smith, who had yet to say a word, nodded, went to a case, and opened it. He pulled out a long-barreled pistol and slid it into a holster under his jacket, while palming another gun, a pocket-sized pistol with a pearl handle. This he handed to Jonathon along with some bullets. Smith's raised eyebrows asked the question of whether Jonathon knew how to use it. Jonathon took the bullets, loaded the gun, set the safety, and put the pistol in his breast pocket.

It was amazing how much could be said by action alone.

"We have to see one more person," I said. "We'll meet you there. Perhaps you can examine the premises?"

Smith nodded and was off down the street.

"One more?" Jonathon queried.

"I'm bringing Reverend Blessing with us."

"And who's that?" Jonathon asked.

"An exorcist."

"Ah, of course."

Chapter 20

A smile crossed the reverend's face when he saw me at the door, and he examined Jonathon and Rachel. "Hello, Miss Stewart. To what do I owe this sudden honor, and what's all this company you've brought with you?"

"I'm so glad you're here. I'm sorry for the emergency call, Reverend Blessing, but that's just it. It's an emergency. This is Lord Denbury and my friend Miss Rachel Horowitz."

As I expected, two heads poked curiously out from either side of the reverend: the tall, elegant greyhounds, Blue and Bunny. Jonathon gasped.

"Well, hello, and aren't you two *beauties*," he said admiringly, his face aglow, reaching a relaxed hand out so they might sniff him as he closed the distance. In one fluid motion he had confident hands on both dogs and was speaking to them excitedly, clearly having some knowledge of their prowess and the sports in which they were used. The dogs were equally thrilled. They circled around him closely, quaking with joy, their tongues lavishing kisses on his hands.

"They like you," Blessing said to Jonathon.

"Well, they're gorgeous," Jonathon exclaimed, remaining on his knees and beaming like a schoolboy, perfectly happy to have the dogs' fond black noses directly in his face as he stroked their short fur.

Rachel, watching, couldn't help but smile at Jonathon too. She turned to me. "I *really* like him," she signed to me. "You'd better keep him."

"I plan to," I signed back, and we shared a girlish grin.

"Tell me your troubles," Blessing called, gesturing us into his parlor. Bunny was lockstep with Jonathon, hardly allowing him to sit. Blue had repositioned herself to stare at Rachel, who did not waver from returning the creature's gaze. The dog padded up closer to her, putting a damp nose directly onto her trembling fingers.

"Ah, my little bleeding heart," Blessing said, nodding toward Rachel and her new friend. "She can tell if something's wrong. Intuitive, intelligent, emotion-filled creatures," he added. "She knows you're here with troubled hearts, so tell me everything."

"Well," I began and listed all that had brought us to this point and what we might expect at the hospital. Even the dogs listened. There was an occasional squawk from some other creature somewhere else in the house.

When I finished, there was a long silence. Blue nosed Rachel's hand. Gingerly, Rachel touched her, and her tensed shoulders relaxed. Bunny had returned to Jonathon. Smitten, she was practically in his lap. She had good taste, that dog.

Blessing, who had listened with a passive face, rose, slid a well-worn *Book of Common Prayer* from a nearby shelf, and stood at the parlor threshold. He looked up at us expectantly. "Well, then, come on. No time to waste."

"And we are to…" Jonathon prompted, hoping Blessing might elaborate.

"If spirits cannot go onward toward their eternal peace, then we must set them to rest ourselves. And if there's a demon, that requires an exorcism, of course," he replied, as if it were the most natural thing in the world.

"Of course," Jonathon murmured. He and I shared a nervous smile. Rachel's lips were thin, her slight frame trembling. If I wasn't mistaken, Blessing had a distinct twinkle in his eye, as if he lived for days like this.

We followed him to the door. His hands stroked the hounds until the last moment out of the house, and even then the dogs strained their necks over the threshold toward him. He grabbed what looked like a black doctor's bag at the door.

"Shall we take a trolley? Hansom?" he asked.

"I need the air," Jonathon said, and we were out for another walk in the light rain.

To explain our group, we had agreed that while Jonathon

was there on "Society business," Rachel would escort the rest of us in for an unrelated séance in her basement office.

Jonathon looked up at the Gothic-style building. "You know, it looks like the House of Usher," he muttered.

"I thought the same thing."

Neither of us commented on the tale being about a body buried alive, which might relate to what we'd encounter.

Blessing pulled a purple silk ascot from his bag. He tied it around his neck to hide his white cleric's collar, but the collar remained there beneath. Like hidden armor.

Mr. Smith was outside on the corner with a carriage parked up the block. He took one look at Blessing, raised his brow, and folded his arms. I took in Mr. Smith's expression and defensive stance for a moment, then stepped forward. I thought of how Mrs. Northe might bring parties together and said what I hoped would be the right words between us.

"Is there a problem, Mr. Smith?" I asked. "I hope you understand the nature of this unconventional mission. We need warriors of two kinds. Physical…" I gestured deferentially to Smith. "And spiritual." I nodded to Blessing.

Smith looked at me a moment, turned, then tipped his hat to Blessing. "Father," he said in a gravelly voice. Blessing nodded in turn.

As we approached the rear entrance of the wing we knew was Preston's, we felt the air temperature drop a few degrees. As we reached the door, it opened on its own. There was no one on the other side.

"Well. Something must be expecting us," Jonathon said. Undeterred, Mr. Smith was the first one in. A cool draft immediately surrounded us as we followed him.

"Quite the welcoming committee," Blessing noted.

The interior was no more welcoming than the exterior, and there were still no patients to be seen, just row after row of neatly made-up white cots down the long hall. Only our footsteps broke the oppressive silence as we waited for someone to greet or stop us. We moved without notice.

At least, no one *living* noticed. The chill worsened, and I glanced at Jonathon as I rubbed my arms. He nodded. We were most certainly in the presence of ghosts. Many.

Rachel turned to me, her face a pained mask. She signed that she "was not welcome."

"Wait for us by the door, then," I signed, gesturing to the front portico. Her face as pale as the neat sheets tucked into their springs, she turned toward the door but then turned back. She shook her head, signing that her comfort was not important now. The look on Rachel's face wasn't something to question.

Jonathon had pulled ahead of us. At the opposite end of the hall was the frosted glass door marked DOCTOR PRESTON. He put his ear to the door.

We all jumped back when the guard, Roth, opened it and stepped out into the hall.

"You again." He narrowed his eyes at Jonathon, then at me. "What's all this?"

"*I'm* here to talk to Preston," Jonathon said as if it was obvious. "This lot is here for a séance. That's the girl's job. Now stop keeping me from doing mine."

"Preston is indisposed," Roth said through clenched teeth.

Mr. Smith evidently had no patience or inclination for diplomacy, for he stepped forward with a lightning-swift motion and threw a punch that made the stocky guard collapse unconscious to the floor.

"Careful, Mr. Smith," Jonathon said. "I probably should have warned you that was a demon."

And then, before any of us could respond or react further, the guard's body started moving. Fast. It was being dragged by unseen hands swiftly, inhumanly down the hall. A basement door flew open on its own, and we winced as we heard the thud of a body down a flight of stairs.

"Oh my God," I said, my body lurching from still to shaking with fear. I wanted to run but couldn't move. Did the spirits just kill that man?

"'Make it stop,' they say," Rachel signed to me. "They want us to end this."

"Ask the spirits if they will end us. We can't help them

if they'll do *that*…" Jonathon gestured to where the guard had disappeared, "to us."

"If they kill us, they won't be set free," Blessing said. He withdrew a silver wand-like apparatus from a pocket of his bag and shook it in four directions, then at each of our heads. Droplets of liquid flicked down upon our hair and foreheads. Mr. Smith scrunched up his face and wiped his eye.

"Only holy water, Mr. Smith," Blessing assured with a smile. "Harmless. Unless you're a demon too."

Mr. Smith snorted a laugh. Blessing placed the silver dispenser in his breast pocket. He turned to Rachel and waited for her eyes to settle upon him. "The spirits are leading us to the basement, yes?"

Rachel nodded.

"Mr. Smith, while we may be preoccupied with spirits, I'd like it if someone kept an eye out for Dr. Preston," Jonathon said, trying to keep his voice steady.

If Smith was frightened he did not show it, but I thought his pale face lost what little color it had as he took up the rear. Jonathon took out his gun, and I heard the click of the safety. At that click, the door to Preston's office swung wide open. Again, by unseen hands. Doors here seemed to be under the spirits' control. No one was inside.

Trying to master my shaking, I strode forward to Preston's desk. There was a note scrawled in a dark red pen. I couldn't help but assume that it wasn't actually ink at all. The note read:

I'm sorry. Make it stop. Room 01.

Beside the note lay a key. Beside the key lay a scalpel.

"Well, then," Jonathon said. "At least we know where to go."

I snatched up the key. Rachel signed the room number with a questioning look.

"Rachel," I assured her, "you don't have to—"

She nodded vigorously, signing, "I must see this through."

It wasn't as if any of us could volunteer or bow out. It was simply a fact that we were drawn into this and had to see how it would play out.

Inexorably we moved down the hall. I glanced at Blessing. His dark skin had a sheen of moisture despite the dropping temperature, but his expression was calm as he removed his ascot, revealing his cleric's collar, and took a small wooden cross from his pocket.

Halfway down the tight stairwell, I paused.

It was *that* basement, of course, the one from my dreams. I gasped in recognition, and Jonathon turned to me, his hand immediately reaching out to steady me.

"I've seen this place," I said.

The long corridor with all the dim rooms. The yellowed hand slamming against the glass. Rachel, the boxes, the body parts. My dream images flashed before my eyes. Would we open a door to a pile of dead, dismembered pieces? Each with a ghost trailing its detached limb or appendage, a most cruel and unnatural tether to this world? I didn't know if the reality we found would be better or worse than that theory.

Room 01 was at the end of the hallway. In my dreams, the end of the hall was where things grew most dire, where I was most startled, where I would be attacked…

Rachel swooned suddenly, and Mr. Smith caught her by one arm. The cold in the corridor dropped another few degrees. "She is most *certainly* not welcome here," Blessing said, gesturing that Mr. Smith should continue to support her. He complied while the rest of us pressed on.

"Where's the guard?" I asked. Jonathon kept his gun raised.

Just then *all* the doors flew open at once of their own accord. We couldn't help but jump. Jonathon smoothly swept the gun from side to side. But no one came out of the rooms. On both sides of us, the rooms were empty and unlit except for the occasional lantern trimmed low. One of the rooms would have been Rachel's "office," I presumed. Still, *something* had thrown open the doors. Was it better to see that something or not?

Room 01 was ahead of us on the right. The room

marked "Morgue" was on our left. The morgue door was open. Room 01 was not.

Which way should we look, and what terrible sight would we see?

I took a deep breath and tried to no avail to keep my dream of the rising dead out of my mind.

Something flew out at us in a flurry of red and white. I'm sure I made some sort of noise, but it was lost in the crack of the gun firing.

The next moment, a bloody sheet lay crumpled on the floor with a bullet hole somewhere in it. The spirits were *certainly* proving themselves active.

We slowly turned to our left. Inside the morgue a body lay on the metal table. It was Roth, his bright suit of an obnoxious pattern ripped open, the golden fabric of his cravat streaming down to the floor, and his head hanging at an odd angle. Perhaps the fall had broken his neck. The fact that the spirits, or whatever they'd become, had enough power or anger to hoist his body up on the table was a feat I considered with terrified wonder.

"Poor sot," Jonathon said, calmly approaching the body to feel for a pulse. He shook his head. As Jonathon stared down at the sternum, he drew back, repulsed. I came closer.

Glancing down, I saw that Roth's sternum and breastbone had been carved. Marked with runes.

Where then was the demon that had inhabited the body?

Was it still trapped within or was it a danger? Jonathon and I stepped back as Smith stepped forward, letting Rachel go for a moment. She steadied herself on the doorframe as Smith came closer and looked down at the body with a satisfied smile.

The movement was swift and fast, but before I knew what had happened, Smith flew across the room and Roth's fist fell back lifeless once more against the table. It would seem Smith's punch had come back to haunt him. Shaking off the pain and wiping his split lip, Smith staggered forward, drawing out his long-barreled pistol and aiming it at Roth's body, which was now twitching in a most unnatural way. "Son of a—"

"No." Blessing cautioned Smith with an outstretched hand. The reverend set down his bag, his cross in one hand and a small, worn, red Bible in the other. "We can't treat this like a human body any longer. Any further anger or violence might encourage it to take you as its next host. It must be banished to the abyss." Blessing began reading a passage of Scripture.

The body shook and black fluid bubbled from Roth's mouth. I heard low, chanting whispers as an undercurrent beneath Blessing's words. Familiar from my dreams, those whispers, insidious and maddening. Jonathon had moved into the hall, examining the sheet that had been projected at us. I stood at the threshold, supporting

Rachel and trying to pay attention, but the whispers were very distracting.

"This may take a moment." Blessing turned to us between Scriptures. The body might have convulsed off the table had Smith not held down the feet, hatred burning in his eyes, his lip still bleeding. "But when I'm finished," Blessing continued, "we'll have to leave the body here. Bodies are the stuff of the police. Souls are our business. We must determine what the spirits want. We must be willing to see and listen."

"I think what they have to say is fairly clear," Jonathon said grimly, opening the death shroud to reveal a bloody message, written messily:

Make it stop.

I shuddered and turned to face Room 01.

"Rachel will have to help you there. There's nothing you can do here," Blessing said. He closed the morgue door on himself, the demon, and Smith as his assistant. There were growls and shouts. I winced and moved to the door, but Rachel urged me back toward Room 01.

"No more waiting," she signed.

Its number was marked in small black script. The door was locked, a sullen yellow light emanating from behind the frosted glass. We moved to it, from one dreaded door to the next.

Jonathon moved ahead of me. "I'm sure this won't be a sight for a lady."

"Oh, I *know* it won't be," I said. I took out the key, unlocked the door, and swung it wide.

We were met by a sharp medicinal smell with an underlying scent of decay. That I knew well from my dreams.

Nothing leaped out at us. Nothing moved. Not at first.

Within Room 01 was a body-shaped mass beneath a white sheet, surrounded by trays of equipment and surgery tools. Upon a nearby cabinet were glass bottles filled with fluids and marked with letters and chemical words I did not recognize. And wires. Wires were everywhere. The room was *dreadfully* cold.

What had my dreams foretold?

"Oh, yes, that's right." I murmured to myself. "This is the part where the body sits up."

Jonathon raised an eyebrow. "Excuse me?"

"Be careful," I said as Jonathon approached the body. "If it moves. It…it might move. Just…to warn you."

At least there wasn't a room *full* of bodies, as there had been in my nightmare.

"Do we dare?" Jonathon asked, one hand on the sheet, pistol in the other.

There was no argument either way, so he drew back the sheet to reveal a tall body of yellowed flesh and a good bit of stitching.

Fine work, really. Smooth and delicate, a steady hand had done up a properly articulated human body, not a rough-hewn rag doll. Patchwork, yes, but it was—it had *been* human. I couldn't really tell if it was male or female. The face was large but somewhat graceful in its yellowed state, almost as if it had been pickled.

The smell of astringent medical fluids was nauseating, and I supposed it was something funerary—embalming fluid, perhaps.

Jonathon set the safety and tucked the pistol in his breast pocket.

I moved to the corpse. There was a small tag on the base of the metal table and a clipboard and notebook hanging from a metal chain. I turned the tag to read it in the dim light, bruised feet with jagged toenails a few inches from my knuckles.

Laura.

"Oh," I said with regret rather than surprise. "Laura."

"That was the name of Dr. Preston's dead wife, wasn't it?"

"Yes," I replied. "Tell me, Laura," I asked the body, "does the Society prey upon lost loved ones, feeding into a sad man's grief so he makes experiments out of the dead? Is that what's going on here, and in other places? Is that what's happening to Samuel?"

"*Why* would someone do this?"

That was the question for which none of us had an answer,

other than perhaps for some remembrance of Laura....
And then I remembered the Society's avenues of experimentation: Soul splitting. Pharmacology. *Reanimation.*

Rachel just stood there staring in horror. I took her
hand, but she didn't even acknowledge me.

Jonathon was examining every inch of the wires and
equipment, writing notes on a small pad with the stub of a
pencil. I was suddenly overwhelmed with sadness for that
poor creature, a patchwork of human parts, a collection
of souls but no true self. An abomination, surely, but that
wasn't its fault. And what made the difference? Between
living and dead flesh?

I should have been disgusted by the foul thing made
of death. Yet when I'd read *Frankenstein*, I'd been more
disgusted with the doctor and the mob than with the actions
of the monster. Mary Shelley had written *Frankenstein*
when she was about my age. Now fiction found life as the
Society turned nightmares into reality, leaving a fine line
between a terrible dream and a terrible day...

I shivered—we all did, as the room became even colder.
Though I could not see them, there must have been at
least as many spirits here as gathered body parts. It was
terribly frightening—not seeing the ghosts, yet knowing
they were there. At any moment they could grab us like
they'd done Roth. Could they understand that we were
here to help?

How did it work, though? There were trays of strange machinery around the body, with wires that attached to various parts and then threaded up into a grid around the ceiling. What was the source, the engine that woke this being?

Then I saw the markings. Fine, bloodless but specific markings across the flesh. Runes again. These ancient letters, stolen and repurposed, had to mean something of life and death for this poor thing…

Rachel startled me by jumping forward and grabbing the creature's hand.

And that's when the creature moved, a hand shoving Rachel aside. I caught her.

With a horrible sound that I'll never *ever* forget, the body lurched and tried to sit up. Wires flew, popping off the body from where they'd been attached around the head and torso, black fluid dribbling out from the wounds. A flash of light rippled over the body, perhaps sparks, perhaps magic…but the scored markings of runes were suddenly red, emblazoning the body with bloody tattoos.

We all screamed and jumped back.

Rachel had suddenly, inadvertently, made it come alive. It may also have been that Jonathon was standing over by the panel of wires and meters, a part of that sparking surge. There were crackling threads of light all along the wires, and the needles on the equipment meters were swaying and vibrating just as the wires did.

"Reverend…" I called. "Something just woke up in here…"

There was an inhuman wail, and the glass of the morgue door shattered.

"Just a moment," Blessing shouted calmly, now visible beyond a jagged glass edge, as if he were making someone wait in a parlor for tea. He said something about banishing to the abyss, something from Jesus's own battles with demons.

The creature huffed, gasping. It made noises but formed no words we could recognize. It made me think of my first moments speaking again, those ugly sounds I'd hated so much I'd preferred never to speak at all. I batted tears out of my eyes. It seemed like the creature was in pain.

Jonathon was trying to read the strange equipment, seeking to understand the levels and the sudden chime like an automated heartbeat.

"I don't know how to stabilize you," he said mournfully. The sparks and wires were dangerous and live with a charge, so he didn't dare touch anything.

Rachel's eyes rolled back in her head. I caught her just before she hit the floor. "Angry," she signed to me, struggling to rouse. "All the spirits. So angry."

The room kept plummeting in temperature. Breath clouding before me, I forced Rachel to focus on me. "Tell us how to help them!"

"The pieces," she signed, an anguished sound leaving her

lips that broke my heart. "So many ghosts." I translated from her fumbling, shaking hands. "My fault they're here."

The body convulsed upon the table. Yes, it was in pain. It had to be. Body language was the one language that never told a lie. It was so terrible and all I wanted in the whole world was for this to stop. Just stop. Make it stop.

"Tell us what to do," I begged Rachel, tears streaming down both our faces.

"They want it to die," she signed.

"But it needs *them* to live," Blessing said.

I looked up to see him standing tall and calm just inside the door. Smith stood between rooms, white as a sheet, a dark fluid spattered over one cheek, looking as if he'd just glimpsed hell in that morgue. Perhaps he had. Blessing tossed Smith a kerchief from his bag and wiped his own face with another. The white cloth came away begrimed with unctuous green-black fluid similar to that I remembered from when we reversed the curse.

Rachel nodded vigorously at Blessing. "But they want me to die with it," she signed to me. "Sacrifice. For the sins of all."

"You're not going to die for this," I insisted.

"The spirits must be the spark," Jonathon said, looking around the room at the wires, at the shaking body. "The electric charge. Together they are a coalescing *animus*.

"Spirits." Jonathon moved to the center of the room and

shielded his eyes as if from some great light, even though to me the room remained dim. "Can you see me?" He spread his arms out. "*I* see light around us. I see *your* light as you make yourselves known. I've come from the other side. I crossed death itself and returned to tell you that you're free. Haunt these floors no more. Here lie only pieces. Dust and ashes. But you can be so much *more* than that. Please choose to be angels, not devils. You can choose."

It was riveting, his speech. He *did* have a light about him, that silvery light I'd seen before when I'd thought him an angel.

"Tell us who you are," he declared. "Tell us your names. The demons like to use your names against you. But *I* say names give *you* power, not them. Tell us who we may honor."

"The names are carved…" Rachel signed. I looked closer at the runes and glyphs on the dead skin.

"Tell us, give us the power of your names," I encouraged. Rachel began spelling out names in a torrent, as fast as her fingers could fly.

I said them aloud as she signed: "Teresa, Bartholomew, Benedict, Ursula, Maria, Sarah…"

All the names of saints. Like those dead in the Five Points. As I spoke each name, there was a resulting sizzle upon the yellowed flesh of the creature, and the runes glowed bright and wept dark, sour blood…The creature moaned, rustling from side to side. It almost sounded female.

Jonathon stared in pity at the face of it, of *her*...

"Jonathon," I begged, "can you—"

"Ease the suffering? I'll try."

He darted to the cabinet full of medicinal bottles and began rummaging, for what I didn't know. Blessing followed him, dabbing holy water into his hand.

Rachel and I repeated the names again, a few more I don't actually recall, each of them saints, and she fumbled for my hand. More sizzling flesh and ignited runes, more restlessness of the body.

Jonathon had seized a towel and was dabbing liquids onto it, murmuring chemical compounds and numbers.

Blessing moved to the head of the body and gently anointed the yellowing forehead, placing one hand on each side of its matted hair and offering the body named Laura a blessing by name. There was power in a name indeed. The milky eyes opened. And if I wasn't mistaken, those eyes focused directly on Blessing, and he stared bravely and unflinchingly back, repeating the benediction. The body seized again in a frisson of pain, and Blessing blinked back tears.

Jonathon, damp cloth in hand, darted to the shaking corpse's side and spoke gently. "We don't want you to be in pain," he said. He placed the towel over the nose and mouth of the creature. It seized in a spasm and then went motionless. Peaceful. Jonathon eased a moment, tension releasing out of his shoulders. And the room was held suspended—an oddly lovely pause when the creature's pain subsided. The sparks stopped crackling over the wires, and the body lay still. We all held our breaths.

And then the screaming began. We all heard it. It was a horrible sound I'll never forget. The body stirred again, roused, arms flung forward, one leg off the table, fighting for life. It was moving, getting up. The spirits may have wanted it dead, but it wanted to live, just like any of us did.

What was making the sound? The creature's mouth was open, and it was like the world was screaming. It was all-consuming, the sound. It was the sound of madness. I wasn't sure if I was laughing or crying. I couldn't hear myself. The sound split our skulls, and one by one, each of us began collapsing onto the floor of Room 01.

I sank to my knees as Rachel dropped heavily beside me, her arm across my lap. Blessing crumpled against the wall, holding his head. I glanced back to see that Smith had collapsed at the door's threshold. Jonathon was reaching for me as we fell, and everything faded to black as the creature began to walk out the door.

Chapter 21

Jonathon roused me. He placed something pungent and acrid beneath my nose. I sat up with a start, my head pounding. Either my ears were ringing and echoing, or the screaming was farther away. Whatever whispers I'd heard earlier, I couldn't hear them now over the distant screams that seemed to be shrieking on every pitch of human hearing.

"How long have we been out?" I asked.

"By my watch, about nine minutes," he replied.

Jonathon moved to rouse Blessing and Smith with the same acrid chemical in a blue bottle, like smelling salts but far more powerful. Once they were upright, he returned to rummage again in the chemicals. "What are you doing?"

"Making chloroform. It subdued the creature before. Well, it isn't quite right, a bit too much chlorine, surely—"

"You're amazing," I said. I looked around. "Where's Rachel?"

She was nowhere to be seen. Smith jumped to his feet and tried all the downstairs doors. Nothing. He returned to help Blessing to his feet.

"Thank you," Blessing said, glad for the help as he'd gone down hard. He stood rubbing his back and leg.

"From that godforsaken sound," Jonathon said as we stumbled into the hall, rubbing our temples. "It's still in the building. We can't let it get outside. Look for Preston and for Rachel." Smith took off ahead of us as we left that dreaded basement behind us.

Ascending to the first floor, we were stopped in our tracks by a trail of blood. It was coming from Preston's office and down and around the corner, then down another hallway.

"Please God, don't let that be Rachel's blood," I cried softly.

We followed the trail of blood. Jonathon had his pistol in one hand, his chloroform in the other. I took the bottle from him, and he steadied his shaking pistol with both hands. The blood led to another door labeled MENTAL WARD.

The screaming was behind that door, along with a soft, pleading male voice. Blessing flung the door open, a cross in one hand, an open bottle of holy water in the other. He flung a spray of it forward as we took in the sight before us.

Dr. Preston lay on a cot, bleeding from the wrists. The creature, tall and yellowed and now a bit peeling from stitches strained by movement, was standing over him, a yellowed hand awkwardly petting his head.

Beside the cot sat Rachel, her hands bound, tears streaming down her cheeks. Three surgical knives hovered in the air, poised to plunge directly into her heart.

The creature turned to look at us with vacant, milky eyes.

The screaming was farther away, and we realized it wasn't coming from the creature anymore. But from the floor above us. The upper floors of the hospital were still active. And evidently, everyone on the upper floor was losing their minds. Quite a bedside manner, this creature had.

"Laura, please," Preston begged, looking up weakly. "Please forgive me." He looked around him, wildly. "All of you, spirits, forgive me. Take me. Not the girl. I didn't mean for this to happen."

Blessing stepped into the room quietly. Jonathon, at his side, lowered his pistol. But Preston pinned Jonathon with bloodshot, wide, and desperate eyes.

"You! Demon!" Preston cried, pointing at Jonathon limply, blood dripping from his wrist. "Leave me be! Tell the Society they can go to hell! Spirits, take out your vengeance on him as you did on Roth. That man is now Society property!" Preston swooned back onto the pillows, pale from loss of blood.

The surgical knives flew toward Jonathon.

I stepped in front of him. The knives stopped short a foot from my flesh.

"Spirits! This is not the man Preston thinks," I cried,

wishing I had somewhere to look other than thin air. "Teresa, Bartholomew, Benedict, Ursula, Maria, Sarah, *please*," I begged. "This man is no demon. You saw him below. Spirits, you saw his light. You know he wants what's best for you, as we all do." The knives seemed unconvinced. They held their targets. "Please," I begged, "Don't kill us. You've no longer any enemies here."

Blessing had moved to Rachel and untied her as Jonathon stepped in front of me, closer to the blades. The furious movement of Rachel's hands distracted me from the knife points.

"The creature and the spirits are enemies," Rachel signed to me, approaching us.

It was true, I suppose. While one lived, the others were enslaved. If the spirits were sent to rest, the creature would die. And then Rachel moved to place herself in front of Jonathon, leaning her thin and shaking body against him as if she'd fall over otherwise. I wondered if the screaming was manifest in her mind, too. Was she hearing something the rest of us could not? None of us could make any sudden moves for the knives reacted if we twitched.

"Laura," Preston said softly, gazing up at the unblinking, parchment face above him. He clung to something once human that resided there and held the discolored hand, his bleeding wrist drenching the yellowed palm and turning it orange. "All I wanted was one more day with you. One more chance to tell you I loved you, a chance I'd been denied. But now, now we must join together and hope that somewhere I may see you again." He turned his head. "And by divine provenance there is a reverend here so that I might be forgiven. Bless me, Father, for I have sinned. Please bless this creature here, she knows not—"

"I already did, Dr. Preston." Blessing came close, placed his hands on either side of Preston's face, and gave him a benediction and his last rites. Everything was still, hesitant. The knives still floated in the air, now directed toward "Laura." Mr. Smith, a step behind me, tried to pluck a knife from the air, but it moved just out of his reach.

"Please, spirits, take me instead," Preston said to the air. "Take no lives other than mine. Stand back, Father."

The surgical knives shifted and dove suddenly into Preston's heart. We all jumped as Preston shuddered, blood pouring from his mouth, and lay still. In that moment all I could think about was Samuel, and I prayed to God that Mrs. Northe had gotten to him in time to prevent something as terrible as this.

As Preston expired, the creature made a terrible keening sound. There was a pause in the screaming above. Then it began again.

The creature hung its head and ran a clumsy hand over Preston's hair once more. Then we watched, breaths held, as it slowly left the room with a heavy tread, its thin hospital shift smeared and spattered with Preston's blood. We quietly followed, and I silently shut the door behind us, keeping an eye out for any stray knives. Mr. Smith moved to shut Preston's door.

It padded down the hall again into its room. We kept a slight distance behind. It turned and looked at Jonathon, and I could have sworn I saw some sort of pleading look there. Without taking his eyes off "Laura," Jonathon reached his hand out and I placed the bottle in it.

The creature lay down upon the table, a few stitches popping. It gasped. It fumbled for Jonathon's hand. Jonathon squeezed it, undeterred by Preston's blood, and his tear fell onto the cold metal table.

Blessing joined his side, offering additional benedictions as Jonathon doused a cloth with the chloroform and pressed it to the slack mouth.

"Stand back," Rachel signed to me, urging me toward the door.

"The spirits still need to be put to rest," Blessing instructed. Rachel ran next to Jonathon, nearly pushing him back, grabbing my hand, and shoving me toward the door. "Back," she signed, her face panicked, shooing Mr. Smith. Whatever she was hearing from the spirits, it really wanted us out of the room.

The sparks began again down the wires and the equipment again chimed. The body again shuddered, hands smacking against the table, the torso trying to raise, the head straining, knees twitching. The entire grid began to hum with increasing power, emitting a high-pitched whine. The body shook evenly and quickly. The crackling sound and the threads of lightning began weaving between the wires, lifting them as if they were hair…Yes, its hair lifted too.

We were captivated by the sight, rooted to the ground…

Rachel shoved us back further, one by one. A wire near the door came loose from the ceiling and burned the back of her hand where it made contact. At the door I turned to see the body burst into flames.

Thank God, it did not cry, nor did it scream. It only gasped and then was silent. I'd like to think it gave a sound of relief, but that was perhaps my wishful thinking.

It was an immediate, all-consuming incineration of the body, as if it were more combustible by its dead weight. Dead wood ignites all the quicker. The fire did not catch beyond the wires that singed and snapped. The metal table bore a body-length heap of glowing cinders in mere minutes.

In the end, the spirits had their say of what they wanted with it. I wondered if the Master's Society would ever understand that: the human soul was not something to enslave, not living, not dead.

I wasn't sure when it had happened, but we'd all taken hands at the threshold, even Smith, forming a chain.

While the room was hazy with smoke, it must have been well ventilated, for the room was not completely overcome. But the smell of chemicals and burned flesh was still overwhelming.

Jonathon shut the door. No one should ever have to smell such an odor. I'll add that to the list of things I will never forget. We stood between two sets of remains behind closed doors.

"Dr. Preston's life-and-death work," Jonathon murmured angrily. "All for what? A new age in the new world," he muttered, words Preston had used when trying to recruit Jonathon as a resurrectionist. "What could drive a man to create such a thing?"

"Why man does any unnatural thing," Blessing replied. "He was driven by love, hate, or fear. What makes this so terrible is that I think this was originally love."

"Why would reanimation be useful to the Master's Society?" I asked. "I'm sure the Majesty is hardly lovesick for some dead princess—"

"Did you see the effect the body had?" Jonathon said. "Not only was it flesh that they might command, but it knocked us all out. It also affected a whole floor above us, and I hardly think that was at full capacity. Let's hope they're not on an industrial scale with their experiments." Surely he thought of Samuel and that Preston had mentioned other doctors. What terrible acts of love and grief may result in scenes like this elsewhere? "A creature like this could wreak havoc in a town, entirely overturning the natural order of things."

On its own, the door to Room 01 opened again, reminding us we were not finished here.

"Not to mention the poltergeists," Blessing murmured, staring ahead into the room. Everything inside—the sheet, the equipment, the bottles, the wires, all of it—floated.

"What *now*?" Jonathon asked wearily.

"Ghosts can affect objects to get our attention," Blessing explained. "It's our attention they want, not the room or you, Miss Horowitz. Their bodies were used for ill, and their spirits pulled from rest. They're scared and confused. We must bury their ashes in consecrated ground. Miss Horowitz..." He turned to her, and I gestured for her to look up at him. "I do not wish to make assumptions, but are you Jewish?"

Rachel nodded.

"The spirits," he said. "Do you have a sense of their faiths?"

"Some Yiddish," Rachel signed. I translated aloud. "The rest, I sense, Christian."

"So for our Jewish friends," Blessing continued, "may they rest in peace, as we move about our tasks. Miss Horowitz, please add anything from your faith you deem appropriate. The more prayers the better, and the more tailored to the needs of the spirit—"

Rachel nodded. She stood straighter, her dazed eyes becoming more focused. I remembered the same shift in Jonathon. When he'd solved a piece of his own puzzle and had a task to do, he was less oppressed by his condition and more empowered, more alive, more effective.

Mr. Smith entered with a box of glass jars. Blessing beamed at him. "Mr. Smith, you read my mind."

Blessing moved to each of us, anointing our foreheads with oil. He offered Rachel blessing in what I assumed was Hebrew. She clasped onto the Star of David tucked beneath the lace of her dress. I pressed my own talisman, a small silver cross gifted to me by the Immanuel congregation at first communion that I often wore against my skin.

As Blessing began to murmur benedictions to calm the spirits, Jonathon winced and hissed, suddenly shielding his face and giving me a start. "Sorry," he said. "You're all glowing."

There was a pause. "What do you mean?" I asked.

"The light again. I see it when someone is about to affect something or become important. Natalie, you've a trace of your colors again. It's beautiful, really."

"You see the truth of the matter, Lord Denbury, the true *spirit* of things," Blessing said, smiling suddenly. "Well, then, let there be light!"

There came a terrible crash as the metal table overturned. Ash flew everywhere, and we all clapped our hands to our mouths and fumbled for handkerchiefs. None of us desired to breathe in the dead. The surrounding equipment shook and buzzed. Sparks flew from whatever still carried a charge. A few bottles of chemicals crashed and shattered against the wall, making our jobs infinitely more difficult.

Mr. Smith had hardly said a word, eerie in and of itself, but he made himself useful by taking all objects that could be projectiles out of the room. The ash was settling enough for us to not breathe it in.

Blessing calmly repeated the Lord's Prayer, then Psalm 23, the verse apropos:

"Though I walk through the valley of the shadow of death…"

And we fell in with him as we all gathered ash into the jars. Rachel had steeled herself, and even though she shook and was surely receiving an onslaught of anger, she remained upright and forced her eyes to focus. She kept pressing the corners of her embroidered handkerchief with symbols on the edges.

She glanced over at me, seeing me squinting at the symbols, and she signed to me: "Hebrew. It means *life*." And she continued breathing in, through *life*, filtering out the ash of death.

As I continued sifting ash into bottles, I repeated the Lord's Prayer as many times as I could. Rachel had tied her handkerchief around her mouth and was signing rapidly. I couldn't make out any of it, so I assumed she was spelling out words relative to the spirits who shared her faith.

"Release your anger and be done with it. Be done with this world," Blessing cried, flipping open his *Common Book of Prayer* to bestow rites. He ducked out of the way of an airborne bottle Mr. Smith had missed.

It was probably only a few minutes in that godforsaken room, but it felt like an hour. The bulk of the ash contained, Blessing ushered us back out. He kept the door open and dispersed holy water. He spoke a message of good news and benedictions of peace in a soothing voice that was not banishing devils but in fact begging for tranquility.

"I go now to take your ashes to hallowed ground, restless souls. Permit us to give you respect."

After a long moment the table stopped shuddering on the ground, the equipment stopped shaking on its hinges, wires stopped swaying. There was silence. No more screaming upstairs. Peace.

No, not silence. Not entirely. There it was again, the whispering, the low, droning chant. It had been there all along; we were just too distracted by everything else. Did the wind pick up? Was there a storm outside? I couldn't tell if I was hearing it in my own ears, like sounds underwater, or if it was external, like thunder. But it was familiar.

"Do you hear that?" I asked, a hand out to steady myself on the doorframe. It was the same noise from my dreams.

"Hear what?" Jonathon asked.

"The murmuring. Whispers. Chanting? It's getting louder. Don't you hear anything?"

"No, why—"

A jolt of pain ripped through my body and I screamed. It felt like someone was peeling my skin from my arms. I dropped to my knees as everyone stared at me in horror. No one else was affected. I saw Jonathon dive for me, and that's the last thing I could remember.

Chapter 22

Some part of me knew I was unconscious as I saw the corridor.

It was the recurring corridor of my dreams. This time it was marked with light and shadowy threads. Thin sparkling vertical lines, thousands of them, each shaded differently. I'd seen this in a dream before with Jonathon, but this time I was on my own. The corridor went on indefinitely, but before I could explore I heard a whisper. Not a maddening cluster, but just one. One soft, kind, loving Whisper.

The Whisper, the one from my mother. This time I heard her clearly. She said, "Hold on."

On each side of the hallway were open doors. Countless doors with windows onto the world, so many choices, thousands of diverging courses. Here a meadow with children running. There a battlefield. Here a family dinner. There a first kiss. Here a brawl. There a last breath. Deep darkness lay ahead of me and darkness lay behind me.

I watched the entities around me, dizzying flickering

lines. Each thread was like a spirit or its own force of nature, weaving in and out around one another and pulsing at these doorways. Then at once they all converged on me, light and shadow.

"Hold on, I'm here," I heard the Whisper say. I didn't want to leave that voice. I didn't want to leave *her…*

A deep breath of something sharp and pungent roused me with a coughing choke.

My eyes opened to see Jonathon before me, only this time he held a fancy bottle of ladies' smelling salts beneath my nose, not some random hospital compound. I was in a boudoir I recognized: upstairs in Mrs. Northe's home.

"Thank you," I murmured and took stock of my body. "My arms hurt." I glanced down at my blue blouse. No obvious damage, but my skin tingled strangely, my arms burning as if wounded under the surface. "What was that about?"

"I don't know. Everything was finally quiet at the hospital, resolved, really, but then you heard chanting and blacked out. Maybe everything we've been through built up like a toxin in your body, all the magic and ritual. Since you'd been subjected to so much already, perhaps your body and consciousness was at a breaking point—"

I grimaced. "Maybe I wasn't fully rid of it before throwing myself back in the center. That must be why a dream could wound me, why magic could reach up like a surging tide to drag me under."

Jonathon kissed my forehead. "I'll never let it take you."

"Where are Reverend Blessing and Rachel? Mr. Smith?"

"Smith helped me bring you here, drove while I held you. Now he's keeping watch on the house. Remind me to ask Mrs. Northe where on earth she picked him up. I still don't know what to think about him."

"Useful, though I think that's why he's around."

"Blessing and Rachel have gone to place the ashes in consecrated ground. He mentioned visiting a rabbi friend of his as well. I imagine that will take up most of their day. How are you feeling?"

I nuzzled against him, kissing his cheek softly with a thankful prayer. He always reminded me of what was good and true in the world against such dark, draining magic. Surely not all magic was dark, though. Love was magic.

"Do you remember anything?" Jonathon asked. "You were murmuring, like chanting, but I couldn't make any of it out."

I told him about what I'd just seen, about Mother's voice, about the entities that turned to swarm over me.

"As you fainted," Jonathon said carefully. "I saw red and gold fire surround you, signs of the dark magic."

I clutched at Jonathon's lapels. "Could the demon still be active? How do you really kill a thing like that? And *why* am I in such pain if I'm not bleeding?" I asked, itching at my forearm. I spoke too soon.

My fingernail came away bloody, a dark splotch pooling upon the light blue linen.

"Oh, God," I moaned. "Jonathon…what's…"

"I can hazard a guess," he said grimly. I knew it too. He tore my sleeves open.

Runes. So many of them. Carved into my arm lightly, on the surface but bloodier than before. It had happened to Jonathon during his curse, and now it was happening to me. And this, this wasn't just a few characters. This was the whole message. It began with the same few runes but now took up both of my forearms. He dashed into the hall.

"Make it stop," I cried, reaching out for him. From the bathroom I heard the rummaging of glass.

Make it stop. I saw those words, saw Rachel signing them to me, saw them emblazoned upon the desk, upon the downstairs sheet all in blood. It's all we wanted, all of us drawn into this mad quest. Just *stop*…It was enough to drive someone mad ten times over.

Evil was inflicted upon me, manifest by forces I couldn't see, forces that wanted to drag me to the depths rather than let me live in the light. I couldn't even bat the tears from my eyes, too scared to bring the bloody markings closer to me. Jonathon was upon me again in the instant, mixing an ointment with a clear fluid on a ball of cotton.

"This will sting," he said calmly, taking my arms and

laving them with the swab. The pain of his tincture wasn't any worse than the pain of the wounds, and I was so grateful for his touch, to have him taking care of me, that I didn't mind.

He kissed my palms. "Come now, Natalie. What did we say to your nightmares? What do we say to devils?"

"I renounce thee," I said. He said it with me.

The markings immediately began to recede. Jonathon turned over the swab that should have been bloody but wasn't.

"Quick, Jonathon, write down the markings before they're gone," I insisted.

We were in a woman's sphere, so the boudoir had a lush Turkish suite made surely for love letters, with cards and a fountain pen. Jonathon snatched up a paper and wrote out the sequence of the runic letters on one arm, then the other. Hardly a love note.

"I renounce thee," I said again to the magic. My breath fell over the letters. With a shimmer of red light, the demons' calling card, the markings, faded entirely as if I'd dreamed them up. I peered closer at my now smooth forearm. I glanced up at Jonathon sheepishly. "Tell me you saw them—"

He held up the paper of markings to prove it.

I threw my arms around him. "Thank you for taking care of me."

"It is my greatest pleasure." He eased me back onto the

divan so he could gaze down at me, stroking my hair with one hand as I kept hold of the other and kissed it. "Care for tea or coffee?"

"Earl Grey, please," I said. "You've made me a fan." I drew him toward me, breathing him in. "It smells of you, and I cannot get enough…"

He leaned in, kissed me tenderly.

"Were you left alone to tend to me?" I breathed in his ear. "We've no chaperone." I nibbled down his neck, loosening his cravat so that I might trail kisses lower. He moaned softly. "Someday we won't have to steal moments like these—"

We were interrupted by a familiar cry from downstairs. "Will someone tell me where on earth my daughter has gone? Again?" came the exasperated cry of my father.

"Hello, Mr. Stewart," I heard Mary say. "She's here. She had a nasty fall. Lost consciousness. Lord Denbury is looking after her."

"I'll bet he is."

"Oh, but he's a doctor, sir."

"Where's Evelyn?"

"Gone to Chicago. On emergency. Her friend Florence—"

"Is ailing. Yes, I know. Oh, that's a shame. I'd have gone with her," he said quietly. He sounded lost. "May I see my daughter, please?"

"Have you woken our fair sleeping beauty, Prince Denbury?" Mary called at the top of the stair.

"Sleeping Beauty was awoken with a kiss," I murmured and drew him down to give me one.

"Yes," Jonathon called finally. "I think I've roused her."

"I'll say," I teased.

"Naughty," he whispered.

"It's your fault," I countered.

Looking up from the divan, I saw my father in the doorway, arms folded. "Well then, what was that about?"

"Did you say there was tea for us, Lord Denbury?" I asked, bouncing to my feet. "Hello, Father!" I kissed him on the cheek and descended to Mrs. Northe's library.

"I see the *good doctor* took quite good care of her," my father said wearily, as if he'd given up on us being found in "proper" conditions. He followed behind me, Jonathon in step behind him.

"I'd give my life for her, sir," he replied.

"Oh, come now. Don't be overdramatic," my father said. "Natalie, what happened? You lost consciousness?"

"Do you want the truth or a lie?"

"The...truth," Father responded, but clearly he wasn't sure what he wanted.

"Lord Denbury, please sit with Father and tell him what happened today while I decipher what the demon carved on my arms."

A sound of shock squeaked from my father's mouth. "Maybe I don't want to know," he said as Jonathon led him into the parlor.

Most New York citizens of fair breeding sat in their parlors and talked about the weather or perhaps a play they might have seen or the new exhibits at our lovely Metropolitan or whether there would indeed be a subway system and whether they would do something about the noise and all the steam. Instead, we talk about omens and possessions as if they were sports teams. Poor Father, I'm sure he went green.

In the library, the volume of runes was lying out for me, as if Mrs. Northe had known I'd need it. I stared at the book and the correlating alphabet, then back at the note card with the message. Dread slithered in my stomach like a snake uncoiling to stalk prey. Roughly, the phantom carvings on my arm translated to: *I am coming for you.*

The book fell from my hands, and I tried not to faint. Twice in one day was already trying enough.

The demon wanted to make sure it was unmistakable. This was separate from the business with Preston and Rachel; this was an earlier vendetta. All the rest was a distraction, deadly for certain, but not as personal. This danger I had no idea how to fight. Was it in my mind, manifesting outward? To destroy it, did I have to destroy myself? I needed water. I needed to sit.

As I entered the parlor with this warning, Jonathon was explaining to my father. "I think it was a message," he stated, trying to put meaning to what had taken me under. "A warning. The demon we bested might still attempt revenge. Natalie awoke with…markings on her arm. Like what was carved into the arms of the victims."

I held up the note card, my shaky translation written below.

"'I am coming for you,'" I said, trying to keep my voice from breaking. "That's what my arms said."

Father stood as if he couldn't bear any more of this. I stared at him. Perhaps my face was haunted. Or calm. Or uncanny. Something about me made him sit again.

"Something's still out there," I stated. "And it's angry with me."

"Wire Evelyn. Get that priest back here," Father choked. "I want you under constant guard."

"The forces the Master's Society called upon aren't necessarily corporeal," I said with a shrug. "Hard to know what to guard."

"Why?" my father asked, trying to process. "Why do what that doctor did? And why this?" He gestured to me, to the ominous message. "Such *devilish* things. Unseen enemies that defy rational explanation."

"The people who…attacked me," Jonathon explained, "were interested in gaining power over me and my estate, yes, but also in the unnatural limits of what they could do. The darkest science is their aim. To what end we can't say."

There was a strained pause.

"This isn't over for you." Father stared at me in awe and pity. "*What's* coming for you, Natalie?"

"A phantom that wants me to believe it has power over me. But we won't let it win," I said with as much conviction as I could muster.

My father stared at me. "You're very brave."

I blushed. "Well—"

And then Father turned to Jonathon, his eyes cold, and he surprised me with his vehemence: "And this is all your fault. If you care for her, Lord Denbury, you should leave her well enough alone. The magic began with you. Your curse. Your entrance into our lives has nearly cost my daughter hers."

I moved to stand between them, my heart in my throat. My voice failed me. There was a terrible silence.

"I understand your concern, Mr. Stewart," Jonathon said quietly, swallowing hard. "I'm not sure what I can say in my defense. If you think keeping my distance will help her…"

"No," I mumbled. I couldn't lose Jonathon. Not now. He was my light, my angel.

"You have to see it's for the best," Father said. "Perhaps some time away—"

"Father, you don't understand," I protested. "We're wrapped up in this together."

"And I will extricate you from it!" Father bellowed. "You have no more say in the matter, Natalie. You are not yet independent."

Tears fell from my eyes. Jonathon stared at the floor.

Father took a deep breath, calming himself. "I'm not saying permanently, but there must be time away. Time to heal. Time for Lord Denbury to solve his own mess. Not you."

"He's right, Natalie," Jonathon said with sad realization. "You're too close. Everyone around me has suffered. I should never have drawn all of you in. The demon could be using you to gain his revenge on me, and I will not have you suffer any more. Surely you will be safer if I go."

Jonathon turned and disappeared into Mr. Northe's study before he could think twice, and my heart went with him, leaving me hollow inside.

Father took me home for dinner. I held back any further tears and didn't say a word. It was like I had no voice again. He filled the silence nervously, talking about nothing in particular. More than once he mentioned "Evelyn" and her thoughts on the various exhibition possibilities.

I glared at him, rising. "You realize, Father, that if Lord Denbury hadn't come into our lives, you'd never have become close to Evelyn Northe. So you'd best *extricate* yourself from her, too," I said, turning on my heel, and I went to my room.

"I love you and I'm scared for you, Natalie," he called after me. "I don't know what to do."

I slammed my door.

The last thing on earth I wanted to do was sleep. How could I rest if I wasn't sure which was safer, reality or dreams? Now that I was entirely on my own.

Chapter 23

After a restless night—but thankfully without any further horrors—I was awoken by breakfast in bed. All my favorites: eggs, juice, and pumpernickel toast. Father sat at my desk.

"How are you feeling?" he asked.

I didn't answer but dove into the eggs. I was starving. Recent events had done quite a disservice to my appetite. I thought about Jonathon and ached, my stomach rebelling.

"Come with me to the Metropolitan today."

"No. I'll go to Maggie's house today," I managed. "It's her calling hours."

"Are you sure? She was…unhinged when last we saw her."

"She's confused. Mrs. Northe doesn't tell her anything. That's the problem. It's made Maggie even more curious than she needs to be. She thinks I've taken her place. Maybe if I try to be a good friend to her, she'll see sense." I glared at Father again. "And if you won't let me see Jonathon, then I need some kind of friend."

Father sighed and went to the door. "Just…don't be alone anywhere. Not with a…curse over your head or whatever."

"I'll try, but you know who I'd be safer with? *Jonathon*," I declared, shutting the door on him. Father just didn't understand. We were a team, and that's what enemies wanted, for teams to splinter so the teammates could be picked off one by one.

Getting dressed into one of the finer dresses Mrs. Northe had given me, I began to wonder if I had the strength or patience to visit with Maggie and try to talk her down from whatever delusions about Jonathon she still believed.

Could I ever forgive Maggie for the advances upon Jonathon? I wondered if she could help it. Obsession did strange things to people. I had to be the better person, but my heart ached. The uncertainty of when I'd see Jonathon again, if Father ever let us be together, was its own terrible pain.

I looked in the mirror and saw Miss Rose. I was in a light, rose-colored gown. Putting the rose perfume behind my ears, I wondered if I was bringing on bad luck by embodying our code word for distress.

If Mrs. Hathorn was taken aback by my unexpected and uninvited house-call, she didn't appear so. She was exceedingly well put together in a cream day gown, as if she simply sat about the house in a perpetual state of expecting company.

"Why, Miss Stewart—"

"Natalie!" Maggie cried and threw her arms around me. I never knew when she wanted me to be her friend or when she wanted to insult me.

"Mother, we're taking tea to my room," she said.

She handed me a cup and saucer of the finest bone china, and I followed her upstairs. She hadn't let me into her private quarters before, so perhaps she had gossip to share. More likely, she wanted to get gossip out of me.

Her room was finely appointed, as I had expected. But it had taken on a flair of abandon. Scarves and fabric were draped everywhere; golden trinkets were lying about; and she'd taken over one wall with an elaborate chalk mural of colored lines swirling around a great eye, dragon wings on either side of it. I found it unsettling.

"Did you draw that?" I asked.

"Yes, do you like it?"

"Yes," I lied.

Even though the day was summer, the room was cold. I felt itchy. There was a distant buzzing sound, a low drone, like a swarm of bees.

"Maggie, I just wanted to explain."

"I hoped you would."

I took a deep breath. "I'm going to tell you the truth. But please take care."

"Finally."

"It *is* Lord Denbury."

"I knew it was."

"Maggie, listen. The nature of his situation is *so* delicate that I don't entirely understand what's going on."

"Because you don't understand that I've brought him to life!"

"Maggie, no, I don't think it works like that."

"Why, just because Auntie says it doesn't? What does she know, really? What does she care about us?" Maggie's voice was calm yet pleading. There was a truth in that. My head felt a bit foggy. All my nerves that had rubbed raw in regards to Mrs. Northe flared up.

"Where is she, anyway?" Maggie asked.

"I don't know. She's gone. Left me to face something really dreadful," I said, my tongue thick. "She makes you feel like you need her…"

"Then she's gone."

Mrs. Northe. She craved to be all things and everything to us, drawing us in so she could save us, a magnificent actress as mother and friend and usurper of my home, of my father's attention. Always a little too sensible, a little too perfect, and we were *far* too beholden to her. We were all her special orphans. And look where that got us.

A foreign anger flared any number of anxieties within me. The exterior drone grew louder.

"She's not my mother," I spat. "*Our* mother. She can't

swoop in every time and play one. Not to me, not to Jonathon, Rachel, all of us 'poor little lost children' beset by demons, and she the vanquishing angel. I wonder if she brings bad luck upon us just to come boldly to our rescue. She could've done right by you, Maggie, but I don't think you're *tragic* enough for her," I said, sarcasm dripping from my words like venom. Maggie seemed as taken aback by my outburst as I was, but thrilled. "I'm sorry," I murmured. "I'm not feeling too well all of a sudden."

"That's okay," Maggie laughed. "I just appreciate that for once you're being honest with me."

I laughed wearily. "I'm not sure about the truth anymore, really. Do you hear that? It's like whispers."

Oh, no. Was the magic coming for me again? I had to warn Maggie. She wouldn't know what to do. She bit her lip, her eyes sparkling at me.

"Can I tell you a secret?" Maggie asked.

"Of course," I said.

"I stole something. Something really important. I've been dying to show it to someone, but I'm scared I'll get in trouble."

"What is it?"

"Do you want to see?" she asked, bouncing a bit in her chair.

"Sure," I said. Maybe that's why she'd been acting strangely. She'd stolen something and was worried about repercussions. Maggie moved to her closet door.

"You're really sure? You promise not to tell *anyone*—"

"Of course."

The drone grew louder. It was chanting. Maggie opened her closet door, and a scream lodged in my throat.

I could hardly have wished that sight upon anyone, and I'd seen it with my own eyes. But to see it again so horribly *reconstructed*…

I was too stunned to say anything. I could only stare at the open door and what hung at the back of the empty closet.

It was the painting.

The portrait that had imprisoned Jonathon's soul within it. Maggie had removed all her clothing from the closet, and only *he* remained, with an altar at his feet.

There was the golden frame, slightly askew. There were the long strips of canvas. Upon release from his painted prison, Jonathon had torn them apart. But now they were side by side again. Maggie had recreated the canvas as best she could. And the subject of the portrait was the terrible, monstrous visage that had been swapped out when Jonathon regained himself, his life, his body.

Below the frame on the floor, Maggie had erected a disturbing shrine. Powder outlined in a pentagram pattern, similar to the symbol she'd made at the museum. I'd been taught that right side up, the pentagram was an omen of protection. But upside down, it could be devilish. There was a candelabrum where candles had been lit, at long hours clearly, for red wax had dripped everywhere in what looked like frozen, bloody strings. Stones were placed in small clumps. Dead flowers were strewn about. Was that a bird's skull in the corner?

"What do you think?" Maggie breathed. "Isn't it wonderful what I've done? It's almost back to normal."

No wonder Maggie thought she'd brought Lord Denbury to life. She thought she'd cast an elaborate spell to draw him out. But didn't she recognize that a charred gargoyle of a nightmare masque stared out from the painting, no longer a handsome lord but a monster in a fine suit? It would have been comical if it weren't so grotesque. The paint was peeling, and there was an odd moisture on the strips that had been carefully tacked together and placed back upon the frame with meticulous care. The elaborate production revealed the deeper seeds of Maggie's unraveling mind. Had someone helped her down this darker path, or by seeking it, had she led the darkness directly to herself?

I stepped forward. Did it move? Did I see the beast's long, gray-clawed finger move?

"Natalie, say something," Maggie whispered. "What? What do you think?"

I could hear it. The demon. He was in my head and around my ears.

The whispers were all around me, like a swarm of biting,

stinging, hissing insects. Just like my dreams. The dark magic was calling to me. It knew I was there.

Its fingers did move! Beckoning. But then they clenched into a fist.

"I thought I was done with this!" I whimpered.

"What do you mean?" Maggie asked defensively. Jealously.

But no, we were never done. There was always something else. There would always be another issue. Then another. That's how it was with people like us. We were really just game pieces. My vision darkened. I felt itchy. Though all the windows were open, it was warm. Too warm. And I was so angry. My edgy nerves crackled like the sparks of spirits down wires of reanimation.

"I mean," I said slowly, "that I've been face to face with this once before."

Maggie's door slammed shut of its own accord. It was just her. And me. And the remains of the portrait. And that was when it tried to kill me.

Chapter 24

The windows of Maggie's room all slammed shut. The gas lamps that had been burning high and bright to banish the shadow of the room guttered entirely, plunging the room into wan, gray light. I tried to cry out, but my voice was cut to the quick. My voice, so often strong for others, proved weak when serving only me.

Maggie screamed. "Natalie, what are you doing? Stop it…Stop it."

"*I'm* not doing anything," I managed to choke out.

The hissing murmurs surged again, crashing over me like a wave dragging me under. My arms seared with pain. Blood pooled on my wrists and wetted the lace cuffs of my sleeves as I was again marked and mauled by the magic. The furniture of Maggie's room shook.

The frame began to glow. The runes carved into the wood pulsed with light and angry power, like a lit heartbeat. My skin throbbed in rhythmic pain. I tried to turn, to move, to run, but I was frozen in place, staring in horror as the eyes of the beast on the canvas began to glow. All the rest of him was peeling, but his eyes were sulfuric fires. I could feel bile rise as I choked, an unseen hand clamping around my throat.

All of this had been foretold in dreams.

I'd been so focused on Jonathon, Samuel, Rachel, and Preston, on that hospital corridor, that I hadn't given my original foe much thought. I hadn't thought what really might wish revenge upon me. Its magic was still fresh and fed by the ignorance of Maggie; it had grown powerful by her doting. This foe knew me. It remembered me, wanted me dead…

"Hello, pretty," came a horrid voice, half in my mind, half a whisper outside my ear, and any sense of reality slipped away.

"Lord Denbury?" Maggie asked meekly.

The shredded portrait shifted, its subject stepping forward, and as he did, the room faded, blackening to one long corridor where the essence of the demon, a dark silhouette that appeared more like a grotesque moving statue than a human, took his dreaded steps toward me. Maggie hovered somewhere on the edge of my vision. My nightmares shifted into reality, or perhaps I simply lost my mind.

"Lord Denbury, come to me," Maggie called. "It's me. I'm the one that's brought you back."

But the demon only had eyes for me. It approached slowly, time stretching into something malleable.

"This is how I come upon the helpless, little girl," it growled, "and always have in my turns around this globe that have made me what I am. This corridor lives alongside you. You and everyone. I wait for a door, a window, a path to open onto you, and that's where I take over. The helpless and the poor in spirit are ever easy to overcome." It turned a skeletal head toward Maggie, snorting derisively.

Blasphemy. My mind screamed, though I could make no audible sound, my voice failing me as I gasped. No. *Blessed* are the meek. *Blessed* are the poor in spirit.

"What are you saying?" Maggie cried, reaching out toward the demon. "Natalie, tell him to look at me. Show him what I've done for him!" Her voice was that of a hurt child. And then she turned vicious. "Why is it you?" she shrieked. "Why is it always you, Natalie? What makes you so special?"

The demon lifted one shadowy arm and backhanded Maggie so hard that she flew across the room and slumped like a rag doll. I prayed she was still alive. She was stupid and deluded, but it was just like the Society to prey on the vulnerable. And goodness if Maggie hadn't given food for the demon. Still, she didn't deserve this. Neither did I.

I renounce thee. I tried to say the words. I couldn't. But the words, even in my mind, caused frissons of light, like spider-silk thin veins of lightning to thread down around me. A sliver of hope, perhaps? Where was my angel now? *Jonathon*, my mind screamed.

The demon's coal black eyes burned in the back of their sockets with yellowish hellfire. This thing was misery and the worst of humanity made solid.

I struggled to move, to breathe. I was *not* as helpless as it thought I was. I'd proven that once, but it knew I was scared. And the first time, I'd had the advantage of surprise. My preoccupation and my pride had underestimated what might still live in the scraps of the painting, lying in wait.

Why has everyone abandoned me? Where was Jonathon when I needed him? Mrs. Northe? Blessing? Rachel? Anyone?

The hissing murmurs became those terrible chants pounding in my head and all around me, thrumming in my veins, shaking my bones. The maid or Mrs. Hathorn would find our dead bodies, and someone would have to tell Jonathon the terrible news.

"You and countless others," the demon said in a gurgling voice. "I will carve your names in blood on your own flesh. Names written in the Book of Death. And when your name is called, you will follow me. The Society will rest upon the shoulders of the restless..."

I renounce thee... I strained in my mind.

A shadowed hand on my throat clamped tighter, even though the demon kept walking inexorably closer and had no actual hand upon me. All the properties of time and space were void. I was between dream and awake, life and death, where truth was suspended. A dangerous place where the dim flicker of life seemed easily snuffed out.

"You cannot stop what has been set in motion," the demon growled. "Your small band of stupid mortals against gathering forces, the futility amuses me. Come, tread this walk as a restless spirit, 'round and 'round the globe. You'll see. There are greater truths than you know."

I renounce thee. Mother…*Mother, if you were ever watching over me, I need you now.*

It seemed as though the beast could have snapped me in half if it wished, but something held it back. Something of my struggle, my fight, my resistance was keeping it from breaking me…

I renounce thee…

A flicker of white. White lace. A quiet whisper. The Whisper. *Her* Whisper. The sound of something loving and beautiful. At the opposite end of that seemingly endless corridor appeared a vision all in white with a face I only recognized from daguerreotypes and my father's stories.

Statuesque and fierce, with dark auburn tresses floating all around her as if she were in water, stood a luminous angel. My mother. And this time when she spoke, praise be, I heard her clearly.

"Demon, unhand my girl! She's not yours and never will be. There are some you can never win. You think you know the tread of the walks. But I know them too. Those chosen to fight are not yours to command!" She turned, as if addressing someone at my side. "Jonathon, if you will, my dear young man, take care of her."

Jonathon? Was he with me? She saw him? I didn't need my voice to call for him after all. After all we'd been through, our souls had language enough.

The tension around my throat eased. I reached out, longing to embrace my mother. But instead I fell, crumpling against strong arms as the demon howled again with that terrible train-like whistling shriek, while red-gold fire crackled.

Looking up, I saw Jonathon, hair wild, eyes bright. He shook and shouted at me. That was my Jonathon, wasn't he? No…his eyes turned dark and full of rage as if the demon had overtaken him once more. No. *No.* Only fear placed the demon in him. The demon wanted me to doubt, to turn us against each other. I fought the image, renouncing the evil that sought to claim me.

Struggling to look at Jonathon again, my vision swimming as though I were suffering the effect of some opiate, I saw him as he was: handsome, concerned, my champion. A veritable halo shone around his strong body. My Jonathon Whitby, lit with angel's fire, shouted the counter-curse we'd used once before and pulled me free.

Oh, yes, the counter-curse! Those ancient words that

ushered evil back from whence it came. Struggling to speak and breathe, I murmured it with him, the words that had been the key to Jonathon's prison.

"*Ego transporto animus ren per ianua...*"

I send the soul through the door. The spell had an extra part, difficult to track, an Egyptian word for "soul-door" that interrupted the Latin. But that frame was a portal for souls, a doorway into a realm I never wanted to see again, a door we must shut for good.

With one more cry of the counter-curse, the corridor seeming to bend around me dizzyingly. With a whooshing crack, the hazy shadows that had extended from outside of the frame like limbs snapped back. Paint exploded onto the floor, and the ugly portal was inanimate once more. At least for now. Maggie's room had returned to normal.

"You came for me," I gasped, my throat still bruised, leaning into Jonathon's hold.

"Don't be silly. I'll always come for you. But thank Rachel. She's the one who got me."

It was only then that I noticed Rachel tending to Maggie, who was still unconscious against the wall. "What happened?" I asked.

"I was writing a letter to the Society when she grabbed me by the hand and dragged me here. I admit I had a feeling something was wrong, but I wasn't sure what. I know better now than to ever ignore the feeling."

I gestured at Maggie, signing to Rachel. "Is she alive?"

Rachel nodded and moved to kneel beside me. I let Jonathon help me to a sitting position, and I threw my arms around Rachel. "I owe you my life," I signed to her.

"We're even," she signed in reply. "Thank your mother. She's the one who told me."

"Thank you, Mother," I murmured. "Mother was there, Jonathon. Did you see her? Wasn't she beautiful?"

"No, I didn't see her. But I heard a woman call my name just as Rachel seized me. We were here in a mere minute. But I had to kick down the door that had locked you in. Gave poor Mrs. Hathorn a fright, charging up her stairs. When she saw her daughter collapsed on the floor and a great breeze in the room, she fainted straightaway."

I glanced at the door, whose jamb had been splintered and the fine pewter knob bent to the side. I grinned at my hero. Claire was caring for the prone form of Maggie's mother.

"What's to be done with the portrait now, though?" Jonathon said. "How can we ultimately destroy it? Remember, Mrs. Northe left you in charge."

I coughed. "I resign."

"Sorry, I cannot accept your resignation," he replied. I sat up and stared at the closed closet door that now seemed so innocuous.

"It's up to us," I said, thinking of what had been deep in

my mind all along. "This has always been about us. The magic is tied to our souls, *our* bodies alone. We're the only ones who can destroy it. You and me. We have to burn it. My dreams were telling me that all along. What appeared terrifying was actually a clue: your burned-out study."

"While that may be, I don't want the ashes in any of our chimneys. The demon, when it used the artist to make the painting in the first place, used powders and ashes for the spell. *Any* remnant of this thing could be dangerous. Whatever we do, it has to be *utterly* destroyed."

"Out above a riverbank. There's a yard a few avenues east. Some of it is used as a scenic outlook, but there are too many mills for it to be very sightly. Burn it there."

"Your father's going to kill me for being with you again—"

"Not when he finds out you saved my life."

But would the creature yet live in my dreams? Would it have any life or strength there? Not as long as I kept to just this side of the light.

Jonathon went to Maggie's side, picked her up, and set her upon her bed, tucking her in. It was a shame she wasn't awake for it; she'd have swooned in ecstasy.

He then went to one of her steamer trunks and tipped it on its side, spilling out petticoats, corsets, and swaths of fine fabric. Then he went to the closet.

Thankfully the Hathorns remained unconscious, allowing us to do what had to be done with no additional histrionics.

The painting frame and torn canvas had disintegrated further. Jonathon unwound the length of his gray cravat, leaving his collarbone deliciously visible, and wrapped his hands in the fabric so as not to touch the icon of horror directly. He lifted the sagging frame from the peg upon which it had been hung, scraps of canvas already falling away and that ugly grime coating the surface.

I joined in, my gloved hands protection enough— sometimes ladies' accessories came in frightfully handy— gathering scraps into the trunk. Jonathon stood on the base of the frame, tore each beam from the other, and stomped upon the carved wood, breaking it into splintering pieces.

I ducked my head into the hall. Rachel and Claire stood at the end to keep any other staff from coming our way. "Broom and dust pail, if you please?"

Claire ducked into a closet, handed me the items I requested, and returned to her post. She crossed herself, not looking at me, as if she didn't want to acknowledge whatever she'd seen here. I wonder what it had seemed from the outside. Perhaps the demon showed differing types of horror to all those who experienced him.

When the shreds, splinters, and pieces of the painting all were collected and deposited into the trunk, I removed my smudged, smeared gloves and tossed them in. Jonathon did the same with his soiled cravat—a shame since it was beautiful fabric—and looked around for something. He found what he sought in a glass table lantern with a bulb of oil at its base and matches at the side.

"I'm not waiting another minute to take care of this," he said.

"Nothing is more pressing," I agreed. He looked at me with a terrible grimace. He plucked another of Maggie's silk scarves and wound it around my neck.

"Quite a bruise you've got rising there."

"I'm sure."

We went directly to the outlook. I'm sure my father wondered about my whereabouts, but he'd get some sort of explanation after this was finished.

Past orphanages, coal depositories, and carriage houses, we made our way. Jonathon was able to carry the trunk on his own, while I held the oil-filled lamp and matches. We were quiet, each in our own reverie.

These battles had become somewhat ritualistic, and though we never knew what to expect, solemn gravity came with taking care of them. Talking about it would only make it more absurd. What we saw defied explanation, but we were still left with evidence.

The late-summer air was humid and warm, but the breeze was refreshing, despite the industrial landscape around us. The deck was more an extension of an industrial yard, but it served well as it was thankfully unpopulated, the nearby ceramic factory closed for the weekend. Those who were out for a promenade stuck to the avenues and sidewalks west of us. Beyond us, the river was far below. Vast, tumbling vegetation stood between us and the East River, filled with countless boats. Queens and Brooklyn stretched out on the opposite bank.

Jonathon broke open the lantern, spilled the oil all over the contents of the trunk, lit several matches, and dropped them in. The hissing fire inside was left to blaze. We let it burn on the gravel plateau and stood back, arms around each other.

"I am sorry, Natalie Stewart," Jonathon said. "I keep drawing you back in."

"I'd not trade you for the world, Jonathon Whitby."

He smiled then, a genuine smile like I'd not seen for a while, and all the shadows that had tinged his expression faded. I did have a good effect upon him.

We watched the last tactile part of the curse burn to ashes, and then we overturned the trunk and watched the ash scatter in the wind. Jonathon then gave the trunk a healthy kick down the bank.

Resolution of our matters seemed to end in fire.

It was fitting then that he turned to me and we engaged in a rather fiery kiss, far from public eye. I wondered how much longer we could go on this way, indulging in stolen kisses as releases of stress and terror. I wondered when we might be able to indulge more properly. And so I dared bring up what I didn't want to have to.

"Jonathon. You know I wish to deny you nothing. But Father…I can't continue flaunting propriety indefinitely. He's going to demand—"

"That I ask for your hand or bugger off. I know," Jonathon said, holding out his arm for me. "And that I prove all dangerous matters thoroughly solved."

"I know we've not had any time," I stammered. "And I understand you want all your affairs in place. It's just that—"

"I can't treat this as child's play. I know. You were a girl but now you're a woman, and society says I must marry you to continue kissing you. And other, more exciting things," he said, trailing a finger down my neck, down the side of my bodice, lifting the edge of the fabric to pull on the laces of my corset. I shuddered in delight. "I don't need a lesson on propriety. Though I admit, I've had some *improper* thoughts about you."

"Oh?"

"Perfectly—" A kiss upon my neck. He trailed down my throat with more. "Passionately—" He pulled at the lace modesty panel across my bosom, revealing more flesh for him to graze with his mouth. "*Improper…*"

I gasped, my ungloved hands raking into his hair and seizing the locks, while I shuddered against him, desperate to give over to seductive abandon. If we disappeared into the copse of trees beyond the deck, would anyone care or find us? But what would happen if I gave myself? What would I have if the reality of our class difference, supernatural fates aside, trumped all? The word "ruined" meant what it meant.

"I'm not of your station," I murmured mordantly. "You're not supposed to marry me anyway."

He glanced up at me, his mouth braised pink from the force of his kisses. He drew back. "I tell you, class is of no consequence! But if you recall, your father isn't very fond of me at the moment, not to mention that I have to play my part. I can't run off and marry you. That would crack my cover wide open, betray my allegiance, and further endanger you."

"Must you still play the agent? Don't you know enough to have others track them? Enough evidence to be done with this?"

"If I disappear, that's just as suspicious. While we might be able to turn some things over to the authorities, the Society will come looking."

The realization that there was no immediate end to his involvement with the Society dawned on me with a new terror. It might take *years* before we could be married. I couldn't continue this. I couldn't feel the way I did about him and not be closer to him in every way. I'd been through so much in the past days that I was about to throw an all-out fit.

"Then…what do we do?" I cried, not bothering to hide my desperation. Jonathon eyed me. The wind caught the waves of his black locks, and his shocking blue eyes twinkled, giving him the look of some beautiful creature in the wild pausing amid a hunt.

"Perhaps a secret engagement might hold everyone at bay until everything can be done with all proper pomp and circumstance."

One moment terror, the next joy. How radically my life changed from moment to moment. I grinned and threw my arms around him as we walked. A secret engagement?

"And no, that wasn't me proposing, Natalie. *That* will be a surprise, and don't you dare go nagging me about it."

I giggled and suddenly felt as if every town-house window-box were as grand as a palace garden and every sound of clattering horse hooves the exclamation of angel choirs.

"But truly, Natalie," he said earnestly, "you've been amazing. So strong through all of it. A lesser girl—"

"I got knocked unconscious. Twice," I protested.

Denbury lifted my chin to look at me with his piercing gaze for a fond lecture. "Natalie, you act selflessly for others without a second thought. You go through paint-ings, spy on murderers, put yourself in harm's way, get on trains, travel across the country without hesitation, stare down dead bodies, face your nightmares, talk to ghosts, stand in the way of knives, and translate sign language, all for people you care for. The world needs women of action, and I've admired none as much as you. Your light shines bright around you, never dimmed. I'm not sure what's ahead, but I do know I need a partner and I choose you."

And that is what I wanted to be more than anything in the world. His partner.

My ecstatic bliss was short lived.

My father must have been watching from the window, for he stormed down the stoop of the town house just as we closed the wrought-iron gate of the garden level behind us.

"Lord Denbury, I thought I was quite clear you were not to see my daughter. No matter what manner of strange circumstance passed between you two, you do not have free rein to escort her about as if you were her husband. I'll not be disrespected like this, and that goes for you too, Natalie. Your voice and your whims alone do not liberate you."

I was shocked that every biddy in the neighborhood hadn't opened her window to listen in. Thankfully Father had enough sense to keep his voice down.

"It's been…a trying day, Father," I said quietly. "Would you like the truth of it or a lie?"

He stared at me a moment, likely wondering how many lies he'd endured. "The truth…Why do you keep asking that question?"

"Because you should always have the option. A lie would be a lot more pleasant than the truth," I said, as I undid the scarf around my neck. My father's hand went to his mouth, tears in his eyes. "Please thank Lord Denbury, Father. He just saved my life."

"Come in," Father choked out, ushering us upstairs.

Bessie didn't appear to be present. That may have been for the best. We sat in the parlor. "What happened?"

I took a deep breath. "Maggie stole the remains of the painting and resurrected it in her room. It had a terrible curse on it. The dark magic attacked me, but Rachel heard the warning of Mother and fetched Lord Denbury to my side. Together, he and I fought it back. We had to dispose of the remains, as only he and I could. The curse marked Lord Denbury *and* me. And we, together, were the only ones to destroy it. Father, any danger I brought upon myself is of my own will. You mustn't blame him," I said strongly.

My father stared at us, part in wonder, part in horror. I reached out and squeezed his hand. "We do try to do the right thing, Father."

He rose, dragging Jonathon up and into his arms in a wide embrace. "I lost my wife. I can't lose my girl." He cried against him. Jonathon returned the embrace in full.

"I told you I'd do anything for her, Mr. Stewart," Jonathon assured him. "I mean it."

Father drew back. He looked at me, his arm out as if

scared to touch me or my bruises. I went to him, and he folded me in the same embrace.

"Mr. Stewart, I appreciate your position very much. I am sorry for any wrong you perceive. Believe me, none of this is how I'd have chosen to court your daughter if I'd have been given a choice. I'll do right by you both as soon as I can in good faith. In the meantime, do I have your permission, Mr. Stewart, to come to call tomorrow evening? There's an event I'd like to take Natalie to, and I'd rather have your permission than sneak about."

"Only *with* a chaperone," my father declared. "Evelyn wired that she's been on nothing but express trains and that she'll return by then."

"Good, then," Jonathon said. He and I opened our mouths at the same time. "Did she say anything about—"

"Yes, she said to tell you that she got to Samuel in time. He's damaged but will be all right."

Jonathon and I breathed a huge sigh of relief. I was suddenly so proud of us, that we'd managed all that we had without her, and so glad we could still turn to her in all our times of need.

"Thank you, Mr. Stewart. I shall see you soon." Bowing to my father and then to me, Jonathon walked off down the street, turning onto Lexington toward downtown and his generous hostess's home. In my darkening mood, when the demon had hold of me, I'd denounced her. I felt guilty at the thought. I missed her, too, her absence only confirming how inextricably linked we were.

"Father, do you and Mrs. Northe plan to court…further?"

He coughed a bit and adjusted his collar. "Provided she doesn't find me tedious, yes, I sincerely hope so. Especially with her gone, I realize how much I like having her around. And you're right, Natalie. Lord Denbury brought us all together, and it's unfair to court Evelyn and deny you. It's just—"

"Been terrifying. Believe me. I know."

"Would my courting her bother you? I…you two seem so close. I assume…She's like family already."

It was true, but I ached. I was worried. If I was at the center of mystery, so was Mrs. Northe, and she was accountable. My heart ached for all that had befallen Jonathon and for Maggie, poor Maggie. Despite Mrs. Northe's protestations, could I have been the friend to Maggie who could have prevented what happened today? And if Mrs. Northe had paid her more attention, I'm convinced things might have turned out differently. I ached for all the things that may yet change.

"You're right. We are close. Mrs. Northe has done so much for me, and it isn't that I'm not grateful. I just don't want her thinking she can take the place of all that we have lost, the whole of us. That's too much space for any one woman to occupy, even as unparalleled a woman as Mrs. Evelyn Northe."

"She's not taking anyone's place," my father said gravely. "There is no replacing your mother. Do you hear me? No one could replace her."

Tears were suddenly in my eyes. And that meant they were soon in his.

"Can we go to Woodlawn?" I asked quietly.

"I'd like that."

Again the train ride up the line, again the haggard old woman with the amazing smile and a cluster of black-eyed Susans. I'd begun to wonder if she gathered them just for us. We made our way through the winding lanes on our usual course. Father had gone ahead of me. I turned the corner of the knoll to see him down on one knee, kissing the stone. He drew back, putting his hand upon the stone and walking away so that I could have my own moment.

I thought about Mrs. Northe's husband, Peter, whom she loved too. No, no one could replace those we had lost. But God made our hearts big and full of many rooms.

The trees rustled in the breeze, as if willing me to make noise too.

"Mother…" I murmured, staring at her name. "Mother, listen. You saw me through today. I glimpsed death and you stood in its way. I want you to be always *in the way*, Mother. I always want your presence in my life known, felt, close. I'm scared. Things are changing—our life, our home…I just want your blessing. I want a sign from you. You are so *alive* to me in my heart, and I don't want you to feel…I don't want to lose you any more than I already did.

"Will you mind if Mrs. Northe assumes part of your place in this world in your absence? She could *never* replace you, but she would be there, in some ways in your stead. Give me a sign. Otherwise I can't be at peace…I can't accept her otherwise."

I stared at the stone. I listened for the Whisper. She'd spoken to me in that corridor just hours ago. But never when I'd asked for her. She was ever elusive. Wild. Walking barefoot through some foreign field on a distant shore…Silence.

I stared at her name and rank as mother and wife carved boldly in old-fashioned script. I stared next at the German phrase carved below her name, a phrase from Psalm 23 that I'd murmured over and over again just recently, while embroiled in spiritual battles:

"Und ob ich schon wanderte im finstern Tal, fürchte ich kein Unglück; denn du bist bei mir…"

"Yea, though I walk through the valley of the shadow of death, I fear no evil for you are with me…"

And then, even lower; a lyric from a contemporary yet much beloved carol:

Westward leading, still proceeding, guide us to Thy perfect light.

I stood a moment thinking about that lyric and wondering why it was there. I'm sure I had the significance written down somewhere. Whatever the case, I'd forgotten. I was always too busy trying to memorize the German.

The sky was darkening and the first star was in the sky. A distinct star.

"Remind me why that lyric, Father," I said as he came to collect me.

"'We Three Kings' was your mother's favorite song. She heard it as a young woman at General Theological during a Christmas pageant, the very first time it was ever performed. She'd sing it sometimes even in the heat of summer. Why?"

I turned away. "I think I have her answer," I murmured, "her blessing." I walked to the carriage, looking up, my thoughts on the chorus of the song: "Star of wonder, star of night."

Above me, glittering in the sky was another famous star that led people to safety as I had been led, and that was the bright, the unmistakable *North* Star.

Chapter 25

I'll have to wait and see what my father does about proposing to Mrs. Northe, about this...*family* of ours.

We had so much to tell her, and we had so much to learn. She'd likely chide me for confronting the demon and disposing of it, not that I'd known it would come to that. But that painting concerned Jonathon and me alone. If I've learned nothing else from classic literature, it's that one doesn't confront destiny with a crowd. One has to go it alone.

And I realized that was, in part, the reason why Mrs. Northe had left right at the confluence of our drama. To prove to us without a shadow of a doubt, that we—that I—could survive without her in our journey, a thought that had once been unconscionable. Still, it would be good to have her back. Soon we'd be a family...Soon I'd have to start calling her Evelyn. Or Mother. That would take some getting used to.

I hoped the demon's spell would be broken upon Maggie, too, bringing her back around to sane and tolerable. That room needed to be cleansed. Scrubbed down with holy water. Nice floral arrangements wouldn't hurt; something *living* and full of light to purge the negative energies that had given the demon another portal of opportunity.

So many loose ends…How can I not be overwhelmed?

Bessie rapped at my door and entered with a rather large box in her hands.

"It's from Lord Denbury, my dear. He says to put it on, that it's 'a must for the evening.'" Bessie affected a fairly good British accent, and I giggled and shared her resulting grin. "He awaits you downstairs. My *lady*." Bessie said with a gleam in her eye.

Within the box lay a gorgeous black silk and bombazine-trimmed dress, replete with onyx beading and tulle gathers that were delicate and frothy along the lines of the bust and fitted sleeves. And, a silk scarf for around my neck. The marks from the demon's stranglehold had faded but not entirely. I gasped at the beauty of the gown. What on earth was the occasion?

"Bessie," I called meekly down the hall.

"Ah, is this one of those dresses that needs help?" she said good-naturedly and whistled when she saw me drowning in the folds and holding the bodice up to my bosom.

"It's gorgeous. But what's he taking you to?" She made a face. "A funeral?"

"A play."

"A play of a funeral?"

I laughed. Before too long I was transformed into the princess of some wild dark tale. Bessie pinned up my hair and left a few curls loose.

It was for the best that my father was at a Metropolitan reception, for he wouldn't have liked how the neckline of the dress plunged, or how I had Bessie lace my corset extra tight to give my womanly features extra emphasis. Bessie whistled again, handed me some tea, and had the audacity to leave me alone in the sitting room to wait for my gentleman caller. I daydreamed of balls, waltzes, stolen kisses in vacant estate rooms…

A voice at the sitting room door startled me, and I looked up to behold a handsome vision all in black, tickets in one gloved hand, top hat and silver-topped walking stick in the other. I rose and curtsied.

"My dear Lord Denbury," I murmured, "My, don't you look—"

"Not half as ravishing as you, my darling Miss Stewart." He bowed, boasting a sly smile that was rakishly delicious. "Her Majesty's Association of Melancholy Bastards has demanded that we stand with them in the galleria tonight as the *very* special guests of Mr. Nathaniel Veil. May I escort you, my lady? Mrs. Northe shall take her box, so we are free to mingle as we please."

It was a striking, stirring look that Jonathon sported,

his blue eyes all the more shocking for the wholeness of black—black ascot, black waistcoat, and the matte fabric of his coattails—down to his trousers and shoes. Was there a faint trace of kohl around his eyes, giving him a slightly haunted visage? Or was I remembering his portrait face? I shuddered suddenly.

"Come now, Natalie. It's all in love and fun—"

"No, Jonathon, I can think of nothing finer than to be by your side and in this exquisite dress!" Still, I shivered. Jonathon reached for me, concern furrowing his brow. "After everything we've been through," I explained, "the chills refuse to quit me."

Jonathon came forward, placing a prolonged kiss upon my cheek. "I'll warm you. I too refuse to quit you."

I smiled then. "To lose our worries in Nathaniel's show will do our hearts good. As he says, 'sweet release.'"

Looking at him, seeing how handsome he was, I had my own ideas about what losing myself in something beautiful could be. Mrs. Northe's driver picked us up. She was meeting us at the theater.

We were handed a program when we entered the gilded auditorium, and as I opened it, a small leaflet insert fell out. It was a picture of a beautiful woman in a dark gown throwing her head back with glee and abandon. The text read: "Lose all your troubles. Miracle cure for your melancholy. Write to P.O. Box 6616, New

York City, for details." At the bottom was a red and gold crest with dragons.

My palms went sweaty and the room spun. "J-Jonathon," I gasped, shoving the leaflet at him. He stared at it.

"Bloody, *bloody* hell," he hissed. "I thought you said Nat turned the devils down."

"He did, but someone must have planted the inserts."

"I've got to get to him, tell him, warn him."

"Follow me," I said and took advantage of the low lighting to run up a narrow stair onto the stage. Our black clothes gave us a bit of an advantage, but a few of the Association members hissed at us.

"What are you—"

"I know where his dressing room is. I paid him a visit, remember."

"You didn't tell me it was in his dressing room."

"Where else does one visit an actor?"

"I don't know, somewhere more public? You can't trust an actor alone."

I laughed and wound my way past scrims and weights. I found that if you moved with purpose backstage and looked dramatic enough, the stagehands didn't question you.

The moment I saw the VEIL raven on the door, I sprinted forward, brandishing the leaflet in my hand. I suppose I should have knocked but urgency got the better of me.

I opened the door to find Veil biting a woman on the neck. She was wearing a dramatic black robe as if she were some sort of priestess. He jumped back at the intrusion, the woman pouting to be released, scowling at me, and throwing daggers with her eyes.

"Why, Miss Stewart!" Veil cried. "Knock next time, would you?"

"Sorry," I mumbled. "It's an emergency."

"I'm sure that's what they all say," the woman snapped, storming off, kicking up black feathers in her wake, and disappearing into the darkness of the backstage. Jonathon just chuckled behind me, stepping into the light.

"My God if it isn't the mythical Denbury back from the dead. Oh, my friend, I've missed you!" Nathaniel leaped forward and seized Jonathon in a bear hug that lifted him off the ground.

"Good to see you too, Nat, but we've got a problem," Jonathon stated.

"Always business with you. Can't you spare a moment for celebration?"

"Those men who came around with their miracle cure," Jonathon declared. "I thought you told Natalie you sent them packing."

"I did!"

"Then what's this?" Jonathon slapped the leaflet on Nathaniel's chest.

He took one look at it and his fury was palpable. "What the bloody hell—"

"That's what I said. That crest is from a society of madmen who keep trying to kill me, who stitched together a body of different body parts and made it come to life, who went messing with Samuel's head, and now they're trying to mess with *your* people."

Nathaniel turned the color of the pale greasepaint on his vanity table. "Why us?"

"I'm still trying to figure that out. Evidently they don't take kindly to being denied."

"They don't," I said. I unwound my scarf to reveal the bruises for emphasis.

"Dear God…" Nathaniel whispered.

"We're all young and talented," I added. "And that gives them extra incentive to make us their toys." I wondered, just then, what my talent was exactly. Well, bravery, I suppose, and the uncanny habit of being in the middle of things. I wrapped the scarf back around my neck.

"So if I were you," Jonathon instructed, "I'd get your Association to go collect those leaflets and pull them from the programs yet to be distributed."

Nathaniel nodded and flung open his door. "Lavinia, darling," he called, "you can't have gone far. Come, love, I need your help." The red-haired woman in the dramatic black robe stalked back to his dressing room, glaring at us. "Don't be rude, L, these friends of mine might have just saved your life and the minds of our whole Association. Someone put leaflets into my programs uninvited. And you *know* I do not tolerate unexpected changes to my show. Have Raven and Ether collect them at either side of the aisles, and tell Mr. Bell not to hand out any more programs with the page in it."

She bowed her head and disappeared into the black velvet wings of the backstage once more.

"You were biting her neck," I said, watching her walk away.

"Gently. I wasn't drawing blood."

"Is that a *thing*? A thing you do?"

"Yes, it's quite exquisite. Have Jonathon try it on you. Or I can, if he—"

"Don't even think about it." Jonathon lifted a warning finger.

"Oh, this is exciting, Miss Stewart. I've always been the one with all the girls. Jonathon's never had anything he's been possessive of. This will prove great sport—"

"I'm no sport," I said through clenched teeth. "I don't take kindly to games."

"Even games of flattery, flirtation, and wit?" Nathaniel asked in his charming way. I found myself fighting a grin. Jonathon set his jaw.

"Don't be cruel," he muttered, and I remembered that plea from my dream. I blushed, recalling the dream I'd had of Nathaniel upon my neck. A little too real here.

322

"I'd only have suffered the things I did for one man, Mr. Veil," I said, sliding my arm through Jonathon's. "So do your worst with your games, but you won't win."

Nathaniel clapped his hand over his heart. "Ah, loyalty. It's so romantic. Come, come, the both of you, out on stage. I'll introduce you to the whole theater as my extra-special guests while the inserts are collected—"

"No," Jonathon and I said at the same time. Jonathon continued: "I'm keeping a low profile, friend, which probably means I shouldn't be anywhere near you."

"Fine, then. Get out of my room. I must prepare."

With a chuckle, we moved to the door.

"Den," Veil called. Jonathon rolled his eyes at the pet name and turned back. "I'm *really* glad you're not dead."

"Me too. Thank Miss Stewart here for that." Nathaniel moved to embrace me. "On second thought, save your thanks for Lavinia. We'll have you over for dinner one night. Keep an eye out for an invitation from Mrs. Northe."

"Will do. Thank you for telling me about the leaflet. You know I can't bear anything befalling my Association. Anything," Nathaniel said, utterly without affect.

"I know," Jonathon said and closed the door behind him.

"*Den?*" I asked with a giggle.

"He's the *only* one allowed to call me that. He has pet names for everything and everyone. It was the only one that wouldn't get me bludgeoned on the street if someone overheard it. If you ever call me that, I will never speak to you again."

I laughed as we sneaked back into our places within the Association. Mrs. Northe was somewhere in her box above, a figurehead of a chaperone leaving Jonathon and I to our glorious freedom. I looked up and caught her eye. I blew her a kiss. She lit up, utterly delighted by the token of affection. I'm not sure I'd ever seen her beam so brightly, and I realized in that moment how much I cared for her. I felt confident she honestly cared for me and for my father just the same.

Jonathon and I were on our own with the crowd in the pit, where we edged our way past black tulle and feathers, onyx beading, and mourning finery at its very finest, carving our own little corner by the velvet-covered railing.

I was giddy with excitement. We looked like we belonged to the most intense, artistic set, the two of us. I didn't know how strikingly dramatic we could be, looking so severe and strangely beautiful. I couldn't stop staring at us in the beveled mirrored sconces that doubled the light of the golden gas-lamps.

Jonathon caught my gaze and slid his arm around me. "Would you look at that beautiful couple? I can hardly *handle* the sight of us," he murmured, a purr in my ear.

"You'd best get used to it," I teased.

"Oh, there are so many things I cannot wait to get used

to," he said, trailing a finger down my back, the bodice line of which was too plunging and exposed to be modest. But then again, it was the height of French fashion, and the French must know how exquisite a fingertip upon a woman's bare back can be.

My giddiness was soon tempered as a man in a fine coat and tails came up the aisle. I thought he was merely taking his seat in the rows behind our standing gallery. His top hat was tipped low over his brow, so we didn't get a good look at him.

But when he slipped a piece of paper marked "Denbury" over Jonathon's hand that rested upon the velvet rail, my eyes bore into him as the stranger turned away. Jonathon snatched the paper, looking after the man who gave it, but he was already lost in a sea of other coattails and top hats, a sea of black satin and white waistcoats.

The small piece of paper read:

They're coming for you.

Sincerely,
A Friend.

I felt sick. When the words came, they came with difficulty. "Will this never end?" I hissed finally, putting a hand on the gallery rail to steady myself. "Will we never be granted *one night* that can just be ours, one night to feel safe? That's all I ask—"

"Tonight," Jonathon said, his nostrils flaring, his pale blue eyes bright. A flicker of white light rippled off him, his defiance made manifest. "This night. I will not have it taken from me. Now. Right now, all there is, is this," he said firmly, placing his hand on my waist as the orchestra began a few lilting, tantalizing notes.

He slid his other hand around to clasp my outstretched hand in his. He bowed his head slightly and began slowly to lead me. The music revealed itself as a slow, lilting, haunting waltz. "Will you let this, us, be all there is right now, my dear?"

"Yes…"

Jonathon moved me slowly, dancing us achingly in a circle, our small steps precise. He was right. We were all there was in the world. Just us, pressed together and moving close in an intimate dance. Just this Association of haunted souls who, for one evening, was made a beloved community. I held Jonathon's hand in mine and would not let go.

Let them come, then, if they must. We are the dark angels who shall block devils' passage.

The pit swayed soft and sweet as Nathaniel sang, the rich strings lifting melody like a lark ascending. His Association, with their mixture of reverence and wit, shared warm glances of appreciation and affection, brought together by darkness but choosing to stand just this side of light, fingertips brushing darkness and coming away with a friend. Hands were clasped in unspoken understanding as Nathaniel took the pulpit of poetry and seared our souls with literary pain and pleasure, encouraging life as we flirted with romanticizing death.

Nathaniel came to a more casual moment of his production, where he commented on the fate of the Gothic in our modern culture.

"Did you hear there's a production of *Hamlet* in the West End where Hamlet marries Ophelia at the end of the play? It would seem we Victorians cannot be trusted with a tragedy. It would seem some directors feel the need to protect us from the truth of pain. What say you?" Murmurs from the audience, hisses from the pit. "I say there's a place for tragedy and a place for a happy ending. We cannot guarantee one or the other, but must let them both live."

A rustle of applause from the Association.

A tragedy. That's what we were caught up in, Jonathon and me. I had a leading role in some twisted tragedy. But while I'd leave Shakespeare well enough alone, I'd be damned if I was not going to write a happy ending for us and live into the truth of it. But just as the witches in *Macbeth* proclaim: "Something wicked this way comes." There's no avoiding it. But that doesn't mean I have to submit.

Some are born haunted. Some have haunts thrust upon them. We greet the dawn with full understanding of the shadows at our backs. Together, we find solace and kindle the fires that will keep us warm and hold us firmly in the light.

Acknowledgments

Thank you, Leah Hultenschmidt, for your guidance and faith. You're a North star. Derry Wilkens, what in the world did I ever do before you were in my life?! Thanks to Carrie, whom I met thanks to Sallie the Romance Puppy, and who introduced me to Bunny and Blueberry—who I think steal the show here. Thank you for rescuing those beautiful creatures, teaching me something about them, and allowing me to nose them into this book. Thank you, Stephen, for clever words. Thank you to Diane and Kristin for your brilliant eyes for detail on these books, and to Aubrey and Danielle for calling me names (you know what), doing your jobs really well, and making me laugh *a lot* along the way. Thank you to the whole Sourcebooks team, every last one of you, from the design to the sales departments. You are magical people who make things look magical and do magical things. Dominique, you visionary you, you are a dynamo of awesome and your support continues to mean the world to me. Thank you Sarah Maclean and Mari Mancusi for always being so helpful and gracious in addition to being rockstar authors. Thank you Saundra Mitchell for the mutual admiration society between our books. Thanks Mala Bhattacharjee for putting me in a magazine, and Morgan Doremus, for putting me on camera. Thank you Nicholas Roman Lewis for dealing with my Drama Queen moments like only you can. Thanks to Marcos, my beloved, for being my strong help in every way. You are my real-life hero, and you've taught Jonathon a thing or two. Thanks, Paul Peterson. That whole H. M. A. M. B. thing is now a real thing. Ha! Aren't we clever?! Thanks Mom, Dad, and Kelissa for being my anchors and harbors. Thanks Aunt Sandy and Jeff for being so devoted, and to my whole extended family for reading and talking up my books. Thanks Marijo—I've *really* needed the brain-cell this year. And last but not least, thanks to the Strangely Beautiful fans who came over and supported Magic Most Foul. I hope you liked those two familiar faces waltzing through Bloomsbury as much as I liked seeing them there.

About the Author

Actress, playwright, and author Leanna Renee Hieber aims to be a gateway drug to nineteenth-century classics. She graduated with a BFA in Theatre and a focus in the Victorian Era. Her debut novel, *The Strangely Beautiful Tale of Miss Percy Parker*, hit Barnes & Noble's bestseller lists, won two 2010 Prism Awards for Best Fantasy and Best First Book, and is currently in development as a musical theatre production. *Darker Still: A Novel of Magic Most Foul* was named an Indie Next List title by the American Booksellers Association and a Highly Recommended title by Scholastic Book Fairs. Her books have been translated into several languages, and her short fiction has appeared in numerous anthologies. Look for her new Gaslamp Fantasy series THE ETERNA FILES coming 2013. A proud member of actors unions AEA and SAG-AFTRA, Leanna works often in film and television and does a *whole lot* of guest speaking dressed in full Gothic Victorian regalia. A perky Goth girl who loves nothing more than a really good ghost story and/or

BBC series, Leanna owns far more corsets and bustles than is reasonable. She resides in New York City with her real-life hero and their beloved rescued lab rabbit. Visit her at www.leannareneehieber.com and follow her on Twitter @LeannaRenee.